HAMSIKKER 3

RUSS WATTS

SEVERED PRESS
HOBART TASMANIA

HAMSIKKER 3

WWW.SEVEREDPRESS.COM

ISBN: 978-1-925342-55-0

This book is for whoever it is that keeps putting these crazy ideas in my head.
And to Karen, for keeping me sane.

"Your faith can be tested, but it's how you deal with it that matters."
Erik Lansky.

CHAPTER ONE

Foul skin sloughed off, falling away like slices of cold ham, sheets of pink rubbery flesh feeling cold and dead to the touch. Bishop withdrew his sword from the dead body, and made a hasty retreat. He had used a lot of energy in repelling their attack, and he knew he needed to get back before encountering another herd. It didn't matter if there were five or five hundred. He knew when it was time to fall back. The hilltop had been a natural place to pause, and there was certainly nowhere better in the vicinity. The surrounding trees provided a natural barrier, and the river on the northern side meant there was only one way up or down the hill. It was a place he had used a couple of times previously without incurring any problem. This time, though, was different.

They had found him.

Bishop hoped to get back to base before nightfall, but with the extra weight, his horse was struggling in the heat. He still thought he could make it and still expected to do so. Nightfall was no time to be wandering around in the open anymore, but it was going to be a slog. The two people he had saved from Du Pue had been unconscious for a long while, and whilst he had wanted to push on, Black Jack needed a break. Anyway, it gave Bishop a good excuse to stretch his legs and refill his canteen with some fresh, cool water. He'd spent enough time on the hill to know the lay of the land, and he used a nearby stream for water on most of his trips. It was only as he was making his way back up the hill that he realized he was being followed. A group of the dead had unwittingly found his little base, and he'd spent the last thirty minutes taking them down.

Bishop could see beyond the tree line that there were more out there, and they wouldn't stop, wouldn't turn around, or wait; as long as he was on that hill, they would keep on coming. A small group of dead had found their way up through the trees, and with his two companions still out cold, he had fought the dead on his own. There was no point in trying to wake the others to help him.

They didn't have the energy to sit up on their own and were certainly in no shape to start taking on any zombies. Bishop trudged back to camp wondering if they were still sleeping. The woman had stirred a few times as they'd travelled, and Bishop had done what he could, making sure she was comfortable and reassuring her that she was safe. Still, she was pale, and looked like she needed a good feed. Since leaving Du Pue, the man with her hadn't woken at all, probably for the best. His injuries were severe, and whenever the woman had woken, Bishop had checked to see if the man was still breathing. He had taken a hell of a beating and needed a lot more attention than was available right now.

Bishop stopped and unsheathed his sword. A branch snapped up ahead close to where he had left the other two under the shelter of a bush and near to Black Jack. It couldn't be a zombie. No way had any of them gotten past him. He knew it wasn't his horse either. He'd left Black Jack tied up securely. No, this was the sound of someone walking, slowly, toward him. Bishop slid himself behind the trunk of a large oak tree and pressed his back against the cold bark. He wasn't about to take any chances and breathed out slowly. Taking in his surroundings, he became acutely aware of everything, every noise and smell that was around him. The patchwork canopy of the trees above provided some shelter from the sun and cast a plethora of shadows across the dry ground that was covered in broken twigs, moss, and crisp, dead leaves. The wildlife had long disappeared from the area. He hadn't seen or heard a bird, and if there were any mice or rabbits, they were safely tucked away in their homes.

"I know, Annalise, I know," he said quietly.

Another crack indicated that whoever was coming was getting closer. Bishop steadied himself. Whoever was approaching was making sure they were doing so as quietly as possible. He knew enough to realize that when someone snuck up on you, it was usually a bad sign. Nobody sprang out to give you a surprise party anymore. He could tell the noise was coming from the east perhaps as little as ten or twelve feet away. A low rustling sound became more apparent, and he realized they were dragging their feet. Damn, he had been so sure he had got them all. Bracing his feet, he wrapped his fingers tightly around the scabbard, and prepared to strike. He wanted to let them get as close as possible so he could take them down with one strike. He counted down in his head, slowly, breathing calmly as he did so. Three, two, one...

There was a slight shift in the air, almost imperceptible, as Bishop swung the sword. It was as if the blade could slice through the very atoms themselves, and if it hadn't been for the scream, he would've taken off the woman's head with barely a sound.

The sword thudded into the oak tree, and Bishop stepped back. "Damn, I thought you were out for the count." Relief flooded through him, though he was still on edge. He had very nearly decapitated the very woman he was trying to save. He pulled his sword free and tucked it back in its sheath. "You okay?"

Dakota was trembling. "Jesus, I thought you were one of them. I woke up and heard noises, and I thought... Jesus." She leant against the tree, suddenly feeling very tired.

"All right, hold on girl." Bishop put an arm around her, helping her stay on her feet. "You know, you really shouldn't be walking around out here. It ain't safe. We did have company, but I took care of it. For now, anyways."

Dakota looked at Bishop's face. It felt familiar, and she remembered he had tended to her over the last couple of hours. She remembered the visions, the nightmares, and the smell of the dead, but most of all she remembered his voice. His warm, deep voice had been soothing, kind; whoever this man was, he had taken care of her.

"Look, we need to get you away from here. You okay to walk?" Bishop asked.

Dakota merely nodded and let him guide her back to the camp.

"Just what were you going to do anyway?" Bishop could see the woman was unarmed. She held a small stone in her hand, but she dropped it as they made their way back up the hill. "You need to rest. You don't need to worry about what's out there in the woods. I've got your back."

"Who...who are you?" Dakota felt like she could trust this man, at least as much as she could trust anyone anymore. Javier and Rose had destroyed much of her faith in mankind, and it would take more than a few kind words to make her accept anyone else at just face value. Still, it seemed like he was good. For now, she knew that she had no choice, and she let him help her walk. The ground was a tangled mess of broken branches, and it would be easy to fall. She hadn't really paid attention to the direction she had come from and was feeling quite disorientated. "Just where are we?"

"Well, the first one I can answer, easy. The name's Bishop. I like to think I'm just a regular guy, nobody special. I'm a survivor, so I guess that make me something, anyway. I don't quite know what else to tell you. There was a time when you were defined by your job or your family. Now that's all gone, what is left? Are we survivors? Killers? When we have more time, I'd be happy to fill in the blanks, but we really need to hit the road. This was just a stopgap. These woods offer us a little protection, but it's no more than a rest stop between A and B."

"A and B?" asked Dakota. She was regretting getting up now and beginning to feel dizzy. If felt like her blood was sluggish, and she hoped they were going to be back to the man's camp soon so she could lie down.

"Well, A is where I found you. Lucky for you, I was close by. That whole area is teeming with the dead. Quite what was going on between you and the others I don't know, but the fellow who drove off in the van sure was happy to leave you for dead. Didn't seem right to just abandon you like that, so here we are." Bishop noticed the woman was tiring. "B is somewhere safe. I'll get us there; don't you worry about that. If we get going, there's no reason we can't get back to base before evening. Say, mind if I ask your name?"

"Dakota."

The path suddenly cleared, and they were back with Black Jack and Hamsikker, both resting quietly, both unaware of the fight with the dead that Bishop had just had.

"And that man you're travelling with?" asked Bishop.

Dakota hesitated. Should she put all her trust in this stranger? What if he was a liar just like Javier? A thousand scenarios ran through her head, all of them involving Bishop killing them in some way.

"That's Jonas, my husband. Everyone calls him Hamsikker."

"I got no argument with that. Well, listen up, Dakota, I'm going to have to get you two up onto Black Jack with me quick sharp. We hang around out here much longer, and…"

"Bishop, right?" Dakota stopped as they neared Jonas. She looked at her husband. His face looked terrible; covered in cuts and bruises, he barely looked like the man she had married. "Bishop, just know this. If you screw us over, if you so much as harm a hair on my husband's head, I will kill you. I promise you that much."

Bishop frowned. "I hear you, and I got no problem with that either. I don't doubt you've been through some shit, and I ain't gonna pretend I haven't too. I'll make you a promise. I'm not going to hurt you or your husband. When I see folk in trouble, I help out. That's who I am. There are enough problems in this world for folks to deal with without me adding to their worries."

"Okay then," said Dakota.

"Okay then," said Bishop, and he smiled. "Dakota, you ridden a horse before? If you're happy to ride with me, I'll make sure your husband is strapped on securely with us. I'll make sure he won't fall off."

Dakota nodded. "I've ridden before, but not so much lately. When I was a girl I used to make my Daddy take me out to this ranch at weekends. We could never afford our own horse, so we used to go and just hang out all day there, so I could feed 'em and ride 'em. There was this one horse, Nancy I called her, and her coat was pure black. I loved her a lot."

Bishop hoisted Jonas up onto the back of Black Jack, and Dakota noticed how he lifted Jonas gently, careful not to hurt him. It seemed like he was genuine, and when he spoke he appeared to be speaking the truth. She couldn't help but feel there was something more, though, that he hadn't told her, something more to this man's story. Why was he riding out alone in an area that he himself admitted was teeming with zombies? Why was he helping them? Was he expecting something in return? Dakota walked up to Black Jack and patted her flank. The horse clearly had a good temper and was standing patiently while Bishop got things ready. Dakota rubbed her fingers through the horse's coarse brown hair and was taken back to her childhood. The smell of the horse took her back to the ranch when she was a young girl. It took her back to a time when her parents were still alive, and life was much simpler. Now everything was complicated, and her friends were dead. She looked at Jonas and grimaced. How could Javier do that? How could he beat a man half to death and leave them? Javier wasn't even human. He was halfway to Canada now, and he had Freya hostage. What a mess.

"He'll be okay," said Bishop, seeing Dakota looking at her husband. He had no medical expertise and really didn't know if Jonas would pull through. "We'll get him back and then see if we can patch him up. I have some supplies back at base. Come on."

Bishop mounted Black Jack, and Dakota climbed on up behind him. She put her arms around Bishop's waist, and rested her head on his back. It was the closest she had been to another man in a long time. It almost felt like holding on to her father again. Bishop was tender and kind, but strong. He spoke well, and she wondered what kind of man he had been before all of this, before the zombies had appeared.

"Why do you keep saying base?" asked Dakota.

"Huh, what's that?" Bishop turned Black Jack around, and they began to trot down the path away from the hilltop. Bishop kept one eye open for zombies. They lurked in the trees and could be hidden from sight right until the last second.

"You haven't said we're going home. You said we're going back to base. Are you a soldier? Is there an army base somewhere nearby?"

"A soldier?" Bishop laughed quietly. "No, Dakota, I am definitely *not* a soldier. There's also no army base near here, least no working ones anyway. They were all overrun a long time ago. There's no army around here. Hell, there's no army left, full stop."

"Oh. I see," said Dakota.

Dakota sounded flat, despondent, and Bishop knew she didn't see. "You realize that what happened here wasn't just a localized event, right?"

"We spent a long time in Erik's house. We figured things had gone bad, but we weren't sure just how bad."

"Erik?"

"An old friend." Dakota wondered how Erik was doing. He would do anything to protect Freya, she knew that, but was he capable anymore? Would Javier just kill him like he had Terry and Mrs. Danick? It hurt to think about it, and Dakota felt utterly powerless. She had lost almost everything. She had lost Pippa, her friends, and now she was stuck on the back of a horse with a stranger taking her God knows where, with Jonas half dead.

"Well, for the record, what happened here, happened everywhere. The dead came back. Boy, did they come back. It was all over in a few days. I don't truly know how many people are still alive, but now and again I come across some folks like you. I help them get where they're going, one way or another."

"So the whole of America and Canada? There's nothing left?" Dakota tried to imagine the streets of New York empty. She tried to picture Disneyland without hordes of laughing children, to see the shopping malls deserted, but she couldn't. She just couldn't believe that everything had gone.

"Dakota, when I said this wasn't a localized event, I meant it wasn't just localized to the US. What happened, hit everywhere: Russia, Europe, Asia…everywhere."

Bishop steered Black Jack down a rough path, and the woods thinned out, the trees gradually disappearing behind them. Soon he would have them back on track, and they would be safely back to base long before evening. He could see the zombies in the fields and on the roads, but he kept them at a safe distance.

"I see," said Dakota. So it really was over. How could this happen? How could He let this happen? Perhaps it would've been better if Javier had just killed her. Instead, she had somehow survived, and now she was going to have to face this. What kind of world was this in which to bring up a baby?

Bishop barely heard her, so quietly did she speak. There didn't seem much point in talking about it. What was done, was done, and no one but God could change that. If there was one thing Bishop didn't like to do, though, it was let depression catch a hold. There was a lot to be depressed about, but he refused to go down that road. There was still so much to do, so many people to save, that he focused on what he could do, not what he couldn't. Some things were just out of his control, and he could tell that if he didn't say anything, Dakota was likely to fall into that downward spiral that had caught him so many times in the past.

"I've got a few places I stay at. Places that are secure and well hidden. I've made them that way so I can sleep at night. You can't spend every night with one eye open. So that's where we're going right now. One of my bases."

"But where's home?" asked Dakota.

"Home? I don't have one. That's gone. I lost a lot of things when the dead came back to life, and my home was just one of them. I don't like to stay in one place for too long. Right now, I'm taking us some place safe. You'll see. Just rest Dakota, and trust me. I'll get you and Jonas there soon. Then you and me can sit down and have a chat about things."

'Trust me.' Dakota physically winced at the words. Trust was exactly what had gotten them into this mess, and now here she was doing it all over again. Whilst Bishop was clearly holding something back, she had to admit that he wasn't like Javier. Bishop could quite easily leave them for dead, and she had to take him at face value that he was only trying to help. What was it he had said, that he helped people on their way? Maybe his base was a giant supermarket, or a canned goods store loaded with guns and ammunition. Maybe he lived with others in a communal apartment complex with high walls and gun towers with people on the lookout for zombies.

"Are there others? Do you have a doctor there, at your base?"

"No, there's no doctor. Look, I'll do what I can for your husband, but I don't want you to get too excited about where we're headed. It's safe, but it's nothing flashy. I get up when the sun comes up, and I sleep when it goes down. I don't live alone all the time, but there's nothing to worry about. You probably won't even meet him tonight. We'll take care of you. Between us we have enough experience to look after your husband."

"So there's no doctor at your base, not even a nurse?"

Bishop's instinct told him Dakota wasn't just concerned for her husband. There was something else in her questions, something he needed to find out. "Dakota, if you've got something to tell me, now's the time."

"That man who beat my husband, the one who killed my friends. He beat me too."

"I can see that, and I'm real sorry about it. Ain't no real man goes beating up women like he did." Bishop had seen the end of the fight, but had been too far away to intervene. By the time he had caught up with them, the monster dishing out the beatings had escaped in a van with others. "Truly, I wish I could've gotten to you five minutes earlier than I did."

"I can live with the beating I took. I can live with the pain for a while, but...I'm worried."

"About what?"

Dakota paused. If she was going to trust this man, she may as well be completely honest. She was reluctant to give too much away, but the truth was that she was terrified. Jonas could be out for days, weeks, for all she knew, and she couldn't wait that long.

"I'm pregnant. I'm worried that my baby might, that what he did to me..."

"You're pregnant?" Bishop was more than a little surprised, but he knew the last thing a pregnant woman needed was for him to fly off the handle. Her hands were around his waist, and he could feel how much she was shaking. After all she had been through, with not even knowing if her husband would pull through, she was going to have a child?

"If you want to leave us here, that's fine," said Dakota. There were some buildings down the road, the outskirts of a small town. "I don't want to be a burden. We can..."

"Dakota, you can stop that right now. I ain't about to drop you in the middle of nowhere and leave either you *or* Jonas behind. Pregnant, huh? Well, I guess we'll just deal with that as best we can. Right now I need you to relax. You're safe now, Dakota." Bishop knew she didn't believe him. He could sense her fear. "I'm one of the good guys. You're safe."

CHAPTER TWO

Perched on a reclining chair with some cold soup warming her stomach, Dakota was finally beginning to accept that she could relax. Bishop had made sure she was comfortable, and it was true; she did feel safe, at least, for now.

She had let Bishop tend to Jonas, clean and dress his wounds, and then they had put him to bed. She tried to make Jonas sip some water, but she couldn't bring him round, and so there was little more they could do now except wait. Bishop didn't seem to think he had any life-threatening injuries, but he had taken a solid beating, and they wouldn't know for sure how bad it was until he regained consciousness. So for now, she was waiting, hoping, and doing a lot of praying. She expected the worst, based on the fact that so much had gone wrong for them lately, but she didn't want it to end like this. She didn't want it to end at all. What she had with Jonas was special, and she knew she had treated him badly of late. There were quite a few things she had said to him in anger and regretted. When he was back with her, she would talk to him, apologize, and make sure they were okay. The last thing she wanted was to be without him, and as much as she was safe, she couldn't face the prospect of going on without him.

They made sure Jonas was as comfortable as possible, and then settled in for the night. Dakota made sure she was never far away in case Jonas woke, and she intended to sleep by his side as far as that was possible in the close confines of the cabin.

"So go on, Bishop" she said as she wiped the last traces of soup from the bowl, "you were going to explain how you ended up here. This isn't exactly your typical family home."

"This? This place was just luck," said Bishop, patting the solid walls surrounding them. "I came across it by fluke really. I wasn't looking for it, or looking for anything in particular. At the time I was just…wandering."

"Wandering?"

Bishop grunted. "You remember what it was like at the start, right? Things turned sour pretty quick. We've all got our sob stories, and I ain't about to launch into one now, but I lost a lot of myself. I lost a lot. Everything and everyone I cared about. I'm not so blinkered that I don't see that all around me though. The people I meet all have horrible tales to tell, memories they wish they could get rid of but that haunt them all the same. So how did I end up here?" Bishop looked across at Hamsikker, sleeping soundly.

"I guess we got plenty of time. My identity was my family, and when I lost them, I lost myself. Now I'm just Bishop. Links me back to my family, but lets me move on. Nobody calls me by my name anymore, not since my wife passed. Annalise was the most amazing woman I ever met. What went down was just…well, anyways, I don't like to talk about her like that. In the past tense, you know? I try to remember all the good times we had. I try to honor her memory. There were times I wanted to give up, times I did, but something always pulled me back. So, yeah, I was wandering. Didn't seem no point in staying at home, so I left. I just started walking and didn't stop."

"And you found this place?" asked Dakota.

"Not exactly. Not at first. I stayed a while in a farmhouse further south. I was living on scraps, whatever I could find. Wasn't much of an existence. There were some fruit trees around the place which kept me going a while. I managed to get some fresh apples and pears, and as sweet as they were, I found the taste quite bland. After I lost my Annalise, I just didn't know how to go on. It was as if the world had turned grey.

"I came across a young kid out in the fields one day. I was trying to find some fresh water, and there he was, clear as day, just sitting on the ground. He wasn't doing nothing, just sitting there looking at me as I walked up to him, as if it was just a regular day. I asked him what he was doing, told him it wasn't safe being out in the open like that, and he just smiled at me. Didn't pull a gun, didn't run away, just smiled at me. I talked to him a while, asked him to come with me back to the farmhouse, that I would help him if I could, and all he did was sit there and smile. It was damn strange. At the time I couldn't understand it. Quite a young guy too. He had a few cuts and bruises. I could tell he had been through the ringer, but he had a lot of life left in him. As far as I could tell, he wasn't seriously hurt. He had no bags, no weapons, nothing. I sat with him a while, but eventually it started to turn cold. I practically begged him to come in with me, but he didn't budge. As I started to leave him, I could hear Annalise in my head telling me to make him come, telling me to drag him if I had to, to force him to come back to the house with me, but I ignored her and went on back. I figured he must be retarded or something, but I never got to find out. Next day I went out to go and talk to him some more, and he wasn't there."

"He'd gone?"

Bishop looked at Dakota, a frown across his face. "They'd gotten to him in the night. All that was left from where I'd found him the day before was a scrap of clothing, and a shitload of blood. I found what was left of his body a few feet away. I never heard a sound in the night, never heard him cry or shout. What makes somebody do that? I think that he'd given up. Something inside of him had made him sit down and just wait for it. Christ, he was so young. I tried to deny it, but I knew when I left him there that he didn't stand much chance. I think I knew what was going to happen, but I didn't accept it, I couldn't. I had a look around for the zombies that had taken him, but they'd cleared out. Must've had a good feed and moved on. I found a small carrier bag on my way back to the farmhouse. I thought at first it was just rubbish, but when I looked inside I knew it was his. There were a few pictures, and he was in a few of them. Some were of a young boy with his parents, and some were later on when he was grown up. The photos were covered in dried blood. There was one of the kid wearing a suit, his arm around this beautiful young woman, and he was smiling just like he did at me that day. That poor kid...

"I buried him, or what was left of him. I put the pictures of his family in with him. Seemed like the least I could do. That's when I knew. I had lost so much, and given the chance to do something, I had turned my back. I could've helped that young man, and I left him to die."

"Sounds to me like he wanted to die," said Dakota. "You offered to help, and he turned you down."

"So does that make it right?" Bishop shook his head slowly. "No, I spent that whole night trying to figure it out. I had myself a good talk with Annalise. She was right. I should've taken him in. I should've made him come with me. I knew full well what would happen if I left him out there alone, and yet I did. As miserable as I was it never occurred to me back then that others were hurting too. I was so wrapped up in my own problems that I was ignorant to what was going on around me. I could still make a difference. I could still *help* people. I swore after it happened that I wouldn't turn my back again. I intended to help people get where they were going, wherever they needed to be. Sometimes I don't know at first where that is, but it soon becomes apparent."

"You've helped a lot of people then? You've taken a lot of people in?" Dakota looked at Jonas. He was still breathing, but it didn't look like he was going to wake up anytime soon. "Like Lukas?"

"Well, not all like Lukas," said Bishop, casting a glance over at the sleeping man. "You see, Dakota, some people need help getting to where they should be, but they don't even realize it themselves. Sometimes I have to step in, give them a little push."

"How do you mean?"

Bishop was about to answer when he heard a noise.

Jonas's eyes fluttered open reluctantly. His eyelids were stuck together through a mixture of sweat and sleep. There was a dim light above him, a yellowy-white that bobbed in and out of his vision. Jonas lifted his arm to his head, running his fingers across his forehead, feeling for the cuts and bruises that the pain told him were there. He tried opening his eyes again, but the light was too strong, and he let them close. There were voices. Muffled sounds in the background, male and female voices almost whispering, too quiet for him to make out what was being said. Had they made it already? There was a female voice, but it didn't sound like Dakota. It was too young, too high pitched. Freya? No, it wasn't her. Janey?

"Water...please," he managed to stutter out, hoping the distant voices would hear him. He heard a faint clattering noise, and then someone squeezed his hand.

"It's okay, honey, I'm here."

It sounded to Jonas like the voice was ethereal, floating in space somewhere above his head, not real. It felt like his body wasn't attached to the ground, as if he were floating six feet above it. He tried to open his eyes again, but they refused to obey. A thin trickle of water passed his lips, and he gratefully sucked it down as more water was poured into his mouth. It was cool, refreshing - clean. They had made it. Something had happened while he'd been out. The others must have picked him up and carried on. God, how long had he been out? They'd only gone into the garage a moment ago, or at least that was what it seemed like. When the zombies had attacked, they weren't prepared. Cliff hadn't scoped the place out correctly. Something bad had gone down, he was sure of that, but what next? One minute the dead were pouring into the garage, the next he was...what? Had he been out so long that the others had managed to get all the way to Canada? He had so many questions.

Jonas brushed away the glass at his lips. "Janey, listen to me. I need to..."

"Shush. It's okay, Jonas. Just rest."

"I should've stayed. Erik was right. I'm sorry, Janey. What Dad did...I'm sorry."

"Jonas, please just rest. Everything's okay now."

"Janey, I left you, and I wish I could take it back, but...I'm sorry, I..."

Jonas wanted to say more, to see his sister, to let her know that he still loved her. He had a lot of making up to do, he knew that. The main thing was that they were together again. How had she coped all this time on her own? The light filtering through his eyelids suddenly grew darker, and the woman's hand holding his slipped away. Shooting stars filled his vision, and then the world went quiet. Unconsciousness pulled him back down, and Jonas heard nothing more as he slept.

*

The next time his eyes opened it was dark. He woke feeling hungry instantly, and Jonas licked his lips. His upper lip was swollen, and he knew eating was going to be painful.

"Dakota?"

Jonas tried to raise his head, but it felt like trying to lift a logging truck with nothing but his little finger. The darkness had begun to formulate shapes in the shadows. Somewhere out of his vision candles were flickering, illuminating the roof above his head in a dancing firelight. The roof above his head was no more than six feet away and seemed to be made of a plastic that was cracked and discolored. It curved away to the sides, and as he tried to turn his head to look at his surroundings, he felt his neck stiffen. Where was he? There were soft thumping noises approaching, and he stretched his fingers, feeling around for his axe. All he found were soft sheets and what felt like an armrest. The bed he lay in was comfortable, if a little small.

"Dakota?"

Jonas uttered her name quietly, fearful that he was someplace strange. Was Dakota even around? He didn't recognize anything and suddenly felt very exposed. What if he'd been left behind? It felt like he'd been run over by a bus, so maybe the others had been forced to leave him behind? They might've tried to make it safe, but the truth was he could be anywhere right now. What if he was surrounded by a hundred hungry zombies? He had no way of protecting himself. He had no way of calling for help. Jonas tried to lift himself up from his bed, but sharp pangs of pain stung his body as he moved, particularly in his head, and he closed his eyes desperately trying not to black out. He needed to know where he was and if Dakota was safe.

A hand grabbed his, and instantly he jerked his eyes open.

"Jonas, honey, I'm here," said Dakota as she rubbed his hand. "How're you feeling?"

Jonas tried to speak, but he began coughing, and was thankful when Dakota held a glass to his lips. The cool water was beautiful, and he looked at his wife. She seemed to be fine. She was sporting a nasty bruise on the right side of her face, but otherwise she appeared to be fine. She was even smiling.

"Dakota, where are we? Are you okay? Are we…safe?"

"Yes. We're safe here. You need to rest, Jonas. You need your sleep. I wanted to be here when you woke."

Jonas let Dakota bring his hand up to her face, and he stroked her cheek.

"Honey, I'm sorry, I…I don't remember. I don't know what happened. Did we make it to Janey's? Did everyone get out of the garage okay? Anna? Tyler? Is everyone here with you?"

Dakota's smile cracked, and he could tell he had said the wrong thing. Her eyes looked away, and then the smile returned.

"Don't worry, honey, we can talk in the morning. It's important that you rest now, got it? The main thing is you're okay. *I'm* okay."

Despite what she said, he could tell she was lying. There was no chance of him going back to sleep without knowing if the others were okay?

"Dakota, tell me the truth. Is it the children? Freya and Mary are all right, aren't they?"

Dakota looked over her shoulder as if checking they were alone. She leant in closer to him. "He said I shouldn't tell you yet. He said it would be best if we waited, but…"

Jonas was alarmed, but he had to know. Dakota's brown eyes looked dark in the dim light. She brushed her hair behind her ears, and whispered to him.

"Jonas, they're gone. Anna and Mary, Tyler, Cliff, Terry – they're all gone. We ran into some trouble. The garage was a long time ago. We met this man who said he would help us, but he turned out to be someone he wasn't. We trusted him, but he let us down. He took what we had, and left us to die. You would be dead now, you *should* be dead, except…look Jonas, it's just you and me now. I hate this, I really do, but we have to stick together. We're all that's left."

'We're all that's left.' The words stuck in Jonas's head like a record going round and round. Was it true? Had he been out so long that he had forgotten all of this? He couldn't believe they were all dead. It seemed like only yesterday that they had been in Erik's house, looking for a way out of the city. He could still remember going into that garage with Tyler and Cliff.

Cliff.

An image flashed through Jonas's mind, a horrible picture of Cliff with his face bashed in, with his eyes burst open, and his teeth smashed to pieces, of his skull cracked open, and his brains oozing out onto a bloody floor.

Jonas felt sick. Dakota was right. Something bad had happened. Not just to Cliff, but to the others too. Why couldn't he remember?

"Dakota, we can't be all that's left, surely? Tell me Erik and Pippa are okay? They've still got the kids, Peter and Freya, right?"

Dakota's lips were trembling, and he could see from the look on her face that they weren't okay. Nothing was ever going to be okay again. He felt cold, despite the thick blanket covering his body. Fear and cold ran through his body.

"Pippa and Peter are dead," said Dakota as tears began to fall from her eyes. "Erik and Freya are…somewhere else. I don't know where, but they're in trouble. Jonas, I'm so sorry. I love you so much. I just want you to get better, and then we can raise our child, find some place safe where we can…"

"Our child? You're *pregnant*?"

Through her tears, Dakota let slip a smile. Despite all the terrible things that had happened, despite all the friends they had lost, she still felt hope. "Yes. I did tell you, but I think you've forgotten a lot. You took some nasty blows to the head. Javier…"

As Dakota continued to talk, explaining what had happened, Jonas felt the dots begin to connect. Somewhere within the recesses of his brain the fragmented memories were being put back together. Javier's face flashed into his mind instantly, and he saw the man grinning at him. There were others too. Pictures flashed before his eyes, the things he had seen scattered across his mind like a jigsaw demanding to be put back together. He remembered Javier shooting Mrs. Danick. He remembered killing Cliff. He remembered a strange man wearing a purple shirt and carrying a sword. It was all a bit of a jumble, but he knew he would get there. Suddenly he felt tired, and the last thing he recalled was Javier laying into him, kicking and punching him as he curled up on the ground.

"I love you too," whispered Jonas. It was as if his mind was overloaded, and suddenly he needed to sleep. His left arm was terribly sore, and it was bandaged up tightly. Had he been shot?

"Hey, man, you should rest up," said Bishop.

The man in the purple shirt. Jonas recognized his face, and the old man appeared behind Dakota with a bottle of water in his hands.

"Glad you're able to talk. For a while I wasn't so sure you were going to make it. I've done what I can. I bandaged you up, reset your shoulder, strapped up some broken fingers, and cleaned out your arm where you were shot. I'm no doctor, but the best I can recommend for you right now is bed rest."

Jonas tried to raise his hand, to shake the hand of the man who had saved him, saved Dakota, but it was too heavy. Everything was too heavy. His legs, his neck, and even his fingers wrapped around Dakota's ached. Bed rest sounded perfect.

"Dakota? Are you going to be okay?" Jonas asked.

She nodded. "Bishop is nothing but a gentleman. I'll be fine. We'll talk more in the morning." Dakota leant into Jonas and kissed him lightly.

As she bent down, Jonas saw another figure lurking in the background, just on the edges of his peripheral vision. It was too dark to make out any of the man's features, but Jonas wasn't sure he recognized him. Who was that?

Dakota must've seen the frown on his face, as she answered his unspoken question.

"That's Lukas. He's cool. Don't worry. Just sleep now. I'm, right here if you want anything."

"Where are we?" whispered Jonas. "Did we make it?"

"We're safe. We're outside of Munroe, and far enough away from the town to not be bothered by anything or anyone. Don't worry. Just get some sleep, Hamsikker," said Bishop, and he retreated from Jonas's vision.

Jonas gripped Dakota's hand. "Dakota, tell me, did we find out if Janey is okay? Did we make it? I thought I saw her, but my head has got a lot of things mixed up, and for all I know, it was just a dream. It was strange. I really thought I was there, at her house in Canada."

"We never made it, Jonas. I don't know how she is. I'm sure she's fine." Dakota needed to ask what Jonas had been talking about earlier when he had thought he had been talking to his sister. "Jonas, I think you were probably dreaming. You said something earlier, as if you were talking to her. You said you were sorry. Something about your Dad?"

Jonas closed his eyes. So it had been a dream. It had felt so real. He could practically see her, yet it was nothing more than a hallucination. Javier had really messed things up for him, for all of them. What had he said? He had started to apologize to Janey, but from Dakota's questioning he could tell he hadn't said much.

"It's nothing. Nothing to worry about at all." Jonas yawned. "I think I'm going to rest some more. Like you said, I feel pretty beat up. Literally."

Dakota could tell Jonas wasn't telling her something, but she let it go. There was more to worry about now, like the baby. She was done pushing Jonas. If he wanted to tell her, he would in his own time. She kissed his lips gently and then lay down beside him on the floor.

"Okay then. I love you, Jonas."

She waited for an answer, but all she heard was his breathing. Evidently he had fallen back asleep which was a good thing. Quite what they were going to do tomorrow she had no idea. She was tired herself. Her conversations with Bishop and Lukas bad been interesting, but she hadn't broached the subject of what they were going to do long-term. Did Bishop expect she and Jonas would stay with them? He kept telling her how he helped people move on, so perhaps he wanted them gone in the morning. She knew she had little choice. This was Bishop's place. He seemed to be on the level. He talked of his wife, Annalise, as if she was there with him, even though she was dead. Dakota guessed it was just his way of dealing with it. She turned over onto her side and closed her eyes. She could feel the tears coming again, but her head was throbbing, and she didn't want to cry anymore. She couldn't help but think about Pippa and Mrs. Danick. They had been killed and left out on the road to be devoured by those things. It wasn't fair. Javier had kidnapped Quinn, Erik, and Freya, and right now was on his way to Canada. Should she tell Jonas? Would he remember anyway? There was so much to consider that her mind wrapped itself in complex thought, her grief for her friends and her concern for Jonas and the baby slowly overwhelming her, and finally she slipped into a restless sleep.

CHAPTER THREE

Jonas took the carton from Bishop and sucked up the warm orange juice through a clear plastic straw. The juice was so sweet that he couldn't help but scrunch up his eyes as he drank. It had been a long time since he had tasted anything with such flavor. As it slid down his throat, he took a tentative step forward. The ground was only a foot beneath him, yet it looked like a mile away. He squeezed the last of the juice into his mouth and contemplated what lay ahead of him.

Since waking he had managed to get up, with a little help from Bishop, whilst Dakota continued to sleep. It was early, but Jonas was restless, and as sore as he was, he didn't want to lie around feeling sorry for himself. Bishop wanted to wake Dakota so she could help him, but Jonas knew she was as exhausted as him, and wanted to let her sleep as long as he could. The peace also gave him a chance to get to talk to Bishop one on one, man to man. Quite what had happened yesterday was still a blur to Jonas. Most of the events had come back to him, and Dakota had filled in the blanks last night. He could remember being beaten by Javier, but between then and now all he could recall was a fleeting vision of Bishop astride a horse, and a brief conversation with Dakota last night. Evidently he had spent most of yesterday sleeping. His body ached all over, but he wasn't about to start complaining. Jonas was lucky to be alive, and he knew it.

"You sure you don't want me to get Dakota up for you?" Bishop looked on with concern as Jonas stared at the ground. He looked unsteady on his feet, and Bishop wasn't sure if it was wise for him to be up on his feet this soon. Hamsikker's left arm was still wrapped in bandages, and he should probably be resting.

"No," said Jonas firmly. "Let her be for a while." As Jonas planted his feet on terra firma he looked back up at Bishop, smiled, and raised his fist triumphantly. "See, nothing to it."

Jonas looked at his new surroundings, and was happy to see no sign of the dead. It was an unusual home, but it clearly worked for Bishop. All around Jonas could see what he could only describe as a desert. The ground was hard and dusty, and a horse was tied up to a wooden fence. Some way off in the distance was the burnt out remnants of the town of Munroe, its buildings reduced to rubble, its roads and sidewalks charred and scarred. Bishop had assured him there was nobody present, alive or dead, and it felt like they were truly alone. The morning sky was a perfectly clear blue, and Jonas patted the side of the airplane.

"Sure is a big beast," he said, impressed at just how large it was when he was standing so close to it. Jonas ran his hand along the smooth grey aluminum. Its flying days were over, and the landing gear was buried somewhere in the ground, but the plane was largely intact, and in good condition. It looked like it had landed on its belly, and Jonas was quite sure they were nowhere near an airport. It appeared as if the plane had come to rest in the middle of nowhere. "I'm guessing it's a 747. How on Earth did you end up here?"

Bishop smiled. "I found it, simple as that. I was looking for a place to spend the night a few months back, and just as the stars were coming out I was getting ready to give up. I thought me and Black Jack would be spending the night out in the open again, which wasn't the most reassuring of thoughts. So I looked around, and I saw the setting sun just bounce off this thing. I checked it out, and lucky for me it was empty."

"No sign of anyone at all? No zombies strapped in their seats? Nothing?"

"No, sir, it was nice and quiet, just how I like it. I figure they ditched it here and everyone left. Don't know whether they meant to or not, but I guess the folks on board weren't sticking around. The hull's intact, apart from a break in the mid-section, so it's pretty secure at night. I can draw the shutters down so even at night I can light candles without worrying about being seen. No one much ventures out here, so I'm on my own by and large."

Jonas scanned the horizon again. Bishop seemed to think they were clear of danger, but it still felt unreal, being able to stand out in the open and not having to watch out for zombies. "What about Lukas? How does he fit into all of this?"

Bishop came closer and dragged a couple of suitcases with him. He sat down, and Jonas sat down beside him. "Lukas won't be with me forever. I found him a couple of weeks back on the fringe of Rockford. Such a shame what happened to that place. After the tornado of 2015 it had only just got back on its feet, and then this. The town suffered badly. There was a war there between the living and the dead, and nobody won. The whole area was decimated. The military, in their wisdom, decided to carpet bomb the whole area. Now there's not so much as a blade of grass left.

"Lukas was in pretty poor shape. Poor kid had been through a lot. Getting out of Chicago took a lot out of him, and he lost a lot of friends. I'm just making sure he gets strong enough to carry on like you. I'm lucky enough to be able to be in a position to help, so why wouldn't I? There's enough shit going on without me adding to people's problems."

"What about family? You been out here all this time on your own?" asked Jonas.

Bishop scuffed his feet in the dirt as he answered. "Not at first. I had Annalise with me. She's still with me, God bless, just not in the same way. We ran into some trouble. Some folks picked us up after the dead started coming out of Chicago, and we thought we were going to a safe house. They told me they could protect us. It was a small military group, about half a dozen of them, so we went along. I should've listened to my gut. Things were bad for a while there, but I managed to turn things around. Anyway, if I can help people on their way, then I do. When I saw you and your wife left like that, there was no way I was going to leave you too."

"Thanks for that. It's fair to say we were fooled too. Ran into some people we thought would help us, but turned out we were wrong. *I* was wrong. My naiveté let a lot of people down, got a lot of people killed. I can't take that back, and to be honest, I'm not apologizing for it. I didn't kill them myself. It has opened up my eyes though. I think I see now. I see it's impossible to live with a group. This world just doesn't allow it. There are too many people to watch, to think about; too many that need protecting. I should be concentrating on my own family. It's easier to be alone. You don't have to worry about anything or anyone. You've got it right, Bishop, just you and your horse, Black Jack. You're better off that way."

Bishop let out a small laugh. "I don't know about that, friend. If you take that attitude, then what's the point in going on? You want to spend the rest of your life alone, without friends, without support, or help, or someone to come home to? You need more than Dakota. When all this was just a bad dream, when you still had a job and a real life, did you lock yourself away with her? Did you close yourself off from the world, not interact? I'm sure you had more than just Dakota in your life. What about Janey? I heard you say something about her last night? You can't shut yourself away from the world. By all means, have your guard up, but don't try and convince yourself that everyone out there is an asshole.

"I don't see this as the end of the world. Nothing of the sort. It's just a reboot; a fresh start for those that are strong enough and brave enough to make it. You just have to be wiser. Don't rush headlong into situations you can't control. There ain't no law and order anymore. No cops. No jury. Not even a pretty young thing in a miniskirt standing outside of Walmart waiting to ask my opinion about chocolate milk or the latest country we invaded. No sir, the end of times meant the end of our way of life. There's good and bad to that. Mostly bad. Let's be honest, as shitty as things were, they weren't as bad as they are now. Once things changed, though, once I lost Annalise and I sorted my head out, I saw a hell of a lot of people around who, quite frankly, didn't deserve to be. Got me to thinking that maybe someone should make a stand."

Bishop cleared his throat before continuing. He had Jonas's undivided attention. Black Jack was standing placidly by the fence, calmly looking around at the rising sun, and Bishop felt good. He was pleased Jonas was going to pull through. Getting through the night was important. He and Dakota seemed like good folk. They had gotten themselves into a messy situation though.

"I talk to Annalise quite a bit now, but the first time I truly listened to her was a good few months back now. I had a run in with a chap who I left to die. I could've helped him but I didn't. I can't do much for him now except listen when she tells me things, and make sure I do my best to help people get where they're going. After my encounter with this man, I was looking for a new place to stay, and this young couple helped me. They took me into their home. Real nice it was; fortified, strong, and apparently safe. The husband had a basement full of canned food. Turns out they were preparing for world war three. Smart move. I was pretty beat up, so I didn't ask too many questions, and they never questioned me. Pays not to be too nosy sometimes. The wife was the sweetest woman you ever met, real cute. She gave me such a good meal, that I never stopped to ask questions. I went with it. Couldn't believe my luck. I guess, like you, I was naïve. So they cleaned me up, fed me, and let me get a good night's sleep without asking for a cent in return. The next morning I woke and found they'd shot through. Disappeared. Funny, huh? So I took a look around their place and found they had an extension built out over the back yard, a sleep-out of some sort.

"They'd got three kids tied up back there. Shit. They were…well I had to put 'em out of their misery. I couldn't let 'em come back, so I found a hammer in the basement, took it back upstairs, and smashed their brains in. I thought one might pull through, but she practically begged me to do it. She told me what her parents had done, both before and after the start of this whole undead thing. You've got to realize, there's no way of fixing broken bones any more. The cuts on their bodies were infected, and…well, that young couple had been abusing them for weeks, I reckon. You would've thought looking at the photos in the house that they were a happy family, but I guess you never know what's going on behind closed doors.

"I found a note on the front step when I left. 'Dear Bishop,' it said, 'we decided to leave you in charge. Don't try to follow us. We need a fresh start.' Some crap like that anyway. Fresh meat was what I was thinking. I wouldn't say I had an epiphany, but suddenly all the things Annalise had been whispering to me made sense. It was like an awakening. I had a choice. I could go back inside, see out the end of days down in that basement, with those three kids rotting away out back, or I could do something about it.

Those parents didn't have the right to call themselves that after what they'd done. So I tracked 'em down.

"They hadn't gotten more than a mile before they'd come across some zombies. They were hiding, poorly, in a house, hoping the zombies outside the front door would leave them alone. So, I did what the girl wanted me to do, and I paid Mom and Dad a little visit. It wasn't hard getting past the dead. I just let them be and slipped around back. Once I got to the husband I broke his legs and threw him outside; I let the dead eat him alive. The woman, well, she should've known better. Pleaded with me for her life, but it was too late for that. She practically threw herself at me, started ripping off her clothes, saying she'd do anything I wanted, just as long as I let her live. How a woman could do what she'd done to her own kids I'll never know. It seemed only fair to give her a taste of her own medicine, so I found a broom, snapped it up into pieces, and shoved into every hole she got. I made damn sure she felt it too. While she was balling, I had a look around the house. I knew I was going to need more than my own cunning to get out of that house and past those damn dead zombies. Whoever lived there had a collection of swords and knives, so I took the biggest one I could find. Then I had me a smoke, found a neat drop of whiskey to steel my nerves, and left her there. I opened the door as I left. Made sure she went the same way as her husband. I can hear her crying now."

Bishop chuckled.

"She deserved everything she got, believe me. Shit. I don't want you to think I'm some sort of sadistic fuck. I took *no* pleasure in what I did. But it was the right thing to do. Annalise agrees with me. I just gotta help people get where they're going. Some go up, some go down; I just give 'em a little push. Lukas is a good man, I could tell right away. I'm glad I was able to help him. Doing what I do, it takes it out of you. Those two deserved what they got, and don't you think otherwise.

"Anyway, after that, I kept my eyes open. Just because the authorities are gone, doesn't mean people should be allowed to get away with shit anymore. It was bad enough back then, what with the corruption, the violence, and those racist bastards giving us a bad name. After what went down with those kids and their parents,

I didn't feel much like being myself anymore. When I lost Annalise part of me died with her, and when I started to focus on what lay ahead, I realized it didn't matter anymore. I can barely remember my real name anymore. Bishop just seemed to fit. Annalise likes it."

Jonas noticed Bishop was grinning. It wasn't the tale he told that made him happy, it was talking about his wife. Clearly Annalise was dead, and yet sometimes Bishop talked about her as if she was right there with him. Jonas didn't doubt that everything Bishop told him was true, yet it was almost unbelievable. He had good intentions, but Jonas was a little nervous knowing that Bishop liked to dish out his own justice. What if Bishop decided they needed moving on too? What if Bishop didn't appreciate the way he and Dakota lived their lives and decided to dispense his own sentence on them?

"I can see you're having a bad time with this, Hamsikker, and that's fair enough. You probably think I'm crazy, right?" Bishop could see the wonder in Hamsikker's eyes. It was a look he had seen several times. "You know, once Lukas wakes, you should have a chat with him. He'll give you his own opinions about me. I've helped a lot of people. Some folks are just lost. There was a group of four I came across a few weeks back, trying to get to the east coast. They thought they could find a boat and skip on down to Florida. They figured they may as well live out their days in a condo with a swimming pool than try to scrape together enough to eat around here. They were solid folks, so I helped them. I gave them directions, some supplies, and gave them a good night's rest in my very own private jet."

"They make it?" asked Jonas.

Bishops shrugged. "Couldn't tell you. I hope so. All I know is I did what I could for them."

Jonas looked at Bishop's sword. "You ever regret helping someone you shouldn't have? You ever get tired of this nomadic lifestyle you have? Don't you ever want to get on down to Florida or go somewhere else?"

"No, sir. I've got a job to do, and I intend to see it through. I've got regrets, who hasn't? But I'm not going to let them stop me doing me what I'm doing. If I abandoned my post, I don't think

Annalise would ever forgive me. It was only a week or two ago I had to intervene with a gang down near Westport. I was just passing through, but I ran into some trouble with the locals. Seems they were having too much of a good time raping some poor young woman."

Bishop shook his head and spat.

"Four fellas forced her. I was keeping an eye on them. Something about the group wasn't right, so I kept my distance at first while I tried to figure out what they were up to. They told the girl they'd protect her Granddad if she slept with them all. I kept an eye on them, thought it was just bravado at first, you know? I thought there was a chance they might do the right thing. I ain't a cold-blooded killer, I give people a chance. I should've known better. They bunkered down in some shit-pot garage outside of Westport. They raped and beat her, all while her Granddad was forced to watch; then they shot the old man and strung her up. I was too slow in getting to the garage to stop it. I wish it could've gone differently, but you do what you gotta do. When I called 'em out about it, they said it was none of my business. So I made it my business. Luke six thirty-one: Do to others as you would have them do to you. People seem to think there's no justice anymore, that they can do whatever the hell they want. I don't see it that way. Some folks call it karma. Call it what you want, but I firmly believe you get what's coming to you. And damn it, if those sorry excuses for men didn't have something coming to them.

"I strung them up. I made damn sure that girl's Granddad got to see 'em suffer before he died. The poor man. I couldn't bring myself to put one in his head. I left him there. Been here and there ever since, looking out for people. Don't pay to stay in one place for too long. I've seen a few good people out there, but not many. Apart from you and Lukas, it's been a while since I found anyone worth saving if the truth be told. Black Jack and Annalise keep me company, so I don't mind so much."

Jonas was stunned. He couldn't decide if Bishop was insane, or the only sane person left.

"I was watching you folk for a little while. I wasn't sure at first. I had my concerns, what with your group having women and children in, but I've seen enough shit to know when someone's being treated well. The kid looked all right, that young girl, you know? I was about to leave when you had that falling out with…what's his name, the skinny fella in the baggy clothes?"

"Gabe – I mean Javier," said Jonas. "His name is Javier." Just the mention of his name made Jonas angry. He had been fooled and hurt. He thought he could trust him, but it would be difficult to trust anyone again. Even Bishop had an edge to him. He meant well, but how far could Jonas trust him? How far should he trust him?

"Sounds like you've got it all figured out," said Dakota as she hopped out of the plane to join them.

"You heard all that?" asked Jonas. "I thought you were sleeping."

"And I thought you were resting," replied Dakota, kissing her husband warmly. She embraced him, and looked him over. "How are you feeling?"

"Like I've been run over by a truck." Jonas smiled. "How are you? How's…" he patted her stomach, "you know? Mini-Hamsikker."

"Mini-Hamsikker?" asked Dakota smirking. "I hope everything's fine, but I guess there's no way of knowing for sure. I feel okay. I mean I've felt better, but…we'll be okay, so long as you come up with a better name than *Mini-Hamsikker*."

A voice called out above their heads from within the airplane.

"Bishop, you want me to get Black Jack ready?"

Jonas looked up to see a young man stood in the doorway to the cabin. He was dark-skinned, sporting a grey T-shirt, skinny jeans, and black sneakers. The boy had close-cropped hair and was probably no more than twenty.

"No, I think we'll take a leisurely breakfast today, Lukas," said Bishop as he hopped up into the cabin. "Let's see what we can rustle up for our new friends. You'll be pleased to see that Hamsikker is up and about on his feet now."

"Pleased to meet you, sir," said Lukas, as he nodded at Jonas.

"Likewise," replied Jonas.

As Lukas and Bishop disappeared into the aircraft, Jonas turned to Dakota. "Are you *really* okay?"

"I'm just pleased you're back in the land of the living. I don't know what I'd do without you, Jonas. Last night was awful. I kept thinking about what was going to happen to you, to me, to our baby...to Freya."

Jonas sighed heavily. "I take it you've been able to talk to Bishop and Lukas. They on the level?"

"For sure. Lukas is a sweet kid. He dotes on Bishop. I know Bishop says he likes to be alone, but I think he enjoys having Lukas around."

"We have to go, don't we?" asked Jonas. The question had been weighing on him, and now they were alone, he had to get it out, to know how Dakota felt. "No matter what, we have to go. Bishop will understand."

Dakota nodded in agreement. "You know Javier took Quinn and Erik with him. There's no guarantee we'll find them, but we have to try. If he gets his way he'll kill them. Christ knows what he'd do to Freya."

"We'll eat, thank Bishop for his hospitality, and then get going." Jonas winced as a barb of pain shot through his arm.

"Maybe we should stay another day," suggested Dakota. "You're in no fit state to hit the road so soon. Maybe we should..."

"No. He's already got twenty-four hours head start. We can't sit back and relax while he's out there with Freya. I know if Quinn and Erik get a chance they'll get away from him, but what if they can't? I remembered something else too. Something Javier said to me yesterday."

Jonas surveyed the landscape spread out in front of him, the dusty ground soaking up the last of the autumn's sun underneath a vast orange sky. Wispy clouds clung to the sky, and a fireball hidden behind the arching hills in the east disguised the sun's rising path. It would soon be overhead, and the day was draining away. Jonas knew he couldn't afford to wait. It would be time to leave soon. Beyond Black Jack, who was snorting and grazing patiently, there was a treasure trove of vehicles. Jonas hoped that Bishop had collected them for a reason. Some of them had to work, surely, and he could part with one couldn't he? Bishop had been good to them, good for Jonas, enabling him to rest, to regroup, to gather his thoughts; to let his wounds heal. Yet it wasn't enough, he could sense that. Janey was out there waiting for him. He had even more reason to hurry to her now: Javier.

"He said he was going to find Janey. He knows where she lives, Dakota. He knows how to find her. If she is still alive, then…"

"Jonas, he wouldn't waste his time on her. He's looking for his brother."

"Can you be sure about that? You know as well as I do, that he's a vindictive son of a bitch. I think he would go out of his way just to make a point. Given half a chance, he'll go looking for her, and then…well we know exactly what will happen. I can't risk it, Dakota. I have to go. For Erik, Quinn, Freya, for Janey; for me. If anything happens to them…"

Dakota kissed Jonas lightly, and forced his face back to hers. She stared into his eyes. "I'm with you, okay? Through all of what's happened, whatever will happen, I'm with you, forever. I swear I must be crazy to love you, Jonas Hamsikker, but I do. So let's eat, thank Bishop for his hospitality, and get going. He says he likes to help people on their way, right? Well he's helped us already. It's time we helped Javier get to where he belongs - in Hell."

Jonas kissed his wife back, and she hopped up into the cabin. "Coming?" she asked, holding out her hand for him.

"Yeah, just give me a minute. I need the fresh air in my lungs."

"Okay, well don't be long." Dakota went deeper into the grounded airplane, looking for Bishop and Lukas.

Jonas didn't know if Javier would truly waste his time looking for Janey, but it seemed like just the sort of sadistic thing he would do. What had become of Erik, Quinn and Freya? Were they still alive? Jonas couldn't just forget about them. He and Dakota would make their way to Janey's house, and hope to find the others on the way. Perhaps he would find them all there. With any luck, Javier would come to his senses, forget all about Janey, and go and look for his brother on his own.

Jonas twisted his feet and hopped up and down, alternating from foot to foot, putting all his body weight on either leg. He wanted to check he wasn't about to crumble. Going back out there meant he was going to have to be able to protect Dakota. If he couldn't even walk, how was he going to do that? Despite the pain reverberating around his body, he felt like he was strong enough. He only had one working arm, but that was all he needed. Dakota could drive, and Jonas suspected that Bishop might have a stash of weapons hidden around the place. Some of the vehicles out there in the compound were military, and he hoped that Bishop might be able to spare something to help them. They were going to need more than luck and faith to catch up with Javier.

There was a mean streak running through Javier's soul, an evil that couldn't see reason, wouldn't let him understand empathy, love, or sacrifice. Jonas knew what he was going to have to do when he caught up with him. Dakota was right. Javier was going to Hell.

CHAPTER FOUR

"I understand," said Bishop, after listening to Jonas and Dakota explain their plan. "I think you need more time to recover, but I can also see why you want to get going so quickly. If that's what you want, then I'm not going to stop you. Lukas and I will join you for the first part of your journey, but I have responsibilities here that I'm not prepared to abandon just yet."

Jonas remembered the garage in Westport and wondered what would have happened if they had arrived there earlier. Would Bishop have even entered their lives? Would he have made a different judgement call? At the time it had appeared to be a horrible crime, that perhaps the men hanging in that garage had been the victims of someone evil. Now Jonas knew that he shouldn't have felt sorry for them. They deserved what they got. Jonas was glad Bishop found them. He was a little unhinged undoubtedly, and the way he talked to his dead wife was unnerving, but his heart was in the right place. Even now, after only just meeting, he was generously offering to help them even further. They finished breakfast and went outside to let the sun warm them up naturally. They all looked at the array of vehicles Bishop had collected.

"Over time I've picked up what I can. Most of them still have gas, and the batteries should be fine. I keep them ticking over when I can spare the time," said Bishop. "Of course, nothing compares to Black Jack. Whatever you need, you can take. I'll travel my own way."

"What about that one?" asked Dakota, pointing to a station wagon. "It's got plenty of space for us, and any provisions we pick up along the way. Once we find Janey we can't guarantee her place will be okay. It could be compromised. If so we're going to need lots of space for her and the kids."

Jonas was pleased that Dakota was finally on board with the whole idea. She had begun talking about meeting Janey and his three nephews. If Dakota did have any doubts, she was hiding them well.

"Nice idea, but it's no good. We need speed, and she wasn't built with that in mind," said Lukas. "We need something with space, and the ability to outgun a pack of zombies. If I'm coming along, I want to be sitting in something with a bit of grunt."

"There," said Jonas. "We might also need something with some power behind it, not to mention strength if we have to batter our way through a horde of those things. How about that?"

Jonas pointed to a black armored van. The truck was unmarked, had a mesh grill at the front, and looked impervious to attack. It would have plenty of space inside and be strong enough to cope with anything they threw at it. Jonas couldn't afford to take any risks now they were on the home straight. It was less than a day's ride to the border and from there only a few more hours to Thunder Bay. He had to make the right decisions from now on. There was no room for error. Javier had a head start on them and that worried him.

"I picked her up in Aurora," said Bishop. "She was sitting there with the keys in, just begging me to take her. Seemed rude not to. This was before I found Black Jack, of course. I thought it would come in useful someday."

"Can I drive?" asked Lukas, flashing Jonas a cheeky smile.

"Actually, yes," replied Jonas, to Lukas's surprise. "I take it you know how to?"

"I know I'm young, but I'm not completely wet behind the ears. I can drive. Never had so much as a parking ticket." Lukas admired the black truck they were about to set off in. "Yeah, that's good. You sure you don't want in, Bishop? I can't see how you can possibly feel safer out on Black Jack when we're in that thing."

Bishop shook his head. "No, thanks. I prefer to be in charge of myself. I trust Black Jack. I'll ride ahead of you when I can; check out what's up ahead. That way, if there is anything, I can double back and let you know."

"Like a scout?" Lukas whistled. "Nice."

"All right then, it's settled," said Bishop. "Let's pack up some gear, and we'll get going. I'm quite sure there's no talking you out of this, is there?"

Jonas looked at Dakota. She didn't need to answer his questioning gaze.

"No. We need to go. Our friends are relying on us. My family is relying on us. We need to hurry."

It didn't take long to pack up what they wanted. Bishop insisted they take some food and water, as he had plenty stored away in the hold of the airplane. Bishop packed up some medical supplies too. Jonas still wasn't feeling great and was prone to dizzy spells, so Bishop threw a variety of pills into a bag for him. There was a question that nobody wanted to ask and seemed to hang in the air, unspoken, uncertain if it wanted to be spoken out loud.

The baby.

Dakota said she felt fine, but Bishop was concerned that at such an early stage in the pregnancy the beating might affect her and might even have terrible consequences. He could do little more than give them support as he knew next to nothing about pregnancy. Having never had children himself, he just hoped nothing was wrong. Dakota seemed fine, but Bishop knew that any problems with the baby she carried might not manifest themselves for a while. He tried asking Annalise for guidance, but she was quiet on the matter. It was as if she couldn't, or wouldn't, help.

When they were ready to go, Bishop opened the rear doors of the armored truck and prepared to load up the supplies. He had given them more than enough. He reckoned they could be in Canada by nightfall if they got lucky and didn't run into any trouble. Problem was that they always ran into trouble. Experience told him that when things seemed easiest, they suddenly got a lot harder than you could possibly imagine.

Jonas joined Bishop. As he picked up a bag, he looked inside the back of the van, expecting to see it empty. "What the hell?" The van had half a dozen sacks in the rear which Bishop began to drag out. As he dropped them onto the ground, they kicked up dust, and Jonas could tell they were heavy.

"I figure there's probably around half a million in each one," said Bishop, as he dragged another sack out.

"Shit, we're rich," said Lukas, as he watched Bishop drag the final sack out of the truck. "And you got us eating canned food? If I'd known you were loaded, Bishop, I would've made you at least take us out for tacos."

Bishop jumped down and saw the surprised faces that were looking back at him. "What? It's not like you can do anything with it anymore. When I run out of things to burn, this will do nicely. If I hadn't kept it in the truck it could've gotten damp. Plus, it's far too heavy to go lugging around the place."

"You realize that you're technically a millionaire, Bishop?" Lukas knelt down beside one of the sacks, and began examining it. "You think they picked this up from a bank?"

"I'd say. The truck was parked up by one when I found her."

Jonas picked up a bag loaded with food and put it in the back of the truck. "Well, you can keep it Bishop. If this world ever comes back to what it was, you'll need it to fix that plane of yours."

Lukas's eyes widened. "Hell, yeah. Then you can fly us down to Miami. I've always wanted to go. Maybe we can get a place by the beach. That would be sweet."

"You can probably put Black Jack out to pasture too," said Jonas, laughing. "Find a nice boy for her, you know? Raise some little Jacks?"

"All right, boys, that's enough. When you've finished dreaming up ways of spending money that isn't even yours, we need to hit the road." Dakota pushed the rear doors closed and looked at Jonas. "Shotgun."

Jonas rolled his eyes in his head. "Damn it. Fine, I'll squeeze in between the two of you. No way am I rolling around in the back of this thing on my own. I want to see where we're going."

Lukas hopped up into the truck and got behind the wheel as Dakota climbed into the passenger seat. Before Jonas could jump up with her, Bishop held onto his arm.

"Hamsikker, take this." Bishop held out a revolver and a cache of bullets. "I've got one myself so it only seems fair you should be armed too. There's a couple more guns in the back of the truck. Just in case, right?"

"Just in case," said Jonas as he tucked the revolver into his pants. Giving him the gun told Jonas that Bishop truly trusted them. It was refreshing to finally meet someone he could trust, even if Bishop was a bit of an oddball. He was wearing another trademark brightly colored shirt, a largely red color decorated with orange flowers. Bishop always seemed to be thinking about the next thing, as if he couldn't just relax and be in the moment. "I'm grateful for your help, Bishop. Truly."

"Don't mention it," said Bishop. "Now get on in there with your wife. We've a long way to go today."

Jonas squeezed in beside Dakota, and got in the middle of the truck so he could talk to Lukas easily. The truck wasn't designed to carry three people, and it was going to be an uncomfortable day.

"Bishop," called out Lukas, "stay safe. We'll see you soon." Lukas closed his door and watched as Bishop jumped up onto Black Jack.

Bishop sheathed his sword, pulled his cape tightly around him, hiding the bright shirt he wore, and then began to ride north at a canter.

Jonas watched Bishop draw ahead of them. "Will be he all right out there, like that?" he asked Lukas.

"Yeah, he'll be fine. I'd bet my life on it. As long as he's got Black Jack with him, he's good." Lukas ground the gears, and then finally pulled off, heading for the nearest road that headed north. They were parked up in a dry, barren field, and at first the going was slow and bumpy.

"Black Jack. I feel like I know that name," said Jonas. "Wasn't that a military horse?"

"Sure was," replied Lukas. "Bishop took great pride in telling me all about her. Apparently Black Jack was present at the funeral of JFK, Hoover, *and* Johnson, and when she went she was buried with full military honors. Bishop told me he found her and named her after the original Black Jack. She's got a fine temperament, and doesn't get spooked easy. Reliable too. Doesn't break down, never complains. I can see why he prefers her to riding in a hot truck."

The truck lurched onto the road, and instantly the ride became smoother. They began to pick up some speed. Bishop was already well ahead of them, but Lukas knew they could take things as they came; there was no need to hurry to catch him. If Bishop wanted to make his presence known, he would.

"So your sister, Janey, she had two kids right?" asked Lukas. If he was going to tag along, he wanted to know what he was heading into.

"Three. All boys. Ritchie, Mike, and Chester," recalled Jonas. He was pleased that he hadn't forgotten their names. Many events of the past few days had been kicked out of his head, but remembering his family was easy. "They're cute as hell. Janey's a good Mom. She's doing it all on her own too. You have no idea how badly I want to see them all again."

"And this place she lives at, it's good? You think it's somewhere…safe?" asked Lukas.

Jonas got the hint. "Yeah, it's a small place, so I'm hoping it's good. Her place is close to the lake, and we should be able to make a go of it. I don't really know you, Lukas, but Dakota tells me you're okay. If this works out, and you want to, you can stay, you know. I get the impression Bishop likes his own space."

Lukas laughed quietly. "You could say that. Look, Hamsikker, the truth is I don't really know what I'm going to do. My life was back in Chicago, so now I guess I'm open to offers. I'll come with you for now. I've nothing else to do, and if there's a chance of a fresh start, then why not?"

Jonas waved his hand, indicating the vast expanse that lay ahead of them, a desert landscape of burning buildings, crashed cars, and dead bodies. "Before all of this, what did you do? Were you married? Kids? You grow up around Chicago?"

"Hamsikker, you leave him be," said Dakota warmly, shooting Jonas a wry smile. "Lukas, don't let my husband pressure you into answering a heap of questions. You focus on driving. Jonas should be resting, not giving you the third degree."

"It's all right, Dakota, I don't mind." Lukas took a deep breath. "Before all of this? I was lost even back then." Lukas smiled at the memory of his previous life. "Teleconferencing, networking, meetings, marketing strategies, matrix strategies for development chart, more meetings, client liaisons, meetings about meetings…" Lukas laughed. "When I think back to it now, it's like a dream. I can't believe how I was so sucked into it. I was raised in Chicago

— well, Highland Park actually. Thought I was going to be the world's best basketball player before I realized I sucked at it. Thankfully my Mom and Dad made me work hard at school, and after I graduated, I landed a job at a telecommunications company. Thought I had hit the big time." Lukas shook his head. "We really lost sight of what we should be doing though, don't you think? I don't miss it slightly. Not the job, the people, or even the money. It was all a waste of time. When the dead rose, we were clueless. We'd lost all sense of ourselves. Nobody knew how to survive, how to really live when the power went off. If it wasn't for Bishop, well, I'd be dead for sure."

"Your parents. Are they..?"

"Gone," said Lukas plainly. "I don't have any family now. I lost my friends too. There's nothing back there for me now."

Jonas knew how painful it was to lose friends. He had lost a lot recently. He'd lost his Mother a long time ago, but the funeral of his Father was still fresh in his mind. Lukas's grief was real, and the tone of his voice told Jonas that it was still too raw to talk about.

"How did you meet Bishop?" asked Jonas.

Lukas swerved the truck around a tanker that had smashed through a fence and come to rest on the side of the road, its rear end still sticking out and partially blocking the way. Checking his mirror, Lukas saw a zombie crawl from its wreckage as they passed. It raised its arms feebly, but was soon disappearing in a cloud of dust as they left it behind.

"That's a long story. At first, when the dead started appearing I stayed in my apartment with my roommate, Powell. We figured it would be best to stay put, and let it all blow over. I kept in touch with my parents, but...Dad got bit on his way home from work. Mum said she was going to look after him as the hospital was closed, and she kept trying to call for help, but none came. I spoke to her before the phones went down, but the last time I spoke to her she said Dad was getting worse. Told me he even bit her when she tried to help him...

"So, anyway, I stayed put, and waited, and waited, and waited, and it just kept getting worse. It wasn't hard figuring out what had happened to my parents. We knew we couldn't stay there forever, so in the end we decided we'd have to get out. Chicago was like a war zone. Thinking back, I don't know how we managed to get as far as we did. We just lived from day to day, trying to get out of the city. It took weeks. Powell almost made it, but…after what I saw, I don't think I want to go back, ever. What people can do to each other amazes me; there are some real sick fucks out there."

Jonas noticed Lukas was gripping the steering wheel tightly. Maybe it wasn't best to talk about this while he was driving. Jonas needed Lukas focused on the road, not distracted by dredging up bad memories.

"So where do we go from here?" Jonas asked. "I mean, I have a rough idea of how to get north, but if we hit a road block, I'm afraid I don't know the area very well."

"If we keep heading this way we're likely to hit Madison, and that is *not* a good thing," said Lukas. "It could be real tricky if we get sucked in. We need to give it a wide berth. Of course, if we head east we're going to hit Chicago or Milwaukee. The whole area is teeming with zombies. There are millions of them, literally. You do *not* want to end up in Chicago, I promise you that."

"We go west, and we're eventually going to run into the Mississippi," said Dakota. "Let's face it, there *is* no easy way to do this. All we can do is keep going north in as straight a line as possible."

"True. I guess if we run into trouble, we deal with it then. Hopefully Bishop will spot it before it spots us."

Jonas noticed that Lukas had visibly relaxed and could hear that the tension had gone from his voice. The mention of trouble up ahead had Jonas thinking again of Javier. He wouldn't worry about detours or running into trouble. He would have gone as fast as he could. He would've taken the easy option and made Quinn or Erik drive. Javier wouldn't put himself in trouble. Jonas knew they had to get to Thunder Bay as fast as possible.

"Stick with it, Lukas. We're on the I90, right? So we go hard and keep our fingers crossed we don't run into any problems. I need to get there, to my sister. We're already way behind him."

"Once we're past Madison, the road should open up a bit. I'm hoping it will be a bit easier then." Lukas drove the truck around another crash, a three vehicle pile-up that had ended badly for all the occupants judging by the amount of bloodstains on the vehicles' windows.

"If we can avoid Minneapolis, I reckon we could make the border by tonight. Why not?" Lukas wound down his window and adjusted his side mirror. He was concerned that if anything began to follow them, he wouldn't be able to see them until it was too late.

"Yeah, why not?" said Jonas. "It's about time lady luck smiled on us for a change." He felt Dakota shift in her seat next to him, and she moaned uncomfortably. "You okay? I can try to move over a bit, but…"

"No, it's fine. I'm just wiped out. I felt fine when we got up earlier. I think I'm not used to the driving. It's like I'm getting motion sickness. I just feel a little queasy."

Dakota wound down her window, too, letting more fresh air into the truck. She pushed her hair behind her ears and turned to Jonas. "I'll be fine."

Jonas could tell she wasn't fine. There was little he could do about their mode of transport, though, and the best he could do was to reassure her and get them to Janey as fast as possible. Once they were there, they could relax. There was no plan after that. Janey was it. He and her boys were all he had. There was the small matter of getting Erik, Quinn, and Freya back from Javier too. He was going to have to rely on a little luck in tracking them down. If Javier changed his mind and took them elsewhere, then Jonas knew he would never find them. After what had happened to Pippa, Jonas wanted desperately to make sure Freya was okay. He knew Dakota felt it too. They were responsible for her, for what had happened; once they had found Janey and her children, Jonas intended to go looking for Javier. He wasn't prepared to abandon his friends again. He owed it to Erik and Quinn to make sure they were okay. He owed it to himself. Jonas couldn't rewind time and change what had happened, but he could try to do something about the future. The next time that he met Javier, he would be ready.

It was a long way to Thunder Bay, and Jonas had plenty of time to think up fantastic ways of killing Javier. They drove in silence for a while, enjoying the peace. No zombies bothered them, and

Lukas drove well, navigating the road with relative ease. It was a short while later that he was forced to stop.

"What's up?" Jonas noticed they were slowing down, and looked at Lukas peering over the wheel.

"Bishop," replied Lukas without taking his eyes off the road ahead.

Bishop suddenly appeared as if from nowhere. He was sat astride Black Jack, casually waiting for the truck to catch up to him. Lukas drew them up carefully and stopped by a blocked culvert. Dirty sludge spilled onto the side of the road, and weeds grew in thick clumps. Bishop drew Black Jack up alongside the open driver's window.

"How's it going in here?" Bishop asked, squinting as he looked ahead into the sunshine. The road disappeared around a bend and then was hidden behind a series of small houses.

Jonas looked around for trouble. Bishop wouldn't have stopped without good cause. It looked as though they were going to pass through a small town, but Jonas could see nothing unusual. There were a few dead bodies in the field beside the road, but dead people were more common sight than the living these days, and they weren't moving.

"Fine, just fine," said Dakota, trying to raise a smile. She had no intention of bringing up how sick she felt.

"What is it?" Jonas knew Bishop hadn't stopped for a chat. Something had made him stop; something that was causing him to look concerned. Jonas hoped he wasn't about to tell them they were going to have to go back.

"I know, Annalise, I know." Bishop drew in a deep breath. "Up ahead. There was some sort of road accident. It's a real pretty mess, folks."

Jonas's heart sank. They were going to have to find a way around. How long would that take? It could cost them hours.

"You'll be able to squeeze past," said Bishop, obviously noticing the look of worry rapidly spreading across Jonas's face. "There's a hole in the wreckage that I reckon you'll be able to get through. As long as there ain't too many of them zombies, you'll be fine. Just stick to the western side of it and aim for the church tower you can see in the distance there."

"Thanks for the heads up," said Lukas. He rolled his neck around his shoulders, and then gripped the wheel, determined not to let anything interfere with the plan. "If there's a way through, I'll find it. If not, I'll make one."

Bishop grunted. "I know, I know."

Jonas saw Bishop look away and mutter something under his breath. It sounded like he was agreeing with something, as if he had someone perched on his shoulder, but besides Black Jack, there was nobody else out there.

"Thing is," said Bishop, "I'm going to have to leave you here. Wasn't my intention to leave you so soon, and I'm real sorry. I know you need to get over the border in a hurry."

"Bishop, I've seen that look on your face before," said Lukas. "Like just before you went out and came back with these two."

Jonas watched as Bishop looked from Lukas, to Dakota, and then finally to him. He felt Bishop's eyes bore into his, and then he understood. Bishop wasn't just leaving them for the sake of it. There was something he had to do. There was someone out there in the town ahead, someone who needed help. Bishop wanted to help someone on their way again.

"Who is it?" Jonas asked. "How many?"

"I'm not sure," said Bishop. "At least one, maybe more. I can't just pass by, though. I have to know. At this point in time, there's no time to sit down and formulate a rescue plan. I'll just do what I can and figure it out as I go. It's real nasty in there." Black Jack snorted, and Bishop calmed her, stroking her black mane. "Once you're past the crash, go straight past the church, and you'll find yourself back on track. Don't get sucked into the town center. It's a mess. Okay?"

"Where are we?" asked Dakota.

"Up ahead that's Janesville," said Bishop. "There's no reason for you to get held up, though. Lukas here will take care of you, right?"

Lukas nodded. "That I will."

"So, we should be okay after we get through Janesville?" Dakota meant it as a statement, but it came out like a question.

"Avoid Minneapolis," said Bishop firmly. "After that, you'll be fine."

All the time they were talking Jonas kept thinking, how was Janey doing? Were Mike, Chester, and Ritchie all okay? Had she stayed at home like she'd promised, waiting for him, or had she given up like he had given up on her all those years ago. Jonas thought of his father, of his mother, and how happy they had been all together. He was pleased his father had died when he did. Janey was better off without him; they all were. Jonas had left Janey once, but he wasn't about to leave her anymore. Bishop was right. Once they were past Minneapolis, they should be fine. The population was more thinned out beyond the city, and as long as they could get through Duluth, there was a good chance he'd see Janey and his three nephews either tonight, or at worst, tomorrow.

"Bishop, what do you need us to do?" asked Jonas.

"I need you to keep moving, Hamsikker." Bishop fixed his gaze on Jonas. "You've a pregnant wife beside you, and a sister who needs you. You don't need to be a part of this. I've done what I can for you. I've got you where you need to be."

"That's just it, Bishop, you haven't." Jonas licked his lips. The sun was streaming in through the window, heating up the cab, and he could understand why Dakota felt sick. Even with the windows down, the air inside was stuffy, and his throat felt dry. He wasn't about to give up on Bishop easily. "We need to get to the border. So until we do, we're in your hands. And if you need to do something here, then we're with you."

"Jonas, I don't know, I think we should keep going," said Dakota. The thought of heading into another diseased town full of the dead was more than Dakota could take. She couldn't do it anymore. Her whole body was telling her to rest, and now Jonas was going to drag her into another fight? "I can't do it. I can't…"

"I'm not asking you to," said Jonas, taking Dakota's hand in his. "You're going to stay in the truck with Lukas, well out of it. I'm not putting you in harm's way again. But if Bishop says someone in that town needs our help, then we can't just leave. *I* can't leave. Remember at my father's funeral? Where would we be now if Erik had driven off? Where would we be now if Bishop had passed by? I have to do this."

Dakota didn't know whether to laugh or cry. She knew it was important to Jonas and he never liked to leave anyone behind. If he could help Bishop, then perhaps Bishop would stick around it a bit longer. It was true that they needed all the help they could get, and the border was still a long way off.

"Go."

She jumped out of the truck, letting Jonas out, and then got back up beside Lukas.

Jonas walked around to Bishop, thinking over in his head what they needed to do.

"Lukas, get my wife somewhere safe. I'm relying on you," said Jonas as he jumped up behind Bishop onto Black Jack.

"The church," said Bishop. "Park up out of sight at the rear of the church. We'll find you there. If we're not back in an hour, get going."

"We're not going anywhere without either of you," said Dakota. "Jonas Hamsikker, you get your ass back in this truck in an hour, or so help me God, I'll come looking for you."

Jonas knew she meant it. "I promise, I'll see you soon," he said. "Love you."

Lukas briefly nodded, and then Jonas watched the truck head on into the town. He trusted Lukas to stick to the plan, and he trusted Bishop when he said there was someone who needed help. But Jonas wasn't sure he trusted his own promise to Dakota. He couldn't afford to mess this up now and resolved to follow Bishop on this one. It was best if Bishop took the lead. Whoever Bishop had come across had better be worth saving. Jonas felt for the revolver Bishop had given him and wished it were an axe. He had always been better with an axe. They proceeded into Janesville, and Jonas steeled himself. He could sense it. He could feel it. There was a fight coming.

He was ready.

CHAPTER FIVE

As they passed the crash site where multiple vehicles had been mangled and abandoned, Jonas could see the convenient hole through which Lukas had driven. The church spire was visible in the distance, and he felt confident that Dakota was safe. Nothing had come crawling out of the wreckage, and the town was quiet. There was a faint murmur in the background, like the humming of electricity, but Jonas couldn't see the source of the noise. They came to a small park with a children's play area fenced off, and they stopped. Bishop dismounted, and Jonas joined him, watching him tie Black Jack to the fence.

"We're on foot from here on. The church is just the other side of this park. It's too dangerous to take Black Jack where we're going." Bishop stroked Black Jack's nose, and the horse responded by nuzzling up against Bishop. "Settle down. We'll be back for you soon."

Jonas looked around. The town was eerily quiet except for that throbbing sound in the back of his head. There was something unnerving about the place, as if it were too quiet. Jonas took his gun out and checked it was loaded. The stores across the road were empty, and the buildings were all bathed in glorious sunlight. So why did he feel so nervous?

"Best not to use that if you can," said Bishop, drawing out his sword. "One shot, and you'll draw the attention of every fucking zombie for miles."

"Well, I've tried asking them to leave politely, but it didn't work. I can't rely on my wit and charm to fight off an army of the dead."

Bishop chuckled and walked across to one of the vehicles that lay at the side of the road. It was some sort of delivery truck, and judging by the blood splattered across its hood and the smashed windshield, the driver had not come out of the crash well. Bishop began pulling at the huge side mirror that hung loosely, twisting and turning the metal until it snapped off. He held it out for Jonas. One side was jagged and sharp, and it would suffice for close hand-to-hand combat.

"This'll do for now. I'm sure we can find you something else, but for now this will have to do."

"What am I supposed to do with this, admire my reflection?" said Jonas taking it, wondering how the hell he was going to kill a zombie with a broken side mirror. No matter what Bishop said, if it came to it, he wouldn't hesitate in using the gun.

"You'll be fine," said Bishop.

Jonas followed him across the road, and they quietly backed up against the wall of a post office. Bishop checked the street ahead and then turned to Jonas.

"Let's go. It's clear."

As they walked down the street with deserted stores on each side it became apparent what had caused the huge crash. The road ahead was blocked completely, and the noise that Jonas had heard earlier grew louder. Soon, he saw exactly what the noise was, and where it was coming from.

A prison bus had come to rest at an intersection, smashing into a second hand clothing store. It had become tangled up with a garbage truck, and evidently whatever had caused the crash had happened quickly. It looked as if all the other vehicles behind had smashed into them, resulting in a huge pile of twisted metal. What had once been cars and trucks had become a magnificent work of art, merging into one, their bodies intermingling, and their scratched paintwork adding a colorful dimension to the scene.

"Jesus," said Jonas as they got closer. Some of the vehicles drivers were still trapped inside, and the humming sound Jonas had heard was the clamor of the dead for freedom, a constant moaning sound that filled the air like a church choir singing a terrible, incessant hymn. As they neared the prison bus, it became apparent that the prisoners were still inside too.

When the prison bus had crashed, it lodged itself firmly into the garbage truck, and there was no way either was ever moving again. Power poles at the intersection had fallen across the bus roof causing the metal to buckle, and yet the front door was ajar. Had the guards not been able to free the prisoners? What had made it crash in the first place? Jonas could only theorize that it had been the dead; that even in this remote town the dead had risen, causing instant death, chaos, and carnage. Inside the bus, the prisoners were still moving, but they were still bound by their chains. Jonas wondered if they were chained to their seats, unsure what the protocol was anymore. Perhaps it depended on the nature of who was being transferred. Dead, rotting, horrible faces leered at them as he and Bishop approached the wreckage. The door to the prison bus was mangled but open wide enough for a man to slip through if he put his mind to it. As Jonas got close to it, the smell hit him.

"Probably a routine transfer that just got caught up in this whole sorry mess," said Bishop, keeping his voice low. "There's a correctional facility over at Oregon. These poor folks were either on their way in or out. Doesn't much matter now, I guess. They got far worse than anything they were facing at Oakhill."

"Why would they bring the bus through here in the middle of homes and shops?" asked Jonas.

"Beats me," replied Bishop. "Could be the shit was hitting the fan, and they made a choice to get off the main road. From the way those men are moving around in there, I'd say they got the shackles off, but not the handcuffs. I'm not in the business of looking too closely at the dead. It's the living I'm interested in."

Jonas grimaced as they passed the door. The stench from inside was foul, worse than anything he had smelt before. It was as if the air's very atoms had succumbed to death, and the putrid smell made his eyes water. The rancid stench permeated his sleeve as he held it over his mouth, and Jonas hurried his feet along. There was nothing he could do for them now.

"We're going to have to go through the store on the corner," announced Bishop. "The only way through the road would be to climb over that car, and I'm not about to risk that."

Jonas saw the car that Bishop was talking about, a dark green Honda with its dead driver still buckled in, thrashing about like a fish on a hook. Climbing over the car would be relatively easy except the sunroof was open, and the zombie could easily reach them. Bishop was right, it was too risky.

"Through here. I think there's another door on the other side, see?"

Jonas followed the direction of Bishop's finger. The coffee shop had large windows, and being on the corner where the two streets met, it did look as if it had another door on the other side. They could slip through and avoid the crash completely.

"After you," said Jonas.

Bishop winked and reached up to the door handle. "I thought you might say that."

Jonas nodded, and Bishop pulled open the door. It was unlocked, and both men slipped inside the shop quickly.

*

As they did so, neither of them noticed one of the prisoners straining at the bus door, leering at them, gnashing its teeth, and pulling furiously at its chains to get out. Having become aware of the presence of the two living men, all of the prisoners had shaken off their lethargy and started trying to free themselves. Fortunately for Jonas and Bishop, but unfortunately for the dead prisoners, the chains held fast, and as the two living men disappeared into the shop, the prisoners began to groan and move around in the bus with more urgency. The one nearest the front tried to escape, and pressed himself up against the door, but with his hands chained together was unable to figure out a way through. Over the months it had spent in confinement, constantly pushing and pulling at the cuffs around its wrists, the zombie had worn away the dead skin on his hands and wrists. The metal handcuffs were no longer rubbing against skin or muscle, but against pure bone, and the cuffs had started cutting into the fragile bone, slowly wearing it down day after day after day. As the dead man strained to get out it kicked its legs and surged forward.

Suddenly it was free.

The bone on its left hand snapped, leaving the dead man with a bloody stump, and a bony, severed hand at its feet. With the handcuffs now dangling free on its right hand, the prisoner swiftly began to force his way through the door. Inch by inch, he managed to press himself through. The other dead prisoners watched on, still locked up in their confined bus, still chained, unable to break free.

*

"Over there. See it?"

Bishop and Jonas were knelt in front of the exit to the coffee shop, a glass door that opened out onto a smaller street, away from the crash. The glass was smeared with handprints and dirt, and the name of the shop was stenciled on it in thick letters. The whole place still had that faint aroma of coffee, and Jonas couldn't help but think of the lazy brunches he used to share with Dakota. Those days were gone, and he missed them. He wished he could offer her more, provide some sort of refuge where she could be safe, but he knew it was still a way off. He just had to get through this and get her to Canada. Once they got to Janey's place, everything would be all right. They could find a sense of normality again, a place they could raise their child. Jonas knew they had to get out of Janesville in one piece before that could happen. He peered through the glass door, looking at what Bishop was pointing out to him, and felt that getting to Thunder Bay was going to take longer than he thought.

"Above the optometrists," said Bishop. "I couldn't ignore it."

"You were right not to," said Jonas, feeling an anxiety growing in his gut. Directly opposite them was an optometrist, and surrounding it there had to be a hundred zombies. They were all crowded around the front, jostling each other for position, clearly trying to find a way in. "How long you think they've been there?"

"Maybe since the crash? All I know is they wouldn't be there if there wasn't something, *someone*, in there that they wanted. The sign hanging out of the window looks old. It's faded around the edges as if it has been in the sun for a long time. Whoever is in there must've been in there a good length of time."

The sign Bishop referred to was a large sheet attached to two upper floor windows. It hung outside, flapping gently in the breeze. In large red letters, it simply read:

HELP

"You see anyone at the windows up there? Any movement? Any sign that whoever is inside is even still alive?"

"No, nothing," replied Bishop.

"Shit." Jonas rubbed his forehead, wishing his headache would go away. "You realize that by going in there we're going to attract the attention of all those dead fuckers. Whoever is up there might not even be alive. We could be wasting our time here, Bishop."

Bishop looked at Jonas. "It's a possibility, I'll give you that. But then when I came across you, I thought you were dead. If I hadn't tried, if I had just moved on, what would have happened to you? You prepared to turn away from this now, after what you've seen? You think a hundred dead folks would still be hammering away at that place if there was nothing inside but a shuffling corpse?"

"Shit," said Jonas again, knowing that Bishop was right. "So, what's the plan?"

"Well, there are two options. One, we cause a diversion. One of us goes out there yelling at the top of their lungs, and runs for it. Take their attention away from that door, so the other can get inside and hopefully pull out whoever is up there."

"Well, I didn't plan on committing suicide today, so what's the other plan? Anyone who goes running out there isn't going to get far. One end of the street is blocked by the crash, and who knows where the other will lead you? For all we know those zombies could be runners. We have one gun each. How many can you take down with them chasing your ass? No, that's not going to work. So, what's plan B?'"

"The other plan? Hmm." Bishop rubbed his chin. "Well, to be honest, I hadn't got that far. I was kind of hoping you would go for plan A."

Jonas sighed. "Shit."

Bishop looked around the coffee shop for inspiration. There was a chalkboard still adorning the wall behind the counter offering breakfast specials and coffee to go. The tables and chairs were a mess with moldy food and dried coffee stains everywhere. The place had been left in a hurry. Perhaps Janesville had been left in a hurry. If they were lucky, the only dead left in town were all crowded around the optometrists over the street. He realized he was asking a lot of Jonas, but now they were here they couldn't give up. He couldn't give up. Annalise would never let him.

"Okay, like you said, they all have their attention on the shop front. I think if we're quiet, we could get over there without them noticing. We could sneak over there, both of us, together. You see the sandwich shop next door? The door's wide open. If we can get in, we can get upstairs and find a way through into the next building to whoever is stuck in there. We could find a fire escape out back, or there might even be a door connecting the two buildings. Often these old places were all connected before they were subdivided into separate stores. What do you say?" asked Bishop. He couldn't see any other way and began to believe it might work.

Jonas checked his gun again. "I say let's do it. I'm not sitting here all day waiting for divine inspiration. Let's get this over with. Before we rush out there like the fools we are, though, how do you plan on getting back out? I doubt we'll avoid all of their attention, which means some of them are likely to follow us into that sandwich place. We won't be able to go back the same way we go in."

Bishop shrugged and smiled. "Something will come up." He put his hand on the door handle, and prepared to run across the street. "You ready?"

Jonas looked at Bishop, and wondered why he trusted the crazy old man. "Shit."

Bishop pulled open the door, and slipped outside onto the street. The humming of the dead filled the air, and he walked quickly. Jonas held his gun with both hands and kept it pointed at the ground as he followed Bishop. He felt terribly exposed and just knew something was going to go wrong. He would trip or Bishop would sneeze, and that would be that. A hundred zombies were ready to eat, and all it would take was the slightest noise to make them notice two living, breathing people were right behind them. Jonas glanced down the street, away from the crowd, and saw the street was relatively empty. A couple of cars and a public bus were parked up as if the occupants were out shopping on just another ordinary day, but otherwise there was nothing. He noticed many of the storefronts were open or smashed in, and he knew they weren't going to find anyone else alive in this place. The town was just one of many that had fallen quickly when the dead rose. Jonas remembered the girl that they had so very nearly rescued a couple of days ago before Javier had effectively killed her. He could feel her fingers touching his, and then he remembered the questioning look on her face before the dead swarmed over her. He wouldn't leave anyone behind like that again. A cold fever swept his body, and he saw that Bishop had made it to the sandwich shop. He was standing inside waiting anxiously for Jonas to catch up.

Jonas heard the sound of breaking glass, followed by a series of bangs, and what sounded like chairs being scraped across a wooden floor. What worried him was that it came from behind him, and as he continued to skip across the street, he glanced over his shoulder. One of the dead prisoners from the bus was emerging from the coffee shop, dragging a broken chair after it, its legs tangled with his.

"You've got to be kidding me," said Jonas. The crowd of zombies also heard the noise, and some of them turned to see what it was. The dead prisoner held no interest for them, but the sight of Jonas running across the street piqued their curiosity, and some began shambling toward him.

Jonas broke into a sprint, desperate to make the open doorway and reach Bishop before the zombies cut him off. If they did that, he would have nowhere to run. Half a dozen began to amble toward him, and as they did so, more of the horde began to realize something was going on. More and more of them began to break off from the swarm and head toward Jonas.

His head pounding, Jonas ran for Bishop, and reached the door just as the first zombie did. As he dove into the sandwich shop, Jonas ducked his head, and Bishop fired his gun twice, dropping two zombies that threatened to grab Jonas's legs.

"Well, they know we're here now," said Bishop, and he dragged Jonas to his feet. "Quickly, through the back. Find a way upstairs."

"Guess I don't need this now." Jonas threw the wing mirror away and scrambled to his feet. He ran for the door marked staff only. He heard Bishop fire once more, and pushed the door open. The doorway led to a small corridor that rapidly opened out to reveal a kitchen and then another door in the far corner.

"This way," shouted Jonas, aware that they didn't have long before the hungry crowd of zombies followed them inside. If they didn't get upstairs and put something solid between them, the zombies were likely to make short work of their skinny bodies.

Bishop swung his sword, taking the head off a young girl, and joined Jonas in the kitchen. "They're coming," Bishop wheezed. A zombie pushed its way through into the kitchen, and Bishop ran his sword through its head, the blade entering through the zombie's gullet, and coming out the back of its skull. The zombie dropped to the floor, and Bishop ran for the exit door where Jonas was stood holding it open.

There was an open door revealing a tiny flight of stairs. The air was cool, musty, and Jonas felt it burn his lungs as he ran upward. The walls were painted a sickly hospital green, only serving to reinforce the feeling they were somewhere cold and horrible. He hoped that Bishop knew what he was doing. As he ran, he could hear the zombies inside the shop. It was clear from the sound of tables and chairs being knocked over and the clatter of pots and pans that they were inside. It was only a matter of time before they found their way to the staircase.

Reaching the upper floor, Jonas turned to his right and almost fell over a large suitcase. It looked like it had burst open, and clothes lay scattered about the room. There was a window on the other side of the room, and it let Jonas see exactly what they were dealing with. The room was quite bare except for a cream-colored sofa in the middle of the room pointed at a large flat-screen TV which was sat on the floor. There were no pictures on the white walls, just a brown beanbag in one corner, and a pile of books in another which were propping up an ironing board. Against the far wall was what passed as a kitchen. There was a small stove, a microwave, and a table piled high with cutlery and plates caked in grease and mold that hadn't been washed in months. Jonas guessed whoever lived here had moved on, evidently not having enough time to take their broken suitcase with them. Despite the light, there was no warmth to the room, and the air was just as cold as in the stairwell. Jonas took a little comfort from the fact that they weren't going to run into any zombies though. He knew from experience that he could usually smell them, and though the air was stale, it was clean. It didn't carry the disgusting aroma that often indicated the dead were around.

As Bishop raced up behind him, Jonas turned to ask him what they should do next. As far as he could see, there was no way into the next building. There was a door he had yet not investigated, but it likely just led to a bedroom. It was wide open, and Jonas could see through the bitter darkness a long shape that was almost certainly a bed.

"Check it out. We don't have long before they figure out where we went," said Bishop. As Jonas went to check out the other room, Bishop ran his fingers over the wooden framework at the top of the stairs. His fingers found small holes at regular intervals, and he frowned. "They've taken the door off." Sighing, Bishop surveyed the small room before him. "Damn open-plan living."

"Nothing," said Jonas, returning to Bishop. "The room's got a bed, a heap of crap, and a small bathroom. There's a square window that opens out onto the street we just came across. It looks like most of those dead fuckers must've followed us in here. The place next door is almost clear."

Bishop nodded, listening to Jonas. "Good."

"*Good*? In case you hadn't noticed, Bishop, we're trapped up here. How is this good?" There was a huge bang downstairs, and Jonas jumped. He pointed his gun at the top of the open stairway. "You'd better come up with a plan B pretty smart, Bishop."

Without saying a word, Bishop left Jonas, and went into the dark bedroom. Jonas kept his gun trained at the stairs and peered down. The door at the bottom was being knocked around, and it was surely only seconds before they found a way to open it. The stairs were narrow, and Jonas figured the dead would only be able to come up one by one. That would give him enough time to pick them off, but once the ammo was gone, they only had Bishop's sword. Would that be enough to kill them all? Jonas began to think he had made a mistake. There probably wasn't even anyone alive next door. They had wasted their time, and he wasn't sure there was any getting out of this.

"In here."

Jonas heard Bishop call to him from the bedroom. He wasn't sure whether to go to him or keep his eyes on the stairs.

"What is it?" yelled Jonas.

There was a splintering sound, like wood cracking and popping on a roaring fire, and at the bottom of the stairway Jonas saw the door burst out of its frame. Suddenly the zombies were through, and their snarling faces looked upward straight at Jonas.

"Oh fu...." Jonas dropped the first zombie, putting a bullet through its brain, but it was instantly followed by more. The dead climbed over each other, pouring forward as they ventured up the stairs.

"Whatever it is, Bishop, you'd better have found a way out of here." Jonas fired again, and another zombie fell, only to be replaced by another. The stairwell was rapidly filling up, and despite the cold air, Jonas felt a bead of sweat dribble down his back. He fired again and then gave up. There was no way he could take them all on, and he turned and ran for the bedroom.

"Ready to go?"

Jonas found Bishop pulling a faded red quilt from the bed, and dragging it over to the window where he placed it carefully over the scruffy carpet, now littered with broken glass. Bishop kicked more broken glass out of the way and beckoned Jonas over.

"It's about six feet across, but I think it'll hold."

Jonas looked through the smashed window and saw what Bishop meant. Beneath the ledge was a small window box fixed to the wall. The sign he had seen earlier was within touching distance and was hanging from a small balcony. They were going to have to jump across.

"Go," said Bishop. "I'll cover you," he said, holding his sword out ready to take down their attackers.

"This is insane," said Jonas, as he climbed out of the window. He placed his feet on the window box, letting it take his weight, and was sure he felt it give a little. He kept his hands firmly on the window-frame. As he looked at the balcony and sized up the situation, he noticed the zombies from below had mostly dispersed. They were funneling into the sandwich shop leaving only a few in the street below.

"Time to go," shouted Bishop.

Jonas heard the unmistakable grunts and groans of the dead, and then something heavy hit the floor in the bedroom. He didn't need Bishop to tell him they were truly trapped now. There was no other way out but to jump for it.

Jonas braced himself, and kept his eyes trained on the balcony rail.

"See you on the other side, Bishop," shouted Jonas. He stretched out his arms and jumped.

CHAPTER SIX

Jonas's fingers caught hold of the cold balcony rail, and he slowly pulled himself up. He expected to find the railing would crumble when he grabbed it or that he would lose his grip, but thankfully he made it, and he pulled himself up and over the rail, collapsing into a heap on the other side. His left arm, where Javier had shot him, was aching tremendously, and Jonas had to concentrate to block out the pain.

"Heads up!"

Bishop's sword suddenly flew at him, and Jonas ducked instinctively. The sword landed with a clatter on the balcony, and Jonas snatched at it before it could roll away and fall down to the street.

Wasting no time, Bishop launched himself into the air, and as he banged into the side of the balcony, the window box gave way. Jonas lunged forward to help him. Bishop grabbed Jonas's arms, and together they got him over the rail to safety.

"Jesus, Bishop, that was a little too close for comfort." Jonas picked himself up, and helped Bishop to his feet, handing him back his sword.

Bishop checked his gun and wiped the sweat from his face. "I've got two left in the chamber, then I'm out. I guess we're not going back for a sandwich. I'm getting hungry. I could really go for some sliced ham and pickle."

"You knock yourself out," said Jonas. "Meanwhile, on planet Earth, you want to look inside this place?" Jonas peered at the glass doors facing him. The apartment appeared to be empty. Nobody had come rushing out to meet them, so if there was someone in there, they were keeping a low profile. Whoever was in there had to have heard the gunfire, so why hadn't they come out? If they did need help, wouldn't they have run shouting and screaming to the balcony? Perhaps whoever was in there was no more alive than the hundred zombies now next door.

Bishop exhaled slowly. "I know, Annalise, I know," he whispered.

Jonas tried the handle, and turned it slowly. The room beyond the glass doors was dark and appeared to be empty, but he didn't want to go rushing in. He had done that in the past and found it was a bad idea. Too many unpleasant surprises could be lurking in dark rooms. "You good?"

Bishop nodded, and Jonas opened the door. He stepped over the threshold, and looked around cautiously, holding his gun out in front of him, ready to shoot. Bishop joined him inside, leaving the frustrated and trapped zombies behind them, clawing at the window box, and filling up the bedroom.

Jonas waved a finger to the left indicating for Bishop to go around the other side of the room. The room was large, another open-plan kitchen-diner, and anything could be hiding behind the furniture. The window on the far side was closed, and wooden blinds kept out most of the light. There were two doors at each side of the room, both closed. Jonas tried to listen for the telltale sounds of the dead, but the only noise he heard were the zombies next door, and the pounding of his own heart.

The two men slowly walked around the room, listening, looking, and waiting for someone to appear. Nobody did.

Upon reaching the other window, Jonas cracked open the blind. He peered down at the alley, hoping to find some way out. All he saw were more of the dead. The alley stretched the length of the street and was full of zombies. They lurched from side to side, festering in the sun, and Jonas knew there was no way out. Even if they could find a fire escape, the alley was so crowded with the dead, there was no route past them. Whoever was or had been trapped in here had been truly stuck. Maybe they ended it all and took a flying leap off the balcony.

"There's no one here." Jonas left the window and joined Bishop at the door on the eastern side of the room.

Bishop looked at Jonas expectantly in the gloom, and Jonas nodded. Both knew they had to check out every room, just in case, and both knew what they had to do.

As Bishop pushed open the door, Jonas stepped inside, his gun raised, always ready. The brightness of the room startled him. The window was wide open, and light streamed in exposing the woman sitting upright on the bed.

"Are you…?"

The solid base of a lampshade suddenly connected with the back of Jonas's head, and he stumbled forward, dazed. Turning to look at his attacker, Jonas saw a tall man step forward from behind the door, and he hit Jonas again, cracking the lampshade across the side of Jonas's head. Jonas dropped the gun, and it fell onto the plush, soft carpet.

"Grab his gun, quick," said the man as he pushed Jonas back toward the bed.

Unable to keep his balance, and with a ringing in his ears blossoming, Jonas felt his legs go from under him. He tried to catch himself, but there was nothing to get hold of, and he fell to the floor. His vision was swirling, and all he could see was the vague shape of the man standing in front of him.

"I wouldn't do that if I were you," said Bishop as he entered the room and pointed the gun at the back of the man's head.

The woman on the bed had her fingers on Jonas's gun, and she was bent over it. She curled her fingers around the gun, preparing to pick it up.

Bishop pressed the gun to the back of the man's head and shoved him forward so the woman could see quite clearly what was about to happen. "Drop it, or your friend's brains will be spread across this room faster than you can say cheese sandwich."

Bishop saw the woman look at the man, her eyes seeking answers about what to do. She looked scared, and not just of Bishop. The way she looked at the man suggested to Bishop that all was not well between these two people.

"I knew you would fuck it up," said the man. "*Why* did I have to get stuck with you?"

The woman looked from the man, to Bishop, to Jonas, and back to the man again. Her fingers were still touching the gun, but her body language showed she was reluctant to pick it up.

"Leave it, Private; they win," said the man.

Jonas picked up his gun and told the woman to go sit on the bed. Bishop instructed the man to go and sit with her. Jonas went to stand beside Bishop, rubbing the back of his head. There was already a small bump forming where the man had hit him with the lamp. He looked around the room at the squalid conditions the couple had been living in. It looked as if they had spent months living in just this room. From the smell, and the look on the two stranger's faces, it hadn't been a pleasurable experience.

"You know, I think we got off on the wrong foot," said Bishop. "How about we start again? My name's Bishop, and this is…"

"I don't give a fuck who you are," said the man, a scowl spreading across his face. "I need you to hand over that gun. You too," he said, looking at Jonas. "I am Sergeant Carlton of the US Army. That is all you need to know. The country is under martial law, and as the most superior serving office in the current whereabouts, I am best equipped to deal with this situation. I need to…"

"You need to calm down," said Bishop. "From where I'm standing, you're sergeant of nothing. You do have a certain amount of influence over your fate, and what happens to you in the next sixty seconds will largely depend on if you can control that mouth of yours. We have a very limited space of time to get out of here, and I don't intend to waste it listening to an idiot like you." Bishop breathed out sharply.

Jonas only then noticed that both the man and woman were dressed in military uniforms. Sergeant Carlton looked angry, and his face grew redder as Bishop spoke to him. The woman looked relieved, if anything, although uncomfortable to be staring down the wrong end of a gun.

"You, what's the deal?" Bishop looked at the woman. "You need help, yes? Was that sign outside just a dumb plan to get a couple of morons like us in here so you could take our guns?"

"No, we do need help. I'm sorry, look…"

"Shut up, Private," said Carlton. "These two men aren't here to rescue us. Wake up. They'll kill me first, rape you, and take what we have. The best you can do is to keep your mouth shut, and wait for this to be over."

Bishop crouched down before the two of them and stared into their eyes. As the room fell into silence, Jonas waited for him to say something, but he continued to stare at them. Sergeant Carlton stared back, clearly unwilling to back down. The woman appeared uneasy and looked up at Jonas. Her long brown hair was tied back in a ponytail, and she had large bags under her eyes. If, as suspected, they had spent the last few months here, she had good reason to be tired. If she had spent it with her sergeant barking orders like that, then she was probably desperate to get out.

"I know, I know. You're right, of course."

Bishop spoke to nobody in particular, and Jonas took a guess that he was having one of those conversations with his imaginary wife. Quite what the two soldiers would make of Bishop, he wasn't sure. The pain going around his head meant Jonas didn't much care, either.

"Private, what's your name?" asked Bishop.

The woman answered smartly, but nervously. Jonas detected just a hint of a Southern accent when she spoke, but it was swallowed up by her trembling voice.

"Private Julie Buri, sir."

"Julie, in thirty seconds, we're leaving. I can see you need help, and I know that sign you put out there was genuine. I'm going to help you folks on your way. None of us want any trouble, do we? So why don't you gather up anything you need to take with you, and go over to my friend, Hamsikker. He'll look after you."

Julie slowly got up and walked over to Jonas. She was tall and quite striking. Her uniform that once clung to her body was now a little loose, especially around the waist, and yet despite her timid manner, she walked with confidence. Jonas noticed that the sergeant's eyes followed her as she walked, though it was hard to work out if he was viewing her with lust or contempt. Her long brown hair was accompanied by large brown eyes, and Jonas wondered if there was more to the relationship with her sergeant than just official. A man and a woman cooped up together like that for months on end could only go one way. Jonas hadn't worked out yet whether it was love or hate.

"I don't have anything to take," she said apologetically, offering Jonas a timid smile. "Just him."

"Sergeant Carlton. I'm going to start over, and I would *really* like you to listen this time," said Bishop. "I like to help people. Truly. You need our help. Every good officer knows when to call for backup, and I'm afraid that we're it. I know you wanted something else. You probably thought the whole of the US Army was going to show up and get you out of here in a Black Hawk. Well, frankly, you *are* the army. You and Julie here are all that's left. I'm more than prepared to help you get out of here. We have a vehicle outside, and we'll get you on your way. But I need to know that I can trust you. If you can follow *my* orders, just for the next few minutes, then you're a free man." Bishop stood up and held out his hand. "What do you say?"

Sergeant Carlton stared at Julie who refused to return his gaze. If he thought he was going to get any backup from her, he was mistaken, and Jonas began to think it must be hate.

"Fine. Whatever. I guess you've got the gun, so what choice do I have?" Carlton took Bishop's hand, and they shook briefly.

"Actually, this is for you," said Bishop, turning the gun around and offering it to Carlton.

Jonas felt the hairs on the back of his neck shiver. "Bishop, I'm not so sure this is a good idea." A minute ago, and Carlton would happily have beaten Jonas to death, and now Bishop was turning his gun over to him? He knew Bishop was a bit off the wall, but this was tantamount to suicide.

Carlton licked his lips, and slowly took the gun from Bishop, an expression of anger on his face rapidly turning to confusion. "But...but..."

"When we get out there, trust me, you're going to need it. There are only two bullets left, so use them wisely. You've more to worry about than me." Bishop drew his sword. "If you do try anything, then my good friend, Hamsikker, will kill you and Julie. Assuming I don't do it first. Do we understand each other?"

"Affirmative," said Carlton checking the chamber. "I appreciate that..."

Bishop waved his hand shutting Carlton up. "Later. Right now, we have to run. Everyone out."

Bishop left the room, followed by Carlton.

"You've been here, with him, this whole time? Must've been fun," said Jonas to Julie.

Julie shrugged. "We went into the other room occasionally, but we figured if we stayed out of there that they might go away eventually. They've been there for…for as long as I can remember. It's just…" Her eyes filled with sadness, and she looked at Jonas. "Never mind. We should go."

She followed Carlton out of the dank bedroom with a perplexed Jonas behind. He wasn't prepared to trust a stranger as easily as Bishop, and couldn't understand how Bishop could do so quite so easily. Jonas wanted to keep an eye on them both, but Carlton especially. Whatever was going on between Julie and Carlton, he wanted no part of it. Bishop could do his thing and get them on their way, wherever the hell that was. All Jonas wanted was to be back on the road to Thunder Bay with Dakota.

"So, what now?" asked Carlton.

They were all stood back on the balcony with the zombies still straining to escape the upstairs window next door.

"That way," said Bishop, pointing down at the street. He straddled the railing. "Down."

Jonas saw half a dozen zombies milling around on the street, but the others had all gone into the sandwich shop. It was crazy, but it was as good a way as anything he could think of. Jonas saw that Bishop had already grabbed a handful of the sheet that hung from the balcony, and was preparing to descend.

"Don't leave me hanging," said Bishop, and then he was gone, abseiling down the side of the building, half climbing and half falling.

"Doesn't waste time does he, your friend?" asked Julie.

"You next," said Jonas, helping her over the railing.

He watched the woman awkwardly clamber down, and then Carlton followed her, waiting until she was on the ground before he started climbing. The sheet wouldn't be able to hold all of them, so they had to take it one by one. Jonas saw that the zombies on the street were already engaged in combat with Bishop, which they were losing. Bishop handled his sword like a pro, and Jonas had to wonder if he didn't have some previous experience. Looking up and down the street, Jonas noticed the dead prisoner from before looking back at him. The zombie's eyes were fixed solely on him. It felt like the dead man was waiting specifically for Jonas to get down to street level. It was like a personal battle of wills, and as Jonas got himself ready to make the descent, he glanced back. The prisoner was still looking back at him, still standing there, staring back, waiting; Jonas knew he was going to have to make his bullets count when he got down there. Jonas said a silent prayer, and then followed them down, eager to get out of town. The sheet was cold to the touch, slippery, and it took barely three seconds to reach the street. As Jonas reached the ground, the knots in the sheet finally perished, and it softly fell at Jonas's feet, exposing the optometrists beneath which Julie and Carlton had been hiding. The moment Jonas's feet touched the ground, he felt someone grab his shoulder, and he whirled around, ready to blow their head off.

"We're fucking surrounded! Where do we go?" shouted Carlton. The man's spit flecked Jonas's face, and he pushed him away.

"Keep it together. There, through the coffee shop." Jonas wiped his face and watched as Carlton grabbed Julie and ran for the other side of the road. Bishop was slicing his way through the zombies, and then Jonas saw what Carlton was talking about. From the very far end of the street more were coming, and the zombies in the sandwich shop were starting to come out too, aware that their prey had circumnavigated a way around them. The crowd down the street disturbed Jonas. Where had they come from? Perhaps they had been drawn by the shooting; perhaps they just knew something was going down: either way, it was time to get out of town.

"Bishop, let's go," shouted Jonas. "We've got to…"

Jonas heard the crashing sound of glass behind him, and then felt huge arms wrap around him like thick tentacles. He elbowed whoever had grabbed him, and tried to get away, but the person behind him had a strong grip. Jonas flung his head back, and his bruised skull connected with soft tissue. He felt something break, and warm blood splattered the back of his neck. The arms around his torso weakened, and Jonas quickly rushed forward, escaping the clutches of whoever was behind him.

In the optometrists, below the room where Julie and Carlton had been holed up, an obese man had been trapped. With the sheet covering the window the man had no reason to go anywhere, with nothing to draw him out. Now, with the street in full view and all the action taking place outside, he had quickly spotted Jonas. The large front window had been no barrier to the man who was easily over two hundred pounds, and he charged through it, running toward Jonas, faster than he had ever run in life.

Staring at the disfigured man, Jonas was sickened. He had broken the man's nose with his head butt, and yet the blood on the zombie's face was not the worst part about him. The fat around the man's gut swung loosely around his body, almost down to his swollen knees, and festering sores covered the man's skin. One side of the man's face had been bitten numerous times, and Jonas could see yellowing teeth through the man's exposed jaw. Shards of glass protruded from the man's face, and one eye had been sliced in half. The creamy, jelly-like eyeball was oozing out, dribbling down the man's jowls. In the zombie's gut, which was so large it could've housed a small family, Jonas saw movement. The intestines moved, and Jonas thought he saw something blink at him, almost like an eye. Confused, Jonas raised his gun to shoot. He swallowed down the bile erupting in his stomach as he watched a rat crawl from the man's gut. Its matted black fur was wet, slimy, and covered in blood and feces. The rat darted down the man's tree-trunk legs to the ground before scampering away back into the shop.

"Runner!" shouted Jonas, thinking that the obese zombie was going to charge after Bishop, but the man was on him in seconds.

"Bishop, I..." uttered Jonas, but he was unable to finish as the huge zombie took him down.

It felt like a bull had charged into him, and Jonas was taken aback by how quickly the man was able to move. They both fell backward, and Jonas slammed into the hard ground, the back of his head smacking into the concrete. All Jonas could see was a shiny blackness, as if he was staring into a vortex. Distant echoes thudded around his head, and bright flashing stars began to jump in front of his eyes.

His assailant had knocked the wind out of him, and Jonas tried calling for help, but was unable to suck in enough air to make any noise except a pathetic wheeze. The obese man was on top of him, and it took all of Jonas's energy to keep his snapping jaws at bay. Black blood spilled from the zombie's throat, dripping over Jonas, smelling of death. The blackness in his head began to clear, and Jonas realized the man was right on top of him, mere inches away, and not going anywhere.

In his peripheral vision, Jonas saw Bishop coming with his sword raised, and knew things were about to get messy. Bishop's sword sliced through the obese man's head, scalping him, and causing the man's body to jerk back. The zombie was so close to Jonas, though, that it was difficult to get a clean strike, and Bishop succeeded in only severing the top half of the zombie's head. Tiny clumps of bloody brain plopped onto Jonas's face from the obese man, and Jonas kept his eyes and mouth shut, avoiding getting any of the man's diseased blood inside him. It was too hard holding the man off, and Jonas could feel his arms trembling as he struggled to fight. The groaning sound of the obese man grew louder, and Jonas knew he was only seconds away from having the man take a chunk out of his neck.

Bishop began to kick at the man, and shoved the hilt of his sword into the dead man's exposed brain. He ground the brain around and around, as if making guacamole in a mortar, turning the lumpy brain tissue into a creamy mush that slopped over the side of the dying zombie's half skull.

The zombie stopped moving, and Jonas finally felt the unbearable weight of the obese zombie slide off him. Bishop's hands grabbed him, helping him up to his feet.

"Move it," said Bishop, thrusting Jonas forward. Broken glass crunched underfoot, and he wiped his face as he blindly followed Bishop.

"You okay?" he heard Bishop ask, and before he could respond, he felt the ground under his feet change. He wiped his eyes, and finally got them open, wiping the blood and gunk from them. He looked around and realized they were back in the coffee shop.

"Is he bit?" asked Carlton.

"No. Now keep your wits about you, this isn't over yet," said Bishop striding to the door on the other side of the shop.

"Look, if he's been bitten, then he's as good as dead. We may as well do him a favor and drop him right here, right now," said Carlton, pointing the gun at Jonas. "I've seen too many of my men go through this. A bite is a death sentence."

"Christ, didn't you hear him, he said he's not bitten," said Julie. "I'm going with Bishop. I can't believe you, Carlton. These guys rescued us, can't you understand that? Get over yourself. Let's just get the fuck out of here while we still can."

The coffee shop door rattled behind Jonas, and he turned to see the dead prisoner forcing his way in. Just as soon as Jonas saw the eyes of the prisoner locked on his, all thoughts he had about Carlton being an asshole were gone. The zombie raised a bloody stump where his hand once was and charged through the door. Still reeling from the obese zombie's attack, Jonas felt for his gun and managed to get it up just in time. He fired, ripping open a hole in the prisoner's shoulder.

I always was better with an axe, he thought as the prisoner barreled into him. Jonas tried to side step out of the way, but his feet became tangled with a chair, and he tripped over, knocking the wind out of himself once more as his stomach rammed into a table. There were more shots as another zombie followed the dead prisoner into the coffee shop, and Jonas knew he didn't have time to get caught up in another fight. Dakota was waiting, and if they stayed any longer in the coffee shop, they were liable to draw a whole army with them. That would make getting out of Janesville *very* difficult. Now was not the time to become embroiled in another fight. Now was the time to hurry the hell out of there.

"Hamsikker, come on." Jonas felt arms pulling him up, and he found Julie dragging him to his feet.

The gunfire stopped, and Jonas saw Bishop holding the exit open. Through the open doorway he could see the street filling with angry zombies; a veritable army of evil all heading in the same direction.

"Thanks. Let's roll." Jonas ran with Julie to the exit, and they turned back to see Carlton stood stock still in the middle of the café. The dead prisoner was at his feet, his head blown apart, and the empty gun hanging limply in Carlton's hands.

"Sergeant, get your ass over here, now," said Bishop. "Can't you see when it's time to leave? Read the room."

"I need to know where we're headed, Bishop." Carlton turned to face the others, his square jaw covered in a slight beard, his eyes fiery and wild. His tone was menacing, and his intentions clear. "Private Buri is under my supervision, and I can't let her just go off with anyone. There is a strict chain of command that needs to be followed, procedures for dealing with the death of any civilian following the discharge of a weapon, protocols that I need to…"

A runner charged into the coffee shop, sprinting unchallenged straight at Carlton so fast he was almost a blur.

"Watch your…" Jonas called, but he was too late. It was impossible to warn the man in time to do anything, and Jonas watched as the zombie suddenly attacked. It sprang toward Carlton fast, and sank its teeth into his neck before anyone could react.

Julie screamed. "Carlton!"

Jonas and Bishop raced to help, dragging the zombie off Carlton who was staggering backwards, his hands feebly trying to stop the blood pouring from his neck. Bishop ran the zombie through with his sword, killing it quickly.

"Carlton?"

As the sergeant collapsed, Jonas put his arm under the man, gently lowering him to the floor. Carlton's eyes were already rolling into the back of his head, and small red bubbles of blood formed between his lips. Jonas put his hands over Carlton's neck, trying to stem the flow of blood that was rapidly leaving the man's body.

"Hamsikker," said Bishop calmly.

"I know. We just need to stop the bleeding. If we can…"

"*Hamsikker*." Bishop put his hand on Jonas's shoulder. "Stop."

Carlton's eyes were closed now, and despite Jonas pushing on his neck, he was slipping away. Jonas knew it, and he hated it. It didn't matter the man was ready to kill him literally minutes ago, he hated seeing someone go like that. They had tried to help, and now Sergeant Carlton was dead. Jonas let him go and stood up. He wiped the warm blood on his pants and looked at Bishop. The zombies were crowding around the café, and there was going to be no time for a dignified burial. They were going to have to skip the pleasantries, too, and move.

"Oh Jesus, this isn't happening," said Julie. "Tell me he's not...he's not going to..."

Bishop put his sharp sword through Carlton's temple, ensuring the man would not get back up again.

"No, he's not." Bishop went to her. "Julie, we have to go."

Julie nodded. "So I'm the last. My division is out there in Janesville somewhere. We were attacked. I thought maybe some of the others had made it out, were still out there coming to rescue us. You don't think we could look, do you? Perhaps..."

"Oh no. Sorry Julie, but I've seen this film," said Jonas. "We get sucked into another rescue mission, only this time we get trapped, and slowly picked off one by one. Well, not this time." Jonas shook his head and opened the exit door. He could see Julie was about to break down. He couldn't afford any more slip ups. They had saved one life, but there was more on the line than the three of them. Janey was at the forefront of his thoughts, and getting to his nephews had never seemed more important. Carlton's death had reminded him how quickly things could turn against you, how events could spiral out of control. What hope did Janey have on her own? Jonas checked the street, noticing the other prisoners were still trapped on the bus. In a few minutes he would be back at the rendezvous, and they could finally get going to Canada.

"Get your shit together. We're outta here."

CHAPTER SEVEN

Bishop found a deserted house for them to sleep in overnight on the edge of Duluth. He seemed to have a good eye for it, picking out somewhere that was untouched by the dead, and clear of zombies. He was always alert. Jonas noticed that little got past him.

They scoured the house from top to bottom, making sure to check every last corner, every pantry, even the outside shed. There was nothing. Three bedrooms upstairs, and a comfortable sofa downstairs for whoever drew the short straw. They all knew it would be Bishop, yet they went through the pretense of talking it out, finally deciding what they already knew: Hamsikker and Dakota would take the master bedroom, Julie and Lukas the other rooms, and Bishop would stay downstairs in the living room on the sofa. He said he would feel better knowing he was able to keep a look out, and Hamsikker was privately relieved. Though he was on the mend, he still felt drained. A night's sleep in a firm bed with Dakota tucked in next to him was just what he needed. The swelling on his head was painful to touch, and every time a barb of pain shot through him he thought of Carlton. Jonas tried to remember that he had been a decent man once and tried to forget the unhinged look in Carlton's eyes when he spoke. Being cooped up inside for weeks or months on end could do that to a man. Jonas chose to remember that the man hadn't deserved to die like that, and that at one point he had been a good man, fighting for his country.

Getting out of Janesville had been a breeze after leaving the coffee shop. They hadn't encountered any other zombies on the way back to the church, and Lukas and Dakota were waiting exactly where they were supposed to be. Bishop had taken Black Jack and disappeared quickly, promising to stop only if he had to. The plan was to meet up again outside of Duluth, the gateway to the north. The truck had been awfully tight with Julie up front, too, but there was no way Jonas was sending anyone to roll around in the back of an armored truck on their own. He tried talking to Julie, but she answered very few questions. Over the next few hours all he managed to get out of her was that she had no family and had joined up after leaving school. She seemed happier talking about Carlton. He was a family man. Born and raised on a small farm in Iowa, Julie told them; he was proud of his two sons, who were on the verge of graduating before the dead appeared. Julie told them how Carlton was adamant the rest of the unit would come back for them, and for a while she harbored the same hopes. After a few weeks trapped above the optometrists, though, it became clear they were on their own, and that's when things got tough. Julie refused to elaborate and asked to be left alone to grieve. Jonas could see she was genuinely upset about Carlton's death and let her be.

Lukas kept them heading north, occasionally asking for directions or checking they were heading the right way. After leaving Janesville, the roads began to clear, and they saw precious little sign of the dead. Occasionally they would come across a crash or a burnt out car, but the zombies were few and far between. It was only as they neared Eau Claire, getting closer to Minneapolis, that the numbers of dead began to rise again. At first they would appear on the roadside or in the fields, and then they began to appear on the road. Lukas hit a couple, but the truck made mincemeat of them, literally, and they kept going with barely a pause. The armored truck had been a wise choice, proving to be an effective battering ram when the dead spilled onto the roads. By the time they stopped for the night, the front grill was full of grisly body parts and splattered with blood.

"Why so many?" asked Dakota as they tried to find a road that avoided any built up areas. "Why here?"

"Minneapolis was hit hard," said Lukas. "I heard they tried to evacuate the city, but like everything else, it turned to shit. The evacuation was a mess. The roads got congested, and when the dead attacked, they had nowhere to go. Almost a million died on day one. After that, the news stopped coming. I guess it didn't take long."

Jonas looked across to the west, trying to see the city. It appeared now and then between gaps in the trees as they drove, but it didn't look like he expected it to. A gray pallor hung over the city, like smog, blocking out the view. Dark clouds gathered around the city, forming in huge clumps for miles in the sky, and frequently Jonas caught sight of a faint orange glow flickering between the tall buildings.

"Containment," said Julie, gazing out of the window. She hadn't spoken for an hour, and Jonas thought she might have gone to sleep. "If the Evac' failed, the next logical step would be containment. Burn the city. Stop the disease getting out."

Dakota leant into Jonas, resting her head on his shoulders. "The sooner we get to Janey, the better. I hate this place."

Jonas had to agree. It seemed like everywhere they looked and everywhere they went they found nothing but death. Was there really nowhere left untouched: San Diego, Dallas or DC? Jonas hoped that perhaps someone had made it, that perhaps there was a pocket of survivors somewhere, but no matter how much he tried to tell himself they weren't the last ones alive, he found it hard to accept. Minneapolis was home to close to four million people. Were they all dead? He couldn't work out how so many had died. The number was so large it was incomprehensible. Surely some had made it out. Lukas had made it out of Chicago, and if he could do it, then so could others. Jonas watched a small orange glow on the horizon spread upward, a burst of flame igniting a building, maybe a gas station or a warehouse of some sort, and then it faded again.

If he truly believed that nobody could survive, then he had to accept the possibility that Janey might not either. Thunder Bay was hardly remote. He preferred to think of it as untouched, perhaps able to escape the touch of death completely, but he knew that was unlikely. If Janey and his three nephews were still alive they would probably have had to fight at some point. The chance of them surviving unscathed was slim, he could accept that, but he also knew that Janey would do whatever it took to keep her children safe. If she said she was going to stay put, she would. It was the not knowing that was eating away at him. Now that Javier was one step ahead, it made getting to Janey all the more serious. Jonas had to hope that Dakota was right. Javier would surely concentrate his efforts on finding his own brother before doing anything else. Even if he did find Janey's place, Erik and Quinn wouldn't let Javier touch her.

Where were they? Quinn was clever, quick, and if there were any chance of getting away from Javier she would take it, although not at the expense of leaving Freya behind. That poor girl had been through so much. Having watched Pippa die, Erik was in no state of mind to look after her. Keeping Freya safe had been difficult enough, but now that her mother was dead, it was an even tougher job. Jonas stroked Dakota's hair as he watched Minneapolis burn. Bringing up a child was going to be a real challenge. It was going to be even harder than fighting the dead. At least Jonas had a lot of practice at that. Killing the dead was something he could do. Bringing up a child was something else. He had no real experience of children, other than Freya, and certainly no idea how to raise a baby. How were they going to cope? He knew Dakota was strong. After all they had been through, she still had faith in him, still had faith in herself; that they could make a go of it. That was why Thunder Bay was so important. It gave them all something to believe in. There was a lot riding on it. Lives were at stake, even those who were yet to be born, and Jonas knew he was only going to get one chance.

Eau Claire slowed them down. The roads were congested, and it took time to find a safe passage around the dead town. By the time they reached Duluth, the sun was long gone, and everyone was tired. The night was just as dangerous as the day, and whilst nobody wanted to say it out loud, they all knew they were going to have to stop.

The house they picked was cold but safe, and they all ate a supper quietly upstairs in darkness. Only faint moonlight lit the room through a large bay window. Once the home of a large family, it was now a temporary refuge for five strangers, brought together through fate and fluke. Julie ate very little and sat on the floor cross-legged. Jonas noticed she would listen to the others talk without joining in the conversation much. She was taking everything in, probably sizing them up before deciding whether she was out of the woods and in the company of people who weren't going to murder her.

Black Jack was tied up out back where she had plenty of long grass to graze on. Bishop made sure she was safe and gave her plenty of water to drink. It had been a long day, taking them several hours to reach the edge of Duluth. Despite the late hour, Jonas had tried to encourage the others to press on. Everyone knew he was worried about Janey, but he also knew it would be futile going on alone or in the dark. Reluctantly, he agreed it was safer to find a bed for the night. Going through Duluth in the dark, across the border at Grand Portage, and then onto Thunder Bay at night, would be impossible. No matter how quiet it seemed, they all knew there were plenty of dangers and zombies out there, and it just wasn't safe to go on. Jonas was drained. The whack on the back of the head that Carlton had given him was still sore, and Dakota was feeling sick again. Lukas had spent all day driving and was exhausted. Jonas was forced to accept they couldn't make it to Thunder Bay that night and reassured himself that Javier was having it no easier. Quinn and Erik wouldn't make it easy for him, and there was no guarantee they had even got this far. They could easily have taken a wrong turn or sucked into a fight warding off the dead. For all Jonas knew, they were ahead of Javier, and would get to Janey first.

"So we set off at first light, right?" asked Lukas. He pulled back the metal ring on a can of apricots and began eating them with greasy fingers. They had emptied the armored truck, bringing all the rations and weapons in with them, just in case. Jonas remembered the warehouse back at Martinsville when they had lost Peter. If they had been better prepared, they could've gotten out of there much easier.

"I know, Annalise, just let it be."

Only Jonas heard Bishop muttering, and again chose to ignore it. As long as Annalise stayed in the man's head there was no harm done.

"May as well," said Dakota. "It's not like I'm going to be sleeping in. It seems like no matter how tired I am, I just can't sleep. I can manage a few hours at best. My back's killing me."

"It'll be better when we get to Janey's. It'll be much better, you'll see," said Jonas. "Her house is real secluded, and right by the lake. If we can keep the area clear we can make it somewhere we can stay long-term. I think knowing you're safe will mean you can sleep without having one eye open."

Dakota snuggled up to Jonas. She was nibbling at a power bar, but it was flavorless and dry. "Tell me their names again?"

Jonas smiled. "There's Mike, Ritchie, and Chester. Man, they're cute. I can't wait to see them. It's been too long. Uncle Hamsikker should've visited way before now. Instead, he waited for the end of the world." Jonas shook his head despondently. "There's a ton of stuff I should've done."

"What about Janey?" asked Dakota. She recalled the plane when Jonas had woken, and in a daze had thought she was Janey. He had said something about leaving her, about something their father had done.

"I owe a lot to her. She's strong, stronger than me. That's why I just *know* she's alive. She's a fighter. She'd do anything to protect her kids. When we were children, we fought like all brothers and sisters, but she always had my back. When I was around nine or ten, this kid tried to bully me at school. Taller, bigger, spottier – anyway, Janey saw him pushing me around and clobbered him. I mean well and truly, she smacked him right in the face. I can still remember Janey's face after she had done it. It was a mixture of pride and fear. I'll never forget it." Jonas laughed. "The kid went home crying to his Mom, said *we* had been picking on him. Of course, we stuck together, said we hadn't even touched him, so nothing came of it. Dad said we did the right thing. He said we should always stand up to bullies. It's a lesson my sister learnt well, but me…well, I guess I didn't quite get the message. Took me a long time to figure that one out."

"Your Mom wasn't around?" asked Lukas, still digging into the canned fruit.

"For a while earlier on. After she passed, though, my father…changed." Jonas shivered. "Is it me, or is it getting cold in here? It's going to be a long night."

"There are plenty of spare blankets up there in the linen closet," said Bishop. "Speaking of which, how are you doing Julie? You need anything else? The bed's all made up, so don't feel like you have to sit around with us morons. If you need to go, just go."

Julie had been listening intently, but saying little. Bishop thought she might be brooding over the death of Carlton. He still hadn't worked out their relationship. Nobody had asked her what she wanted to do. She had gone along with them and showed no commitment to staying or going.

"I'm fine, thanks," replied Julie, yawning. "Maybe I'll turn in. You want me to help take watch? Maybe if I could just get a couple hours sleep first? I'm happy to…"

"No, we've got it covered between us." Bishop had already worked out that he, Lukas, and Jonas would take watch a few hours at a time over the course of the night. Despite the isolation of the house, and the fact it was so quiet, they couldn't take any chances.

"Julie, before you go," said Jonas, "we need to talk."

Julie stood up and raised her eyebrows. "Can it wait? I'm beat."

Bishop couldn't help but smile as he watched Lukas admiring Julie's long legs. He was a young kid and still had natural urges. Still, Bishop knew that if Lukas wanted to get inside Julie's bed, it was going to be a long wait. The woman had showed little interest in anything since being rescued. Often she seemed to sink into her own thoughts, almost forgetting she was in company.

"This will only take a minute. I don't need to know what your deal was with Carlton. I can tell you're a decent person. I would like to know what you're planning on doing tomorrow though. You've heard us talk about Thunder Bay and getting to my family. You know you can join us if you want. We've enough food and water to last us all. You shouldn't feel obligated to come. I understand if you…"

"Canada sounds good to me. I've nothing else. Carlton was all I had."

Bishop noticed she said it as if he were her husband and not her sergeant.

"He was over-zealous, pig-headed, controlling, and paranoid. But if it wasn't for him I'd be dead, I know that. Being stuck with him as we were, we got to know each other well. Days turned into weeks, and weeks into months. We were just about ready to give up, you know? When we heard the shooting, we didn't think it was a rescue. There are people out there, *bad* people, who would kill us just for wearing the uniform. So, I'm sorry for the way things started out between us, but please don't try and tell me I'm a decent person. I get the insinuation. Carlton was an asshole. Maybe he was. But he was also a good man who always tried to do the right thing no matter who he offended in the process."

"I'm sorry," said Jonas standing up. "I wish he were here with us, with you, but…I can't change that now."

Jonas looked at Julie. Her brown eyes softened when he apologized. He supposed it had been a backhanded compliment. Jonas hadn't taken to Carlton, but that didn't mean he was pleased he was dead.

"Look, I have no family, nothing to go back for. If this Thunder Bay place is where you're heading, then I guess I'll come along for the ride. What else am I going to do, right? Until things get put back together, it's all about survival."

Julie said goodnight and then disappeared off to her room. When she was gone, Dakota spoke first.

"*Until things get put back together*? I don't know what that woman's been through, but she's got a shock coming to her if she thinks things are going to go back to the way they were. She needs a reality check. I don't mean to sound horrible, she seems fine, but are you sure about her Jonas? Do we even *want* her along with us?"

Jonas rubbed his eyes. They felt grainy, tired, and all of a sudden he felt like sleeping for a thousand years. The beating Javier had given him meant his body still felt heavy, and the bruising had yet to subside. His head ached, and no amount of sleep was going to cure that. He had to get up in a few hours to take his shift on watch and relieve Bishop, and from Dakota's tone, he could tell she was about to get into it. He couldn't face an inquisition now. "We can hardly kick her out, can we? Her sergeant, her friend, was killed today. She's harmless. In fact, being military, she's probably got some skills that will help us. Let's just help her as best we can for now. We can help her get where she's going."

"Now you're talking my kind of language," said Bishop.

"Trouble is, she doesn't know where she needs to be," said Dakota.

"No matter. We'll help her get there," said Jonas. "Right, Bishop?"

Bishop drew his jacket up to his chin, feeling the cold too. "Right. But don't force it. Things will happen for her. Her head's a mess right now. I'm quite sure Sergeant Carlton would have run a tight ship back there in that place they were shacked up in, and now that's all gone. She's lost everything she knew: the army, her security, the man she loved, and all in one day."

"Loved? What makes you think that?" asked Lukas. "I thought she was a Private. That sort of thing isn't allowed, is it?"

"I don't think the rules apply anymore, Lukas," said Bishop. "If she wanted Carlton dead, she had plenty of opportunity over the last few months. No, she wanted him alive. Now she has to start over, and all she has is us. You, Hamsikker. You're the one leading us now. This is your game. I've got you here, but after Duluth you're in charge. I don't know the land. I can't help you get to Janey."

Jonas felt the weight of responsibility fall upon him, and he accepted it. He was a father now, and it wasn't something he could shirk. He had run away from it in the past, but running away wasn't an option anymore.

"Bishop, I'll relieve you in a few hours; Lukas you can get some sleep and take the last watch. I want us up and out of here by six. We can get started as soon as the sun's up. We'll take the truck and get on the I61. It'll lead us all the way to the border and Thunder Bay. There's no stopping once we get going—not for anything." His comment was aimed at Bishop who he knew would want to stop if he saw any sign that someone needed help. "We don't stop until we get to Thunder Bay. My sister's house is on the edge of the lake on the western edge of town, so we don't need to actually go right through the city center."

"Very good. So long as you have it worked out, I suggest we get some sleep," said Bishop. "I don't know about you, but I can hardly keep my eyes open. These bones are quick to let me know when they've had enough." Bishop stood up and began arranging the blankets spread out over the sofa. "I'll go check on Black Jack and check around outside. Any sign of trouble, I'll get you, don't worry. Have a good evening, folks," Bishop said.

Jonas and Dakota made their way up to their bed for the night.

"So are you going to tell me?" asked Dakota, as she followed Jonas upstairs into their bedroom. The room was cold, but otherwise quite pleasant. The bed was comfortable, and had a thick quilt spread over it that looked almost brand new. Dakota quickly stripped and slipped beneath the covers.

"Tell you what?" asked Jonas as he joined his wife in bed. He figured they had about six hours until dawn, and at least a third of that he was going to have to be up on watch: so much for a good night's sleep.

"What happened to you? Why did you leave home? Don't tell me that you wanted to broaden your horizons. I know you and Erik were tight, so why'd you go? It has something to do with your father, I know that much, but I don't know why you won't tell me. After everything we've been though, we should be able to tell each other anything."

"I know, I know, it's just that after Mom died, things changed. We were happy, but Dad just couldn't cope. It was hard for him. It was hard on all of us. What's the point in dredging up the past anyhow? We should try and get some sleep while we can. You said so yourself, you're not feeling the best."

"Jonas Hamsikker, you are as stubborn as your old man. And stop trying to change the subject. You want to raise our child with secrets between us?"

Jonas sat up, shuffled his pillow around, and lay back down. "No, of course. I just haven't talked about it before. To anyone."

"Okay, so how about I start," said Dakota stroking Jonas's head. "Let me see…when I was in college I smoked pot. Like, a *lot*."

Jonas laughed. "For real? You?" He couldn't picture Dakota getting high. Since he had known her she had never so much as smoked a cigarette.

"See, you don't know everything. Now, your turn."

Jonas thought for a moment, pondering how and where to start. He was struggling to get the image of Dakota sitting around a college dorm smoking. He wasn't used to opening up, not about the serious stuff. "I left town because I couldn't take it anymore. It was never-ending. Nothing changed, and nothing was going to change. The beatings, the arguments, the constant fucking miserable atmosphere that hung around our house; it stopped being a home after Mom passed. Erik stopped coming around. I began to hate myself for letting it happen."

"Your father beat you?" asked Dakota quietly. She continued to stroke Jonas's hair. She could feel his body was tense, that he was struggling with letting it out.

"No, he never laid a finger on me."

Dakota put her head on Jonas's chest. His heart was racing.

"I should've stopped it, said something, done something, anything, but I didn't. Christ, it breaks my heart to remember what Janey went through. I can't explain it. I was a coward. I know that now. Hell, I knew it back then. I was scared of him, same as Janey was, and I guess I thought that if I got involved he would start to take it out on me too. So in the end, I ran away. If I could change things, I would, but I can't. All I can do now is try to make amends with her, try to help her with what's going on now. Nothing's going to stop me feeling guilty about what I did. Or rather, what I didn't do."

Dakota had grown up in a stable family, and had only heard of such things going on in other people's families. It was hard to imagine Jonas going through it. "So your father abused Janey, and nobody picked up on it? Not Erik, no one?"

"No. He made sure of that. I'm glad he's dead. My father was a mean bastard: a mean, lonely, disgusting old man."

"So that's why Janey wasn't at the funeral?" asked Dakota.

"I'm glad she wasn't," said Jonas. "He took everything from her. Nearly destroyed her. I could hear her crying at night.

Sometimes he went into her room when he thought I was asleep. The crying didn't stop though."

"Did he…?"

"I think so."

"Oh, God."

They lay together in silence for a while, and Dakota processed what Jonas had told her. It was obvious now why Jonas was so protective of his sister. He clearly felt responsible for what happened when they were growing up, but it wasn't all on him. Maybe he should've done something about the abuse, but that was easy to say with hindsight. Would she have done anything different?

"I love you, Jonas. I love the fact that I'm having your child. And I'm going to love Janey and her kids too," said Dakota.

"I love you too," said Jonas. "I love Janey, but I hate myself for what she went through." He felt relieved that Dakota knew the full picture now; the history of what his sister had gone through.

"What's past is past. In a few hours, we'll be over the border, then we'll find Janey, and Mike, and Ritchie, and Chester, and then we'll find somewhere safe to raise this child of ours. Okay?"

"Okay," agreed Jonas. He felt more awake now than he had all day. He always knew deep down that Dakota would understand, but admitting everything out loud, actually talking about it, hadn't been easy. "Let's get some sleep. Sun'll be up soon."

Dakota kissed her husband. "You're too tense to sleep," she whispered in his ear. Peeling back the covers, Dakota climbed on top of her husband. "Let me help you sleep," she said, and she slowly began to descend his body, kissing him all over.

As they made love for the first time in months, it felt like they were a couple again. So much had happened recently that they had almost been driven apart. Now Jonas felt as if he was making love to Dakota for the first time. It was as if they were lovers, still relishing in each other's bodies, instead of a couple who had been married for years. Jonas also felt relief that they could connect again. He loved Dakota so much that he knew she was right. Finally, in just a few hours, they would be in Thunder Bay. He would be reunited with Janey and his nephews, and he would raise his son or daughter with Dakota by his side.

Jonas eventually drifted off to sleep, satisfied that finally things were going well, and confident that everything was going to be all right. It was all going to be over soon.

CHAPTER EIGHT

The sun had barely risen above the horizon, but he was ready to go. He enjoyed the crisp mornings, and up here, further away from the fires and the dead, there was something special, almost magical. Bishop sucked in the cool air. It was so fresh, so devoid of pollutants, that it almost made him dizzy. Not only did it tell him that there were no dead close by, but that the others were going to make it.

"I know, Annalise. It's time." When he spoke his breath hung in the air, briefly forming small clouds that dissolved in front of his face. "They'll be fine."

Bishop's husky voice cut through the air, and he pulled his jacket tight. He had enough provisions loaded to see him through the day. He could ride faster if he wasn't laden down, and he needed to get back to base. He didn't like to leave things unattended for too long. He stared out at Duluth, for once the quietness of the city reassuring instead of unsettling. There was an aura of calmness about it, as if Duluth was taking care of itself now, able to breathe, free of traffic and people. Bishop could see that the Lake was close, and he felt good about what lay ahead for all of them. The few people that had lived in Duluth were gone. He could feel it. The city felt hollow, empty. Whether they had left on their own feet, or been carried out on the back of a truck in a pile of corpses, the people had gone. Hamsikker would get them to Grand Portage and across the border. From there the road to Thunder Bay should be relatively clear. There were no major population centers then until they got to Thunder Bay. Bishop had done what he could. He almost wanted to whoop with delight.

Sometimes things went bad, like yesterday when they had lost Carlton. Sometimes he helped people, one way or another, and sometimes he couldn't. Today was a good day. He knew he had helped as much as he could, but now it was someone else's turn to take control. Annalise had told him as much, and he had to admit she was right, as usual. It was time to go.

Bishop turned back to face the house where the others were sleeping, or waking, or at that place just in between where dreams blurred with reality. He grinned at Lukas.

"It's good to be alive, son. Don't ever forget that."

"Sure is," replied Lukas, a little confused, still rubbing the sleep from his eyes. He couldn't help but admire Bishop's outlook. He was always positive, always looking for survivors, always dressing himself in colorful, flamboyant clothes as if he didn't have a care in the world. Bishop was practical, too, knew how to handle himself, and had lived out on his own for far longer than he should have. Lukas got the impression there could be a nuclear holocaust, and Bishop would be the last man standing. Lukas saw that Bishop was fully dressed, and Black Jack was stomping his feet on the ground impatiently. When had Bishop brought him around from back? Black Jack's saddlebag was already loaded, and then it dawned on him. Bishop was leaving.

"You know, you don't have to go back," said Lukas. "These guys could use your help. At least let me wake them so they can say goodbye."

Bishop pouted, and sighed. "Never did like goodbyes, Lukas. I know what you think, that I should see this through, but it's just not my style. They don't need me for what they're doing any more than you do now. There are plenty more people who could use my help, and I think Hamsikker and Dakota know what they're doing. I've got you to Duluth. I've done my part. Besides, they've got you and Julie for company. Catch and release, Lukas, you know how I work."

Lukas watched Bishop jump up onto Black Jack, who snorted and bridled with eagerness as Bishop patted the side of her head. Lukas was going to miss being around the both of them. He also knew that Bishop wouldn't be persuaded to stay. He had been around him long enough to know that he did as he liked—or as Annalise liked.

"You take care of yourself. And don't ride Black Jack too hard. She had a long day yesterday. It's a long way back, you know." Lukas patted Black Jack, then reached up and gave Bishop a handshake. "Not everyone around these parts is friendly."

"Don't worry. I've got my ladies. Annalise and Black Jack will take care of me. I've been here a while looking at Duluth. I think you're in the clear. I reckon once you get to the other side of the city, past the harbor, you folks have got an open run to the border. You should take every opportunity you can." Bishop patted his pockets and frowned. "Damn. Say, would you mind grabbing my canteen? I left it inside. Try in the dining room. I think that's where it'll be."

"Yeah, hold on." Lukas jogged back to the house in his bare feet. It was still early, and a fine dew covered the grass that flanked the crooked path up to the front door. Lukas quietly entered the house, not wanting to make any noise that would wake the others. Bishop was right about that, they needed their rest. They would be up soon enough. He also knew that if he tried to wake the others to say goodbye, Bishop would not thank him. By the time he had roused everyone, Bishop would probably have hightailed it out of town anyway.

Lukas checked the living room, just in case the canteen was there where Bishop had spent the night. The table was just as they had left it, still set for dinner by the occupants of the house, and the room was exactly as it was when they had come to it yesterday. He wandered into the dining room. He searched the room, scanning the floor, the chairs, every corner and bookshelf, but he was unable to find it anywhere. Maybe Bishop was mistaken, and he had left it upstairs. He hadn't spent long up there, but it might have fallen from his bag without him realizing. Lukas was going to have to either go upstairs to check, and risk waking the others, or explain to Bishop that he couldn't find it. He decided it would be better to go out with something, and grabbed a bottle of water from their supplies. He quickly slipped on his sneakers, and then trotted back out of the house. When Lukas reached the front gate, he could feel something was wrong. He rounded the corner, and instead of finding Bishop there waiting for him, he found himself looking at the armored truck. There was no sign of Bishop.

"Bishop?" Lukas looked down the street, confused. Seeing nothing, he turned around, and went across the road to check the other side of the house. There, in the distance, he saw them. Black Jack was trotting down the street, and Bishop sat astride her as if they didn't have a care in the world. Just as Lukas was about to call out to him, Bishop turned the horse around, raised his hand in the air, and waved. Lukas thought he saw the man smile, but he was too far to make out clearly, and so Lukas just raised his hand and waved back.

"Catch and release, huh?" said Lukas. He realized then that the search for the canteen had just been a ruse. He could be angry with Bishop, could be annoyed with him, could even chase after him, but ultimately Bishop was his own man, and there was nothing wrong with that. Lukas took it as a sign of respect that Bishop didn't want to say goodbye to him.

"See you around." Lukas returned to the house. A wry smile crept across his face as he walked up the garden path. If it wasn't for Bishop, he would be dead, there was no doubt about it. Now that Bishop was gone, he felt excited. He was sad that Bishop was gone, and scared too. He worried about what the future held, but he was happy too. It was as if he had been released, as though Bishop had set him free. Lukas had learnt a lot from Bishop about survival and intended to use his knowledge as best he could to help Hamsikker and Dakota.

Back inside the house, he slumped down on the sofa, opened the mineral water, and drank. Bishop was gone. They were on their own now. It was an odd sensation. Lukas was sad he had lost his friend, but knew the future ahead was promising. If they could make it to Thunder Bay, they had a chance to start again. Doubt pinched him as he thought about where he might be later. Would Hamsikker and Dakota even want him around? It was Bishop who had led them here, so perhaps they would want Lukas to go too. Would they cut him and Julie free? He had been with a couple before. When he was in Chicago he had only survived by working with a young couple he had been trapped with. It hadn't worked out so well for them. Maybe Hamsikker and Dakota would be better off alone, but where would he go? Lukas didn't know the area, and had no real plans of his own. The idea of getting to Thunder Bay had crept into his head, drawn him in, and now it was all he thought about. Lukas kept drinking the water, thinking about what he was going to say, what they needed to do, and how they were going to get out of Duluth. He was so lost in his thoughts that he didn't even notice as Jonas came down the stairs and crept up behind him.

"Morning sunshine," said a smiling Jonas as Lukas leapt out of his seat.

"Jesus Christ, you nearly gave me a heart attack." Lukas looked at Jonas with his eyes wide, and water spilt down his shirt. "Hamsikker, you do that again I'm liable to take your head off."

Jonas chuckled. "Sorry, I couldn't resist. I promise not to do it again. Today."

Lukas smiled, and offered Jonas the water. He could see Dakota in the dining room and heard the clatter of pots and pans.

"Breakfast?" asked Jonas. "Not sure what's on the menu, but we can make it work as long as you like it cold."

"Yeah, I'm starving." Lukas hadn't even realized how hungry he was until Jonas had mentioned food. Now he could feel his stomach turning over, and they walked together through to the kitchen.

"Is Bishop outside? Black Jack's okay, right?" asked Jonas. "We should get him in here so we can plan how to best get to Grand Portage. Janey's…"

Jonas knew from looking at Lukas's face that something was amiss. He helped Dakota spread some tinned tuna and cherry tomatoes on a plate, and then pulled out a chair to sit down.

Lukas said nothing, and sat down at the table opposite Jonas. He emptied the bottled water into three glasses, and waited for Dakota to join them. When she sat down, pushing three plates of food in front of them, Lukas opened his mouth to speak.

"He's gone, hasn't he?" Jonas knew the answer to his question, but he wanted to hear it from Lukas.

"Yeah," said Lukas quietly. The doubts were back, and bigger than ever. He felt responsible for bringing them bad news, and hoped they wouldn't hold it against him. They might be angry with him for not waking them up, or they might throw him out, preferring to be on their own. He steeled himself, preparing for the cross-examination.

"Lukas, there's more tuna if you're hungry," said Dakota. "We've still a couple of cans left, so don't hold back. Then again, I don't know for sure when we're next going to eat, so you may as well get a good feed now."

"Well, I wish we'd had the chance to say thank you, but I guess he has his own life to live," said Jonas. "I knew it would come eventually, I was just hoping he would come with us to Canada. I guess I was just ignoring it; pretending it wouldn't happen."

"More tea, vicar?" asked Dakota, as she poured more water into Jonas's glass.

"He'll be all right, you know," said Lukas, relieved that he wasn't being interrogated as to why Bishop had gone or where.

"Oh, I don't doubt that," said Dakota. "I'll miss him, but we've still got you, right?" Suddenly a look of panic spread across Dakota's face. "I mean, you're not leaving too, are you? You're coming with us, right, Lukas?"

Lukas opened his mouth, unsure of how to answer. "I...I thought..." He hesitated, unsure if they really wanted him along on their journey.

"Course he is," said Jonas. "You're not going anywhere, young man."

"Any chance of a coffee?" asked Julie as she entered the room.

"Sorry, Private, not unless you take it cold and dry," replied Jonas. Julie looked tired, and he wondered if she had slept much. Her long hair was a tangled mess and her skin pale. He could also tell that Lukas was attracted to her, and he noticed how Lukas's eyes followed her around the room when she walked. She had to be a good few years older than him, and Jonas suspected Lukas had no chance with her.

Julie pulled up a chair, and the four of them ate, discussing Bishop, and how they might get to the border. Lukas relayed what Bishop had told him, that Duluth appeared to be clear of the dead, and they agreed to take the truck as far as they could. Jonas didn't press Julie for more information, and she never offered any. She said she would go with them, and that was that. Jonas could see that Lukas was more than happy with Julie's decision, but Dakota seemed less so.

"Julie, you mind helping Lukas get the truck ready? I think we should get going." Jonas was exhilarated. They were so close now. He put his dirty dishes in the sink, and stared out of the window. It was streaked with dirt, but through the grime, Jonas could see the future. Stretching toward Canada, the light blue sky had never looked so clear. Beads of dew on the grass sparkled like diamonds in the beautiful early sunlight, and Jonas watched as a lone bird flew high in the sky above. The air up here was so fresh, so pure, so brittle and cold, that Jonas almost wished they could stay. He knew that it was a false sense of security though. It would be cold enough to snow soon, and they knew nothing of the area. At least Janey would know more about how to survive the winter at Thunder Bay. They had to keep going. So Bishop was gone. Good luck to him. He had helped keep them all alive, and now it was up to Jonas. There was no going back, no more alternatives. Just one thing left to do. Everything he wanted lay right ahead of him, and in just a few hours it would all be over. "Lukas, you happy to drive again?"

"Aye, aye, captain." Lukas grabbed up a bottle of water. "Come on, Julie, let's get this sorted. Five minutes, Hamsikker?"

Jonas nodded and watched Lukas leave the room with Julie. Dakota waited for them to leave, and then joined her husband at the sink, putting an arm around his shoulder. "You okay? You're not going all quiet on me now, are you?" Dakota tried to catch Jonas's eyes, but he was looking outside, lost in his own thoughts. "I can tell something's eating away at you."

"I'm just thinking about what's going to happen. What we might find." Jonas didn't want to admit it, but as much as he wanted to find Janey, as much as he was so desperately looking forward to seeing her again, there was a part of him that was terrified. What if he had dragged Dakota half way across the country for nothing? What if Thunder Bay turned out to be another Janesville or worse?

"You're worried about your sister, that's fair enough, but there's nothing you can do about it now. What will be, will be. If she's survived this long, another few hours isn't going to make any difference."

"That's just the problem," said Jonas. "That's exactly what I'm worried about." Unable to let it stew inside anymore, Jonas let his emotions out, his thoughts and fears coming out in a torrent. "What if Javier found her? What if I'm too late? She might have been safe, probably was, and I led Javier right to her. I was supposed to be there for her. I'm her brother, I'm supposed to look after her, but I'm too late. He had a head start on us. He'll be there by now. If he's harmed her children, if he's so much as threatened them..."

"Jonas, you don't know what's happened with Javier. For all you know a big ass zombie took a chunk out of him, and right now he's in a ditch with a bullet in his head."

"Or maybe he's terrorizing my family, having fun tormenting Janey. For all I know he's killed Quinn and Erik and Freya, and..." Jonas threw his hands up in the air. "Not knowing is killing me. I know that today, whatever happens, we *will* get to Thunder Bay. I'm going to get us both to Janey's house."

"Not just us, remember. We have a couple of strays with us now."

Jonas turned away for the window and looked at Dakota. "They seem like good people. They certainly don't pose any threat to us. Are you okay with them? If not, you need to tell me now."

Dakota pushed her hair behind her ears. "Lukas is fine. *More* than fine, even. I just..."

Jonas knew Dakota was worried about Julie. "Look, I know she's a bit of an unknown quantity, but we can't just leave her, can we? And she said she wants to come along, so what choice do we have? You want to give her a bottle of water and send her off on her own? She's got nothing. The only person she knew died yesterday."

"You're right, I know. I guess I don't know her well enough to judge." Dakota shrugged and put her hands on her belly. "But we'll get to know her. Things will work out, you'll see."

Jonas leant in to kiss Dakota, but as he did so, she recoiled.

"What's wrong?"

"I just…I feel a little off this morning. I think the baby isn't fond of tuna. Oh, shit…"

Dakota bolted out of the room, and as Jonas contemplated following her, he heard Dakota throwing up in the bathroom.

"Hamsikker, we're all set," said Lukas, suddenly reappearing in the doorway. "It looks fine out. You two good to go?"

"Thanks, Lukas. Just give us a moment will you? We'll see you out front." Jonas watched Lukas go and then went to find Dakota. He had to make sure she was up to the journey. Sometimes he almost forgot she was pregnant. He hoped the strain wasn't too much. It wasn't easy for any of them, but being pregnant was putting Dakota under even more pressure. Until they got to Janey's there was little he could do for her. Jonas hoped Dakota could just hold it together until they got over the border. Once they reached Thunder Bay, everything would be fine.

It had to be.

CHAPTER NINE

"Pipe down," said Javier as he tightened the binds around Quinn's wrists. He yanked them hard, ensuring there was no way out.

"You're like a loaded gun," said Quinn. "You're always on edge, always sleeping with one eye open, just in case someone slits your throat in the middle of the night. How do you live like that? How can you even operate when you're so tightly wound up? What happened, Mommy didn't love you enough?"

Javier grinned. Quinn's hands and feet were tied, but he resisted the urge to gag her. She obviously had something to say, and he was keen to hear it. Erik was quiet to the point of morose. Losing Pippa had hit him hard; not that Javier cared much.

"My Mom didn't make me who I am. *I* did. I learnt how to survive the hard way. Being nice gets you nowhere in this world. How can you live the way you do? The way you did?" He looked at Freya, sleeping in the corner. "Playing happy families? Birthday parties where everyone is nice to each other, even though half of the guys are fucking their neighbor's wife, and the women can't wait to get home so they can resume drinking and watching some mind-numbingly retarded reality show on TV? Pretending that anyone in power actually cares about you? Pretending that you like brunch, saving up for the family saloon, taking your parents a bunch of Christmas presents that they're only going to give away as soon as you've left? Please." Javier leant closer to Quinn. He could see she was on edge, itching to smack him in the face. "I've got the whole fucking world in the palm of my hand. I can do whatever the hell I want. Now *that* is freedom. Why would I want to change that? You should try it. Why do you care what happens to Erik? You think if he had to make a choice between you and

Freya, he wouldn't let you die in a heartbeat? There's only one way to get by now Quinn, and that's to look out for numero uno. But..." Javier sighed. "Forget it. You don't get it, do you? I can tell from the look on your face. You've been sucked in just like everyone else. Mortgage up, vote Republican, vote Democrat, text in for us to hear your opinion, sign up to a lifetime contract for a free coffee, and let us shit all over you. Until you wake up, you may as well be dead."

Quinn let a healthy pause build up. She watched Javier sit back triumphantly, as if he had won her over, defeated her like no doubt he had defeated so many other people. He was so used to getting his own way that he never considered that someone else might want to counteract him. "You done?" she asked.

"This the part where you tell me that I'm wrong, Quinn? This is where you tell me how wonderful it is having a nice home, complete with in-home surround sound music system, high-speed broadband, and Egyptian cotton sheets? This is where you tell me I'm wrong, that until you've had a child, made a life-long friend, or achieved that promotion giving you an extra five grand a year, even though you have to work sixty hours a week to get it, that I've missed out? Come on. I've heard it all before. It was bullshit then, and it's even more bullshit now."

Quinn burst out laughing. "I'm sorry, that wasn't...look, Javier, I'm sure you've given that speech a few times in your life. Who knows, maybe it impressed a few girls back in the day and got you laid. The whole nihilistic attitude, this anti-hero thing you've got going on - you're wasting your time with me. Don't misunderstand me. You are wrong, so *totally* wrong it's not funny really. Families and friendships, love, having a nice home – actually they are wonderful things. But it's not something I truly got to experience before all this. I was married to a decent guy, but we got caught up in some trouble. I've had my brushes with the law too. I wish I could tell you that BBQ's with your neighbors and taking your kids to school for the first time is an experience you'll never forget, but I didn't get that chance. Roger didn't want kids. I kept telling myself we would do one last job, and when we got out he would settle down. I think we could've made a go of it, too. He was a good man deep down. Unfortunately, our last job was his last job."

Javier listened to Quinn. He had nothing else to do but wait while Erik checked the place out, and Quinn was proving to be far more interesting than he had given her credit for. She didn't shy away from him like most women he met. In another time, when he was younger, he had screwed a black girl, on and off, for a few months. She had carried herself with a certain attitude, a bravado that Quinn had too. Still, he had no intention of screwing Quinn. Once they made it to Canada, she was dead meat. Until then, she was a good ride purely in the platonic sense. He let her go on, listening to her speak.

"He murdered both my parents. I had to kill him. I didn't even fully realize what was happening. I certainly had no idea he was, you know, a zombie. I thought he had freaked out, took some bad shit or something. Anyway, the day it happened, I woke up with a serious hangover. I go downstairs, and I find Roger standing over the bodies of my parents. He'd slaughtered them with his bare hands. When I found him, he had my Mother's tongue in his hands and her spleen in his mouth. My Father was...unrecognizable. At first I thought it was all pretend. I thought they were all going to burst into laughter and let me in on the joke, but, of course, my parents weren't getting up anymore."

"What happened to Roger?" asked Javier.

"He came at me, of course, but I've been in situations before when I've had to be quick on my feet, so it wasn't difficult getting past him. I ran into the kitchen, grabbed the first thing I saw. We had a whole drawer full of knives, but no, I grabbed the toaster. I beat him around the head with it. I beat him as hard as I could. He slowed down, but no matter how much I pushed him back, he wouldn't quit. Finally I got him pinned down beneath me, and I kept on at him. I think by the end, the toaster had broken up into tiny pieces, and I was just bashing his head in with my own hands. I lost everything that day. I still don't know if I love my husband or hate him for what he did. I keep telling myself it wasn't his fault, that he was unlucky to get bitten, that it could've been me; yet if it had been me, would things have gone any differently? Perhaps Roger would be sat here now talking to you instead of me.

If he was, I'm quite sure he would know what to say to a monster like you. The guys we worked with could be assholes, but they knew where the line was. You don't even have a line. You should have been locked up in a psych ward a long time ago, but somehow you slipped through the net. Now you have this fucking God complex going on, and you think the whole world is at your beck and call. I used to be confident, so sure that we were invincible, that with Roger I could do anything. That's what will get you in the end, Javier. That arrogance that you think is so charming, so self-assuring, that one day you'll forget something. Something so small and insignificant that you won't even know it until you're lying dead in a gutter, wondering just how the hell you got there."

"Oh, I'll know how I got there. You and Erik. You're going to help me get to Thunder Bay. The rest is my own business."

"So what's the plan, genius? We somehow magically find your brother, and then what? We drive around killing anyone that isn't Diego?" asked Quinn.

"That's not bad," replied Javier. "However, we don't have an unlimited supply of bullets, so we'll take it one step at a time. First of all, you're going to get us to Canada. There's no need for any more digressions or distractions. After tonight, we carry on up to the border. You don't need to worry about what comes after that," said Javier. "We get over the border, and you get me to Thunder Bay. I can take it from there."

"Oh, *you* can take it from there. Yes, sir, sorry, I see now. So, what, when we get to Thunder Bay you're just going to let us go? Maybe me, Erik, and Freya can live in blissful happiness while you go looking for your brother." Quinn feigned shock and gasped. "Maybe, and this is just me putting it out there, but maybe you can *kiss my black ass*."

Javier looked at Quinn. "Funny. You know, I don't need two drivers, so keep it up. I'm sure Erik has plenty of experience of driving. I guess it's a bit much to expect the girl to be of much use. Y*et*."

Javier looked at Freya who was sitting in the office swivel chair, twirling a key chain around and around.

"You touch her, I'll cut your balls off and shove them down your throat," said Quinn.

Javier jammed his gun into Quinn's side, causing her to wince in pain, and draw in a sharp breath. "Just you remember who's in charge, Quinn. You're only breathing because I let you. Remember that. Your smart mouth amuses me, but don't forget that it's *me* who gives out the orders around here."

"Okay, okay, I got it." Quinn rubbed her side where Javier had jabbed her. "You know, I can't wait until Hamsikker catches up with us. He's going to kill you for what you've done."

"Hamsikker? Please. He's dead."

"Really? He's resilient. You know for a fact he's dead?" asked Quinn.

"Last I remember he and that cunt of a wife of his were surrounded by a bunch of zombies. I'm quite sure there's nothing left of them but a pile of bones."

"Maybe, so." Quinn knew it was unlikely Hamsikker was still alive, but she held onto a faint belief that somehow he would make it. The thought of him and Dakota being eaten alive was horrifying. If one of them had woken up, there was a chance wasn't there?

"Say you're right, Quinn. Say that somehow, miraculously, they survived. So what? They won't find me. They won't find you."

"Maybe," said Quinn again. She could see she had at least made Javier think about the possibility he wasn't completely free yet.

"Fine, so what if Hamsikker made it? What if he's out there still intent on finding his sister? You think I'm going to make it easy for him?" Javier leered at Quinn. "Maybe I should leave him a message just in case he's right behind us. Hmm? Perhaps we should think of something we can all do together that would slow him down? We could scare him off. Perhaps start by sticking your head on a spike on the road to the border. Think he'd like that?"

Quinn shuddered. "Do what you like. I'm not helping you lay some stupid trap for Hamsikker. He's probably dead anyway. I'm not doing your dirty work for you. You're a parasite, Javier. You're not worth me wasting any more of my time on."

Quinn reminded Javier of Rose. Sometimes Rose would find some anger in her, too; a fiery hidden piece of her that would rise up out of nowhere. It usually didn't last long. Javier pointed his gun meaningfully at Quinn.

Quinn's brown eyes stayed locked with Javier's. "Shoot me." Quinn looked at Freya and wondered if she had any concept of how much danger they were in. Erik was doing a check of the building, making sure they were safe and secure for the night, but he was unarmed. She knew the chances of him finding a gun were small, and even if he did, she doubted he would do anything with it. While Javier held his daughter, Erik wouldn't risk anything. Right now, they had little option but to go along with Javier's insane plan.

"Not today," said Javier. He approached Freya who had been spinning a chair around while she waited for Erik to return. Javier put his hand on the chair and stopped it.

Freya ignored him, and looked at Quinn.

"She needs the bathroom," said Quinn. "Untie me, and I'll take her."

"No. She can wait until Erik's back."

"I know you think you're a God, but one thing you can't control is a little girl's bladder. So unless you want things to get very messy in here, I suggest…"

"Yeah, yeah, okay, I get it," sighed Javier. He bent down to Freya. "Honey, close your eyes for a second will you? Just count to five, and then open them again, and you can go to the bathroom."

Freya closed her eyes, and Javier turned to Quinn. "Sorry about this." He brought the gun down sharply on the back of her head, and knocked her out. Quinn was sat on the floor, and as she fell into unconsciousness, she slumped against the wall.

"Right, Freya, come with me," Javier said as Freya opened her eyes. "I'll take you to the bathroom, and when we get back I expect your Dad will be back. Quinn's fallen asleep, and then it's your turn. We have a long way to go in the morning."

Keeping the gun at his side in case they bumped into Erik, Javier led Freya out of the office. They were to spend the night in a tattoo parlor, and were currently in a small back room that seemed to serve as the shop's office. Their van was parked up right outside the front door, positioned perfectly in case they had to make a quick getaway.

"In there," said Javier. Down the hallway from the office was a bathroom. "I'll wait for you." He ushered Freya inside, and then turned around. The stairs leading to the upper floor were quiet, but there was noise coming from above him. That was Erik checking they were alone. He was under strict instructions to not come back with anything other than the news they were safe. It was in his daughter's best interests not to try anything, and Javier was sure he would comply. As long as Erik didn't come back accompanied by any zombies, they were in the clear. They had been driving for hours since leaving Hamsikker and his wife to die. Javier wanted to put as much distance between them as possible. His goal now was simply to get over the border. As long as he had Freya, he could control the other two and use them to all the shitty jobs he hated doing.

A click behind him caused him to turn back around, and the bathroom door opened. Freya walked out.

"That was quick. You good?" he asked.

Freya looked up at Javier with big, blue innocent eyes.

"What's that behind your back?" Javier asked her. He could sense something was wrong, that the girl was different somehow. She never spoke a word, but her eyes gave a lot away. She was hiding something.

Freya stared at Javier, shrugged, and said nothing.

"Well? You've got nothing to show me?" Javier took a step closer to Freya, and then bent down to her level. "I thought you and me were buddies?"

Freya lifted her arm and then swung the hammer at Javier. She had taken it from the floor of the van earlier that day and kept it hidden inside her sweater. She had been waiting for a way to get it out without him noticing, and now was her chance. Freya aimed for Javier's head, knowing that it was the only way to stop the bad man. He was horrible, and she wanted him to go away.

Javier ducked and easily stopped her, catching Freya's arm mid-swing. He held it there, looking at the hammer in her hand. "Now, that's not very nice. You were going to hit me with that. Why?"

Freya shrugged, and tried to pull her arm away, but Javier kept a firm grip on it.

"You want to hurt me? To kill me?" Javier wrestled the hammer free from her, and threw it into the shadows. Freya tried to break free, but the more she struggled, the more he squeezed her arm. "Stop squirming around, you little shit."

He slapped her across the face, and instantly Freya stopped moving. She froze, rooted to the spot. "That's more like it. You think you can go around hitting people? Attacking *me*?" Javier shook his head. "Did your Father put you up to this? Quinn?"

Freya shook her head again, and lowered her eyes. Her blonde hair hung over her forehead.

Javier reached out to Freya's other arm, and he snatched the key chain from her hand. Instantly she started wriggling again, trying to get it back from him, yet the whole time not uttering a single word. Javier pocketed the key chain and raised his hand to slap her again. "If you don't stop moving, I'll hit you again, harder this time."

Freya looked at him with hatred, and Javier smiled. "That's better. If you don't like me, just be honest about it. Don't pretend like we're friends. I'll be honest with you. You're not getting that stupid key chain back until we're in Canada. If you try anything like this again, I'll go and cut your Dad's heart out right in front of you. Got that?"

Freya's bottom lip dropped, and she nodded.

"Good. I'm going to let you go now. We're going back to the office where Quinn is where you're going to be quiet, and you're going to go to sleep. It's way past little girls' bedtime."

Javier grabbed a handful of Freya's hair, and frog-marched her back to the office. He was amazed that Freya had tried to attack him. He thought it was only Quinn and Erik he had to look out for, but it turned out the girl was going to be a pain in the ass as well. Back in the office, he shoved Freya to the floor.

"Stay there." Javier closed the door, left the room, and locked it. He put the key in his pocket, and wandered into the front room. The street was quiet, and with only the moonlight to see by, it was dark. They were in some quiet backwater town where most of the residents had been zombies before they became actual zombies.

As he waited for Erik to finish checking upstairs, Javier admired the artwork on the walls of the shop. He crossed over to a display case full of books and picked up a worn folder. He flicked through the pages, letting his eyes scan the photographs and drawings, not really taking them in. Animals, symbols, and all manner of different things jumped before his eyes, but there was one that caught his eye and made him stop turning the pages. There was a rose wrapped around a nail, in simple black and white, adorning a woman's tanned arm.

Javier knew he shouldn't have left her like that. He was angry with her, bitter at the way things were heading, but he knew he shouldn't have left her behind. Those things would eat her until there was nothing left, not even her tattoo. He hadn't meant for things to work out that way, but Rose should've listened to him. It wasn't his fault she had ended up dead. If only people would just listen. It was small consolation that Hamsikker and his wife were dead too. He hoped there was nothing of them left to prove they were ever alive.

Javier traced his fingers along the outline of the tattoo, remembering how he used to do the same with Rose's tattoo. Maybe he was better off alone. Rose had been itching to settle down, and eventually something would have driven them apart. All Javier needed was to keep moving and find his brother. He closed the book and set it back down on the table before returning to the foot of the stairs. There was no point in dwelling on the past. He had to look forward now, forget Rose, and find Diego.

"Well?" Javier asked Erik, watching the man descend into darkness.

"Nothing," Erik grunted. "It's clear up there."

Javier pointed the gun at Erik's face, who looked distinctly unimpressed. "Right then, best we get you back to Quinn and Freya. You can…"

"There's something else," said Erik, pausing on the last step.

"Something else? You want to take a leak?"

"Out there, across the street. There's a light."

Javier looked at Erik with disdain. "What a fascinating story, big man. Be sure to save that for dinner parties; it's a real conversation starter. 'There's a light.' Any more to add? Was it, by any chance, a big white circle in the sky? I don't know, big enough to be a moon perhaps?"

Erik stared at the gun. Javier always held it just far enough away that he couldn't reach it. He ignored Javier's sarcasm and explained. "In the house, opposite. There's a light on in the window. Someone keeps turning it on and off at regular intervals. It's not just random, and I'm *not* imagining it. Someone's doing it on purpose. I guess they're signaling for help. Thought we should check it out. They might need our help."

"Yeah, I don't think so, Erik. I think you've got enough going on without worrying about who might be out there. You should be thinking about your daughter and the millions of zombies who are just waiting to take a bite out of her young, supple flesh. Who cares who's over there?"

Erik stepped down off the stairs and looked at Javier. This was the man who had killed his wife. This was the man responsible for the death of his son, of his best friend, Hamsikker, and was holding his daughter at gunpoint. "*I* care. I care because if I don't, who will? I know you think we're scum and that we're nothing to you, but believe it or not, I still care. I care what happens to you. I care about my daughter, and I care who is over the road trying to signal us."

Javier smirked in the half darkness. "Erik, be my guest," he said stepping aside. "You want to save the world? Go ahead."

Erik rolled his eyes, stepped into the tattoo parlor, and looked outside. The streets were practically deserted, he knew that. Upstairs he had looked from the window and made sure it was safe, noticing only one or two zombies. If he could get into the building opposite, he saw no reason why he couldn't be over and back in no time. Whoever was over there needed help, and if Erik could get them on side, they could be crucial in helping to wrestle control back from Javier. Still, he wasn't happy that Javier would be left alone with Quinn and Freya. "It would be easier if there were two of us, you know?"

Javier burst out laughing. "I think we've already established I couldn't give a rat's ass about who is over there. No, you want to go, you go on over, I'm not going to stop you. I've got my driver and my bargaining chip, so really you're kind of surplus to requirements anyway. We'll be leaving in a few hours, as soon as the sun's up. If you want to see your daughter again, I would suggest you're not late."

"I'll be here. Just be ready." Erik needed revenge for Peter and Pippa. His family had been destroyed because of this man, and he wasn't about to let Javier leave without him. He knew Javier was a coward at heart. He wouldn't leave in the dark, and he wouldn't want to leave without Erik. Javier liked having his bodyguards, someone to do the hard work for him. Erik just hoped he could bring back someone who might be able to help him.

"Erik, I know I'm sending you out there empty handed, so I should also point out that I expect you to come back that way," said Javier. "You turn up with anything more than what you have now, and the first thing I'll do is put a bullet through Freya's skull."

Erik nodded at Javier. Charming as always. Javier had to have the last word. If Javier killed Freya he had nothing. Quinn would refuse to help him, and so would Erik. She was the only reason they were still alive. Erik strode toward the door, feeling the temperature drop as he neared the exit. As much as he hated leaving Freya, he knew Quinn would look out for her. He was lucky he had managed to get Javier to agree to let him go at all. Erik just hoped he wasn't wasting his time. They needed some luck, and whoever was on the other side of the street might just prove to be that someone.

CHAPTER TEN

Erik hated being unarmed, but he had no choice. Stooping as he left the tattoo parlor, he ran to the van and used it as a shield to hide behind so he could check the street. It still appeared to be empty other than a few cars bathed in moonlight. The town was perfectly silent. Seeing the way was clear, Erik jogged across the street and into the open doorway of a sporting goods shop. It was directly beneath the window where he had seen the light flicking on and off. Moving inside, he looked around. It looked as if the store had been looted. Empty boxes and broken glass littered the floor, display cases had been turned over, and the cash register lay in pieces behind the counter at the far end. He hoped he might find a hockey stick or something he could use as a weapon in case whoever was up there wasn't friendly, but other than three soccer shirts still hanging on a rack, there was nothing left. He looked for a way upstairs, and found a door behind the counter that led into a storeroom. There were no windows, and no source of light, so Erik had to use his senses to guide him. He ran his fingers along the painted wall, finding only a useless light switch. His feet scuffed the wall as he carefully went deeper into the back of the store. He found himself at the end of the wall, and abruptly tripped over a pile of boxes, causing them to scatter their contents.

"Damn it," whispered Erik. He picked himself up, and carried on edging his way around the room until he found another door. Opening it, he saw a staircase leading up. At the top there was an intermittent light coming from underneath a closed door. Erik stealthily began climbing the stairs, hoping the noise from his accident in the storeroom hadn't alerted the person upstairs to his presence. Once he was outside the door on the upper floor, Erik took a deep breath. It had been almost too easy.

He was going in unarmed, and had no idea who or what he might be facing. What if it was a trap? What if the light was just on some sort of timer, and the room was full of zombies? Erik had to know. He wanted to find help, and getting a moment out of Javier's sight was a rare opportunity. There was no time to think, to plan, or to grieve. Even now, it was hard to accept Pippa was gone. She had been taken away from him so quickly that it didn't feel real. She was so much a part of him that he would never let her go. He wanted Freya to remember her, too, and once this whole sorry situation with Javier was resolved, he would make sure he taught Freya everything he could about her mother. In the meantime, he had to focus on staying alive and getting Freya way from the murderous psycho who currently controlled their every waking moment.

Erik watched the light beneath the doorway flickering, and then suddenly it stopped. He waited, hearing nothing but his own breathing, hoping the light would restart, but it didn't. Had he been heard? There was no backing out now, and Erik slowly turned the door handle. He began to inch the door open slowly until it was wide enough for him to get through. He eased himself through, keeping his back against the wall. Once fully inside the room, he stayed still, listening for a sign of who was in there with him. The room was pitch black, and he couldn't see or hear a thing. Surely he hadn't been mistaken? He was sure the light had been coming from this room. He knew he could go exploring in the darkness, but he could walk into anything, or fall over and hurt himself. He was going to have to take a chance and hope he wasn't wrong.

"Hello? Anyone here?"

Erik waited for a reply, but he heard nothing.

"I thought I might be able to he…"

The bat smashed into Erik's midriff, and he fell to his knees, clutching his stomach. He was winded, and it hurt like hell, but he knew better than to wait for the follow up knockout blow, and he rolled to his side as the bat swung again. He heard it smash into the wall where he had been, punching a hole in the plaster.

"Stop," Erik rasped. "I'm here to help." He rolled away from where he thought his attacker was standing, and cursed as he rolled over something wet and sticky. It smelt like something had died in here, but he knew zombies didn't use weapons, and he took a moment to catch his breath. The situation could still be resolved. He had faced plenty of confrontational situations in the past that he had managed to control, and faced plenty of angry assailants who could be reasoned with.

"Who the fuck are you?" shouted a shrill voice. "I'll shoot you. Answer me!"

Erik couldn't see the owner of the voice, but he knew better than to take on someone unarmed. They obviously knew the layout of the room, and had a distinct advantage over him. He stayed where he was, lying on the floor, now covered in filth with his clothes absorbing the damp.

"Please. My name's Erik. I saw your light."

Erik heard a creaking noise and sensed something was coming toward him again. He really didn't want another hit like his stomach had just taken, and he waved his hands out in front of him to ward off any attack. In the darkness it was impossible to know from where his attacker was coming, and it was unnerving.

"I saw your light," he said again. The creaking noise became louder, and he braced himself. Whoever was in there was close, close enough to hit him. He began to think he had made a terrible mistake coming up here. Not everyone could be reasoned with.

A glaring white light suddenly shone on his face, blinding him. He tried to shield his eyes, but it felt very much like he was being interrogated.

"Don't move. If you move, I'll blow your head off. What do you want?"

It seemed to Erik that the voice had softened. It sounded actually more like someone was trying to scare him, to ward him off, but the tone of the voice was calmer now. It was likely that whoever shone the light on him was just as scared as he was.

"Look, if you're going to shoot me you may as well get it over with," said Erik. "And if I was going to shoot you, trust me, you would be dead by now. So let's start again, shall we? My name is

Erik. As you can see I'm unarmed. I saw your light and thought you might need help."

Erik waited for an answer, but none came. The light in his face moved down his body as his interrogator checked him over. Once the light had swept down to his feet and back up, the light flicked off, and Erik heard the person sigh heavily.

"I'm sorry, but you can't be too careful these days."

The room was abruptly filled with a dull light. Erik looked at the person who was talking to him. They were holding a battery-powered lantern over their head.

"It switches to a torch function that I used to signal out of the window. I'm running low on batteries so I only do it every other night now. Lucky you were coming past when you did."

"Sure, lucky me," said Erik. The woman speaking to him was young, pale, and very thin. It looked as if she hadn't eaten in days. It wasn't hard for Erik to figure out why she might be running low on supplies. The woman rolled her wheelchair forward.

"Claire. Sorry about that," she said as Erik stood up holding his stomach.

"Forget it. I've had worse." Erik looked at Claire. She was so thin that her clothes hung off her. Her cheekbones were pronounced, and her attempt at make-up only served to heighten how skeletal she appeared. This woman was in no state to help him, and his spirits sunk. He had hoped to find someone who could help him take on Javier. All he had done was disturb this poor woman from a slow lingering death.

"You got a gun?" Claire asked.

"You?" countered Erik.

"If I did, I wouldn't be hitting you with this crappy bat, would I?" Claire put the baseball bat in her lap. "It's all I got since that shithole Mart left me here."

"Mart?" asked Erik.

"My husband. *Ex-husband*, now that he's a shambling zombie. Asshole."

"Right," said Erik, looking nervously around the dirty apartment. "This Mart, he's not here is he? With you?"

Claire raised her face to look at Erik. "You think I'm braindead?"

"No, right, of course he's not. So…"

"So he ran out on me. Left me stuck up here. Look at me," said Claire.

She spread her arms wide, exposing her frail body and the metal wheelchair in which she sat. From the smell of her, she had spent quite some time in that chair, and Erik suspected it doubled as her bathroom.

"Can't get down the stairs can I? Asshole left me. We were only visiting my sister, Niamh. I've been at her for years to get a freaking stair-lift installed, but do you think she'd listen? No. So now I'm stuck here. My sister took off to find help and never came back. Mart went after her, promising he'd be back, 'cept that was months back. Wouldn't be surprised they had a thing going on. I always wondered why he was so keen to visit Niamh, you know what I'm saying? What am I supposed to do now? So are you the rescue party, or what? You with the army?"

Erik looked around the apartment. The woman had no gun, no food, and couldn't walk. He had wasted his time coming here, and despite her obvious bitterness, he could understand why she was so angry. She had been deserted, left to wallow in her own filth and fend for herself. He suspected he had slipped in a pool of vomit, and had no intention of looking at where he had fallen. Whilst Claire couldn't help him with Javier, he could hardly leave her behind. She needed help, and it seemed he was all she had. If he left her, she would undoubtedly die up here.

"Can you walk at all?" asked Erik. He was worried that if she left the light on too long, it might attract the zombies outside. If he was going to get her back over the road, he would need to move quickly.

Claire stared at Erik. "Not since some asshole drunk ploughed into me on a crosswalk when I was seven years old. He got some piss-ant fine and a suspended sentence. I got a lifetime in this fucking thing." Claire rolled her chair back, freeing up the space between Erik and the exit. "So I figure you ain't military then. You a loner? You got family? You got any friends waiting down there or what? Spill it."

Erik had to admit that for everything that she had been through, Claire still had a lot of fight left in her. She certainly wouldn't like taking orders from Javier. "Here's the thing," said Erik as he approached the door. "I'll be honest with you. There's just me and my daughter, and a friend, Quinn. We're travelling with someone. A man. Javier. He's…not pleasant. He killed my wife and some friends of mine. He has the only gun between us, and he's in charge. We're heading for Canada. At some point between here and there, we have to get that gun from Javier. If we don't, we're dead. He *will* kill us. I can't promise you safe passage. I can't promise you anything. It's your choice. You can stay here, or…"

"Stay here, are you fucking kidding? I started eating the wallpaper yesterday. I have nothing left. I stay here, I die. I'll take my chances with this Javier if you don't mind."

Claire gripped her bat, and Erik smiled. "Okay then. Let's get out of here. We're just across the street."

Claire rolled herself up to him, and Erik bent to take her bat.

"No, sir. That's mine. Looking at the size of you, you can handle yourself without any help from me."

"Whatever you say," said Erik, and he put his arms around her. He picked Claire up out of her chair, and it trundled backward as he lifted her out. She was so light that it felt like he was carrying nothing but a bundle of clothes. Erik was reminded of the last time he carried a woman in his arms. Pippa. The thought of her now only made him angry. He was angry at himself for not protecting her, and angry at Javier for taking her away from him.

Erik tried not to inhale too deeply as he carried Claire. He took her to the door, opened it, and then carefully began making his way down the stairs. "The street was clear when I came in, so we should be fine. I'm not going to find Mart waiting outside for me, am I?"

"That asshole? If you do, you have my permission to beat his head to a pulp."

They made it back out onto the quiet road, and Erik was pleased when he saw their van. He was worried they would run into some zombies, and now that he was carrying Claire, it would be difficult to run or fight back. She still had the bat, but she had no strength left to fight off the dead. Her arms hung around Erik's neck, but they were like a whisper, just gracing his skin like the soft touch of a feather.

As Erik rounded the van, he jumped. A zombie appeared, staggering toward him with menace. It was between them and the door back to the tattoo parlor, and he was going to have to get rid of it. If he skirted back around the van, it might work out where they were and follow them inside. He couldn't risk it getting in where Freya was. He had to deal with it. Erik backed up quickly, and sat Claire on the hood of a nearby car.

"Wait here a second," he said.

"Yeah, like I'm going to run off," said Claire shivering, giving him a look of disdain.

Erik had barely turned away from her, when the zombie attacked. It cast its arms forward, and Erik grabbed them, swinging the zombie back around. All his training sprang into motion, and as if he were dealing with a street thug, Erik put the zombie in an arm lock, and marched it away to the other side of the street. He found an unlocked car, and threw it inside, slamming the door shut, and trapping the zombie permanently.

Erik watched as the zombie clawed at the glass, desperate to get out. He knew it wasn't going anywhere, and decided to leave it where it was. It couldn't hurt them, and it was easier than trying to destroy it with his bare hands. As the zombie continued to scrabble at the car windows like a dog scratching to get out, he heard Claire's voice from across the road.

"Niamh, is that you?"

Erik turned and was suddenly wrapped in a zombie's arms. It had him in a bear hug, and the stench of the thing that held him was sickening. The zombie had long strands of blonde hair protruding from its scalp, and the patchy skin was putrid. The woman's face had rotted away, revealing the bones underneath. Now that the dead woman had her arms around Erik, her face was right in his, and he could see her teeth shining in the moonlight. The woman had become a monster and was about to take a nasty chunk out of him.

Erik couldn't think what to do. He had no weapons, and Claire wasn't able to help. He couldn't shake the woman off, and in literally two seconds she was going to give him a bite that was a death sentence. There was no way out. He had nothing to fight her with. He had turned his back for one second, and this thing had snuck up on him. He hated the zombies, hated them for what they had done, for everything they had destroyed. Now Freya would be alone with no family. He couldn't let that happen. He couldn't let Freya down. Erik screamed once, and then thrust his jaw around the dead woman's neck before she could do the same to him. Erik pushed himself forward, thrusting his face into the woman's dead flesh, and he ripped out her throat. Thick blood filled Erik's mouth but he spat it out along with the rough skin he had chewed off. He took another chunk from the zombie's throat, trying to rip off its head before it could get its teeth into him. Like a wild dog, he sunk his teeth into her skin, ripping it apart ferociously. He could think of nothing else but to use the only thing left that he had to kill it — his own life. Erik recoiled as the zombie began to buck wildly. He spat the woman's blood into the gutter, and felt her arms around him lose their grip. He pushed her away and wiped his mouth. The foul taste made him want to vomit, but he wasn't finished yet. Although her neck was open, and her head lolled sharply to one side, the woman was still standing. Erik knew that the zombie wouldn't quit until it was dead. He had done nothing more than shake it off.

He charged at it, and shoved it down to the road. The woman fell back, bringing Erik with her. He landed on top of her, and the woman's neck flopped backward, sending her head smacking onto the tarmac with a loud crack. Straddling the woman, Erik buried both his hands deep into the opening in her neck. Her body was cold, and he curled up his fingers, gripping whatever he could. He began to pull in opposite directions, and heard a tearing sound as the woman's flesh began to rip apart. The hole in her neck widened, and Erik continued as the zombie bucked beneath him. He pulled with all his might, until with a cracking sound, he pulled the woman's head from her shoulders, and he held it up aloft like a trophy. The body beneath him twitched, and then stopped moving, but the head in his hands was very much alive. The woman's eyes turned to look at Erik, and the jaw worked up and down slowly as if still trying to bite him. Erik spat on the woman's face, and then he hurled the head into the air, as far away as he could.

"Rot in hell." Erik spat again, desperate to remove the fetid taste of death from his mouth, and got to his feet. He was shaking, scared, and knew the noise he had made might bring more. He had to get Claire inside and get them both out of sight off the street.

"You okay?" asked Claire as Erik returned to her.

Erik nodded, and scooped her up into his arms.

"I didn't see her until the last second. I thought it might've been my sister, but…"

Claire stopped talking as Erik carried her into the tattoo parlor. She could see the blood on Erik's face, and knew well enough that if he had been bitten, he was not going to be around much longer.

"Look, if that thing got its teeth into you…"

"It didn't. I got my teeth into it. It's dead now, so forget about it."

Erik reached the office and pushed open the door with his feet. He found the light was dimmed, and Javier sitting on the desk.

"My, my, that was quick," said Javier.

Erik gently lowered Claire into a seat. "If you give me that gun, I'll show you what else I can do quickly." Erik went over to Freya who was curled up beside Quinn. She put her arms around Erik when he bent down to her, and he looked her in the eyes. "You okay, honey? He didn't hurt you?"

Freya shook her head and looked down at Quinn.

Erik noticed the blood stain on Quinn's neck. She was alive, but sleeping off whatever Javier had done to her.

"So, are you going to introduce us?" asked Javier, swinging his legs down off the desk and planting his feet firmly on the floor.

Erik glared at Javier. He was arrogant beyond belief. Hitting Quinn around with Erik gone was pathetic. Did Javier really think he could do whatever he wanted? "She's…"

"I'm Claire. I take it you're the leader, Javier?"

Javier kept the gun trained on Erik, walked over to Claire, and held out his hand. "You know, it's rude not to shake someone's hand when you first meet. Aren't you even going to get up?"

Claire gave Javier a sullen gaze. "I can't."

"You can't?"

"She can't walk," said Erik. "I carried her here. Claire's been trapped in that apartment for months."

"Looking at the state of you, Erik, I assume it wasn't all plan sailing." Javier noticed the blood on Erik. "I trust nobody got their teeth into you? Not even a nip?"

"No," replied Erik. He looked at Freya, her tired eyes drooping, yet still full of fear. "I'm fine."

"So all you found was this?" Javier pointed the gun at Claire.

"Charming," said Claire. "You remind me of my ex-husband."

"Ignore him," said Erik. "He's armed with a blind faith that he's in charge. Just do what he says, and you'll be fine."

Javier reached down and took the bat from Claire. "This is something I suppose. Here." Javier held out the bat to Erik. "Keep it safe, and we'll take it with us in the van. It could come in handy."

Erik took it, and laid it on the hard floor beside Quinn. Freya wriggled free from Erik's arms and lay down on the floor beside her. Erik told her to stay there and look after Quinn.

Javier looked at Erik. Despite everything, the man still thought he could win this. Javier could see the anger burning in Erik's eyes. Maybe going out there had stirred something in him, awoken some kind of hope. That wouldn't do, not at all. "Why'd you bring her back here? You could've set her free. You could've taken off at any point, yet you came back. Why? I would've run the second I got the chance."

"That's the difference between you and me. I don't leave my friends behind. I'm not going anywhere until you let Freya and Quinn go." Erik was amazed how Freya was handling it all. She still hadn't spoken a word, but sometimes her eyes gave away what she was thinking. She hated Javier too. He had seen it enough times. Freya understood at least some of what was happening. He hoped that having Claire here would add to the stress that Javier must be under. He had to make a mistake at some point, and then Erik would be ready.

"Well, Erik, as much as I had hoped to spend some quality time with you tonight, I'm afraid your little adventure has brought some attention to us. I haven't exactly been idle myself. I saw what happened out there. You know there are more coming now, don't you? I saw movement out there, further away, but they'll get here eventually, so we're going to have to find somewhere else for the

night. We'll have to keep going and stop where we can, *if* we can."
Javier looked at Quinn and smiled. He picked up a bag and pointed
the gun at Erik. "Get going then. Take Freya and get the van ready.
Quinn's a little tied up right now."

Erik suspected that more would come. It wasn't such a bad
thing that they were on the move again. He hated driving at night,
but it was better than waiting to be surrounded by zombies. He
looked at Claire. She was worried; that was obvious. He had saved
her from a lonely pathetic existence, only to bring her into this. He
still wasn't sure it was a great idea to bring her back here, but it
was the best option. Without help she would undoubtedly die.
They had food, and surely even Javier could see that Claire needed
help. "Come on, Claire, you can ride in back with Freya," said
Erik as he scooped up the bat. He would take Claire and Freya out
to the van and come back for Quinn.

"Slow down there, Erik, you're not in charge of this little group
yet. You're just the chauffeur, remember?" Javier raised his
eyebrows. "I need to talk to our new friend here for a moment."

Erik bristled. "Javier, we don't have time for this. Claire can
ride in the back; she's not going to *do* anything. She's harmless.
Look at her. She's damn near starving. What's the problem?"

Javier swung his gun toward Claire. "Can you drive?"

Claire shook her head. "You really are an asshole aren't you?
Do I look like I can drive?"

"You held a gun before? You ever done any shooting? You ever
took out one of those zombies?"

Claire shook her head again and stared defiantly at Javier. "No,
never had the chance. Plus, I don't much like guns. My father
always taught me to steer clear of them. Said they were
dangerous."

"Right, well your father was a wise man." Javier looked at the
gun in his hands and then back to Claire. He could spare one.
"Erik, get in the van and start it up will you? We're going to have
to hit the road very soon."

"So, we good here?" asked Erik. He wasn't going anywhere
without Claire. He knew he had to get her safely in the van before
Javier did anything. He had begun to like Claire too. She didn't
cower down before Javier but actually stood up to him.

Metaphorically speaking. He could tell that Claire was feisty, and began to think that despite her disability, he might have struck lucky. She would be more than prepared to help him when the time came. "Can we all just go now?"

"Claire, you ever been to Canada? Reckon you could do some navigating at least. I mean Erik would be driving, but perhaps you could help him. We're heading for a place called Thunder Bay." Javier smiled. "We're going to look up some old friends."

Claire shivered. She looked to Erik for reassurance and then back to Javier. "What's with the twenty questions? Look, Javier, I won't be any trouble. You can tie me up like your friends if you want. I promise..."

"Answer the fucking question." Javier raised the gun and pointed it at Erik. "Answer the question, or I'll shoot him right here, right now."

Erik spoke to Claire, but his eyes never left Javier's. There was no way he was going to buckle this time. Javier was nothing but a bully. He enjoyed playing games. This was just another one; a charade to prove to Claire that he was in control. Once they were all in the van, Erik would talk to her, make sure she knew that she was safe with them. "It's okay, Claire, go on. Just answer his stupid questions."

Claire could sense that Javier meant business. Erik had been right about him. She twisted her hands together anxiously. "Last spring break I went to New York for a vacation. Cost us a fortune. Other than that I've not gone far really. Kinda hard in my condition."

"Focus, Claire. Do I look like I care about New York? Canada. Big country. Cold. Ever been?" asked Javier again.

"No. I wouldn't know how to get there if my life depended on it." Claire tried smiling at Javier to see if she could break down his bravado. Hiding behind that gun was a lost boy, and she thought maybe she could appeal to the real Javier. "I could try if you like? But I've never been to Canada."

"Shame," said Javier. "That's a real shame."

Javier quickly moved the gun from Erik to Claire and pulled the trigger.

The noise of the gunshot echoed around the office, and Freya's scream bounced around its four grey walls. Claire's body slumped back in the chair, and Erik dropped to his knees. He looked across at Claire's lifeless body. Javier had put a bullet right between her eyes.

"She was useless," said Javier calmly. "Let's roll."

CHAPTER ELEVEN

The way to the border was clearly marked, and Lukas had no trouble in navigating the truck into Duluth. The roads were largely clear, and it seemed that most people had gotten out in time. There were very few vehicles around and even fewer zombies. They spied a couple wandering around a small park, and there were a few dead bodies littering the surrounding streets, but other than that, the city was unusually quiet.

"You think everyone just left?" asked Lukas as he picked his way through the deserted roads.

"Maybe they got enough warning," said Julie, knowing it was unlikely.

"You remember how fast it all happened," said Jonas. "I'd like to think the people of Duluth are safe and sound somewhere, but somehow I doubt it."

Red and maroon buildings shimmered in the dawn, and thin trees lined streets devoid of life. As they climbed up a steep street, Dakota spotted a tall, stone tower in the distance. It blinked in and out of view as they made their way between the city's buildings, and she wondered if they were alone. Had the city been evacuated, or were they all dead? The truck came to a halt, and Dakota read a street sign pointing the way to Canal Park. Beneath the sign was a stroller that had toppled over and fallen under the wheels of a blue car, dented and scratched all over as if it had been in a fight with a bigger car and lost. A gray fleecy blanket was trapped beneath the front wheel, and a small jacket flapped on the ground beside the stroller which was bent out of shape. Dakota put a cold hand over her belly. Her fingers were so cold that her wedding ring was loose, and she tugged it on firmly. She had seen a fire in Jonas's eyes earlier, and in his mind he was already there with Janey, moving on. He didn't see what she saw. A city didn't just vanish. Tens of thousands of people had to go somewhere. She tried to quell the uneasy nausea growing inside her, and wished she could just snap her fingers and make everything all right.

"Look," said Lukas, as he pulled the truck around a crash, and began steering them downhill. "There's a ship. See it? It's huge."

As the truck rolled through the empty city streets, they all glimpsed what Lukas pointed out. A massive ship was docked in the harbor. It was a gray color, yet difficult to see as the visibility was poor. It revealed itself bit by bit, appearing between gaps in the houses, and it was only as they neared the bottom of the hill when the harbor opened up before them that they could get a clear sight of it. The ship was tall, majestic even, proud and calm as the figures raced around its decks. Even from afar, Jonas could see people on board, scurrying around, looking busy, and waving their arms.

"Jesus, that is one big boat," said Julie.

"Why is it still here?" asked Lukas excitedly. "You think we can get a ride? You think they know somewhere safe to go? That's why there's no one here." Lukas began to laugh. "I'll be damned. We can get out of here. I knew it. The military sent a rescue ship. They probably go from port to port looking for survivors. We should get down there before they go." Lukas swung them toward the ship, carefully picking a way through the discarded cargo containers and delivery trucks across the industrial harbor toward their awaiting rescuers.

"Lukas, turn us around," said Jonas. "Turn us around, right now."

"Hamsikker, this is a way out of here. Don't you see?" Lukas accelerated, and the huge ship seemed to become impossibly large as it got closer. "We miss this ride, and who knows when it'll be back."

"Lukas, stop. Turn us around," said Julie.

"You too? No way. You ever seen so many people before? I'll bet they've got the whole city on there. Look, Hamsikker, I'm sorry about your sister, but we can't afford to pass this up. Who knows when they'll be back around here? Maybe Janey is already on board, maybe…"

"Lukas." Dakota reached over and gently tapped him on the arm. Up ahead she could see two gangplanks stretching from the ship to the pier. One was empty, the other full of people. They seemed to be standing still, neither going up nor down. They were jostling each other, as if dancing almost, but going nowhere. When she spoke to Lukas it was with kindness and humility as if she were talking to a child. "Lukas. Look at it. Look at where you're taking us. Look at those people. Please, Lukas, turn us around."

Lukas let the truck slow down, and as they approached the ship, he finally saw what the others saw. The hull was drenched in blood and riddled with bullet holes while the back of the ship's hull was charred and black from where a fire had broken out. The deck above and the gangplank ahead were full of people, thousands of them. As he looked closer, he realized there wasn't a living soul amongst them. He saw men and women, boys and girl, black faces, white faces, and everything in between. They were all dead. The freighter was nothing more than a floating morgue. Narrow and long, it was humming with zombies, and Lukas wondered just how long they had been there.

"Shit," Lukas whispered as he brought the truck to a halt. He leant forward over the wheel, staring up at the ship. All around the deck, pressed up against the railings, were the dead. They were stuck up there, unable to find a way off. "Shit," he said again, deflated. "I thought we'd finally got lucky."

"I guess they came to get people out," said Jonas, reading the name on the side of the hull. "The Nanjing Equinox. That thing must be nearly a thousand feet long. I guess they dumped their cargo and tried to pick up survivors. There must be hundreds of them up there. I guess they tried to get too many people out. It would've only taken one infected. One person with a bite or a scratch, they bite someone else, and so on, and so on, until there's no one left, not even anyone to take the ship back out onto the lake."

"Whatever, it's going nowhere. The boat's useless to us now," said Lukas. He noticed a few of the dead on the walkway had found their way down to the pier and were starting to come towards the truck. The figures stumbled as they walked, their stiff legs and arms jerking as though the bodies were being shocked with electricity.

Lukas shifted into reverse and turned the truck around. They left the harbor behind and resumed looking for a way over the border. "I guess we stick to the plan. Thunder Bay, right?"

Jonas could hear the despondency in Lukas's voice. It was understandable. The thought of rescue was exciting. More than that, it would mean there was somewhere untainted by the dead, clear of zombies and death. Did such a place exist? Could it? Had anyone gotten out of Duluth, or were the last survivors trapped on the freighter, destined to spend an eternal death on its exposed deck until the snows came and froze them solid?

Lukas charged the truck around a pile of containers and punched the wheel. "Fuck it. I just thought, you know, that maybe there was something out there. I thought someone might have made a go of it. After Chicago, after Bishop picked me up, I figured there had to be some place left to go, you know?" Lukas shook his head. "Whatever, man, whatever."

"Forget it," said Jonas. He needed Lukas to calm down before they reached the border. There was no guarantee the city was going to stay empty or that the roads would remain clear. Lukas had to be focused on driving, not distracted or driving angry. "We all hoped for something better, Lukas, but never say never, right? In the absence of any rescue or sign that other people are out there making a go of it, then we stick together, and we stick to the plan. If we stay alive, then who knows? One day, perhaps, someone will come along. I bet you never thought you'd run into Bishop, right? So who's to say we won't run into someone else, someone in authority, someone who is trying to actually *do* something about this. Don't give up on us yet, Lukas. I've been there. You have a lot ahead of you. One thing at a time though. Get us over the border into Canada. Short steps, okay?"

"Yeah, let's try and stay positive," said Dakota. "Maybe Air Force One landed in Bermuda, and the President is sipping cocktails with the President of Russia trying to figure out this mess."

Lukas snorted, and couldn't help but smile. "Oh, yeah. Did he remember to pack his speedos? Gotta work on that tan while figuring out how to save the planet."

Julie burst out laughing. "The President in speedos? Now *there's* an image."

"Ew," said Jonas, noticing that Lukas was relaxing already. The harbor was behind them, and so were all thoughts of the freighter full of zombies.

Dakota rapped the dashboard and put on a mock serious voice. "Mr. President, here's your bloody Mary. Oh, and we just received word from Washington. The bad news is the body count is approximately 300 million, but the latest polls have you up five points."

Everyone burst out laughing, and when the laughter had died down, Julie shook her head. "That's my Commander-in-chief you're talking about."

"Right, right, sorry, Julie," said Dakota. "What was I thinking? The President would never drink a Bloody Mary. He's more of a Spritzer type of guy."

Julie burst out laughing again. "Sure he is. I always go with a Spritzer when it's the end of the world. I save my cocktails for general homicides, invading third world countries, that sort of thing."

The truck suddenly swerved and bounced, causing them all to hit their knees on the dashboard. Jonas's head hit the roof of the cab, and he grabbed Dakota.

"Sorry, my bad. Dead horse. Didn't see it till it was right in front of me," said Lukas, steering them back onto the road.

Jonas looked at Dakota, who in turn looked at Julie. Immediately they all burst out laughing again.

"It's not even funny," said Jonas as he wiped his eyes.

Swallowing her laughter, Dakota tried to apologize to Lukas, but could only utter the words "a dead horse" before exploding into more laughter.

"I don't see what's so funny," said Lukas. The laughter of the others was contagious, and though he tried to act upset, all he could do was smile. "All I said was I didn't see it. I didn't. What do you want me to say?"

"How about, look out, dead horse ahead?" suggested Julie, giggling.

Dakota was pleased to see Julie joining in. She was still a bit of a mystery, but was beginning to relax around the others.

"Look out!" shouted Lukas.

"Exactly, just like that," replied Dakota, missing the urgency in his voice.

The truck banged up against the side of a trailer, jack-knifed across the road, and slammed into the sidewall of a coffee shop. Lukas wrestled with the wheel, and managed to get them back under control, before hitting the brakes. They came to rest in the center of an intersection.

"Everyone okay?" asked Jonas. "Dakota?"

"Fine, fine," she replied.

"I'm good," said Julie.

Lukas peered through the windshield. They had come to rest inches from the back of a multiple crash. "Sorry, it just—"

"Came out of nowhere, right?" Jonas looked at Lukas. "Maybe you should ease off for a while. It's a couple of hours drive to the border crossing, and I think we'd all like to make it in one piece."

"My bad. I should've been concentrating. Sorry guys." Lukas sighed and began to move the truck cautiously around the crash.

"No need to apologize, Lukas," said Julie. She was shaken by the close call and immediately felt guilty for laughing. Carlton had died less than twenty-four hours ago, and she was already moving on, laughing at nothing.

"It's us who should be apologizing to you, Lukas. I guess we got a bit carried away there," said Jonas. "You okay to drive, or do you want me to take over?"

"No, it's all good. It wouldn't hurt to have a second pair of eyes on the road though. I'm doing my best here."

"I appreciate it. We all do. I know you probably feel like a fish out of water now that Bishop's gone, but we'll look after you."

"Really?" asked Lukas. He winked at Jonas. "I thought it was me looking after you."

They continued on out of Duluth and found Highway 61 leading toward the Canadian border. The Duluth University buildings on their left dissolved into suburbia, and then the buildings disappeared completely. Lukas noticed a large sign advertising cheap fees at a golf course, and then a small sign promising great views of the Lake from a park on his right. With the zombies far behind, he was tempted to stop and take a look. He had never been this far north, and not spent much time at Lake Michigan or any of the other Great Lakes. If it wasn't for the fact that they had somewhere to be, he probably would've stopped to check it out. He consoled himself with the fact that, if they reached Jonas's sister's place which was right by the water, he was probably going to live out his days looking at the lake anyway whether he liked it or not. He guessed he was also going to have to get used to eating a lot of fish.

The highway quickly narrowed as they left Duluth, and it hugged the edge of Lake Superior. Lukas hoped they didn't come across any major crashes. If the road became blocked, they were going to face serious difficulties getting any further. As far as he knew there was no way around. To his left was what looked like a thick forest, and to his right, the massive expanse of Lake Superior. There was no end to it as far as he could see, and it reminded him of the ocean. The water was flat, calm, and the low clouds gave it an eerie feeling. He could imagine the huge freighters crossing it loaded with tons of cargo.

"Or zombies," Lukas said.

"Huh? What's that?" asked Jonas.

"Oh, nothing. I was just thinking about something."

"You ever been to these parts?" Jonas asked Julie. As they had some time before they reached Grand Portage, he figured he may as well try to find something out about their new friend. If she was from the area, she might be able to help. When they reached Thunder Bay, all Jonas had to go on was Janey's address and a picture in his head. He hadn't visited his sister before, and he would take any help he could get. "Were you stationed here, or...?"

"No, I grew up in Vermont and moved to Minneapolis with my parents when I was still a kid. I lost them soon after I joined up. Some idiot fell asleep behind the wheel of a semi. He took them out after they'd been out for a meal to celebrate their anniversary. The bank took the house, I lost my home, and I've made the army my family ever since. Sergeant Carlton took good care of me; took good care of all of us. My platoon respected him. We were doing some training exercises at the Reserve Center in Madison when we got the call. It didn't take us long to get to Janesville. I never thought I'd be stuck there as long as I was though. Carlton never really adapted to the situation. He liked to control things. He was good at his job, and yet…

"So to answer your question before I went and side-tracked myself, no, I haven't been to these parts. I always wanted to go to Canada. Never thought it would be under these circumstances."

"I'm sorry about Carlton," said Dakota. "I'm sure he was a good man."

"He was. Before we lost everything, before we lost the platoon, the communication, our weapons, before any of that shit, he really was a good man. When we were trapped, though, in that awful fucking place in Janesville, he began to lose it. I'm sorry he died, but I'm not sorry I'm not with him anymore. He was driving me crazy. He needed to maintain control, keep the illusion going that his rank actually meant something. He still believed the army were coming to get us."

"We all have to cling to hope," said Jonas. "If you give up on that, what else is there?"

"Okay, okay, let's not start getting sentimental," said Lukas. "Sorry about Carlton, Julie, truly. Nobody wanted what happened to him, but Hamsikker is right. We've got something good here. Another hour or so, and we'll be at the border. We gotta start thinking about the future now."

"That's the last obstacle in our way," said Jonas with some trepidation. "The border." He didn't know what to expect. Maybe they could just drive on through. It wasn't going to be manned anymore, and they certainly didn't need their passports.

Lukas began to hum a tune quietly. "We'll worry about it when we get there. For now, let's just enjoy the view."

The sub climbed higher, and the lake spread out before them, like a shimmering oasis in a desert of death. It was truly beautiful, and Jonas could understand why Janey had chosen to live up here. It was far away from their father and the bad memories that accompanied Louisville, yet if all she had wanted was distance, she could've gone anywhere. No, this part of the world was stunning, and even knowing that at either end of the road were probably hundreds of zombies, it still felt untouched. Watching the lake as they drove north affirmed Jonas's mind that they were doing the right thing. Thunder Bay was going to be the perfect place to raise their child, and he would make it work. He was under no illusion that the impending winter was going to be hard, but it wasn't as if they were moving to the depths of Siberia. Life went on up here no matter how cold it got. Life always found a way.

After a while of contemplation, Jonas noticed that they were slowing. The road itself was fine and in good repair, but there was a queue of cars all along the highway, and Lukas was lucky that there was nothing coming the other way. Signs began appearing indicating that there were major road works ahead, and Jonas hoped the road was still passable. Nearly all the doors of the stationary cars were open that they passed, suggesting the occupants had long gone. But north or south? If they had headed back to Duluth, then there shouldn't be a problem. If they had gone north, then Jonas knew they might find the road blocked or a worksite teeming with zombies. Going back to find a different route would cost them hours.

"Castle danger," said Lukas eyeing up a signpost smeared with what he assumed must be blood. "Sounds lovely."

"You'd better take it easy," said Jonas. The long line of cars was thick, bumper to bumper, and up ahead he could see a crane. As they drew closer, he could see the cause of the trouble. The right hand side of the road had been dug up, and a digger was parked up on the verge. Temporary traffic lights at either side had stopped the flow of traffic and reduced it to one lane opposite the hole in the ground. Jonas looked for any sign of zombies, but there was none. It was deathly quiet.

Lukas stopped the truck just ahead of a barrier and several cones that had fallen over. "I think we can get past," he said. "Once we're past this damn hole in the ground, the traffic is single file again. There's a small gap between the barrier and that digger that I can just about squeeze through. If we can just pull the barrier out of the way, I can get us through."

Jonas knew he was right. Two of them should be able to move it, and they would be on their way again in under a minute. "Okay, let's go. Lukas, stay here and get ready to move the truck through when me and Julie have the barrier out of the way."

"What should I do?" asked Dakota.

"Stay here. Keep an eye out for trouble, and let us know if you see anything."

Jonas got out of the truck and went around to the back. Opening the back doors, he pulled a gun from one of the bags they had thrown in the day before. Bishop had left them plenty of food and water and a couple of extra round of ammo. Jonas didn't want to go anywhere unarmed.

"That for me?" asked Julie.

Jonas passed her the gun. "Actually, it is. It's fully loaded."

"I can see that," said Julie checking it over. "Not exactly what I'm used to, but it'll do the trick. Thanks, but what about you?"

Jonas crossed over to the verge, and picked up a twisted piece of metal. "I'm not much good with those things. I prefer a blunt object over a gun any day. Something I can hold with both hands, and I know I'm not going to miss with."

Julie smirked. "When we get across the border, I can give you some shooting practice if you like? I have a feeling we're not going to be short of targets."

"Sure. Dakota too. I want us both to know how to use a gun. Just in case."

"Just in case." Julie crossed to the verge where Jonas was standing. She looked out over the still lake. The air was cold, and it looked as if the clouds were growing darker. The lake was flanked by greenery, and the sound of the water lapping at the shore reminded her of better times. Vacations had been rare when she was younger, but her parents had made sure she could swim and invariably took her somewhere where there was at least a beach. "Sure is beautiful, isn't it?"

"Cold, but beautiful," agreed Jonas. "Let's do this. Just watch your back. It looks quiet, but you can never be entirely sure."

Together they waved at Lukas and Dakota, and then proceeded ahead on foot to the road works. Jonas kept one eye on the cars. Even though it looked like they were alone, he wasn't sure. There were just so many cars, so many trees, that a zombie could be hiding anywhere. Jonas noticed a set of tracks in the grass leading around the work site. He followed them until they got lost down the bank, and then spied a couple of cars in the water. "Looks like someone tried to gun it and lost control."

"Patience is a virtue," said Julie. "I guess they had no choice. When it's life or death you do crazy things."

A vision of Cliff's battered face sprang into Jonas's head. "You sure do."

As they neared the hole in the highway that had been dug and then abandoned, Jonas looked down into it. There was an exposed pipe, a pool of water, and a dead body. It was face down, and bloated. It wasn't moving, and Jonas knew it wasn't a zombie, just some unfortunate soul who had met his end out here on a lonely road. Even if it were a zombie, there was no way it could get out. The sides of the hole were nothing but dirt, and it wouldn't be able to claw its way out no matter how much it tried.

"You ever think Janey might have left home, tried to make her way to you?" asked Julie.

"No, absolutely not. She has three young children. There's no way she would try anything so stupid. No, she promised me she would stay put, and she wouldn't change her mind. No, she's there all right."

"Cool. Just wanted to make sure I wasn't riding with someone who hadn't at least considered all the possibilities. Good to know. This whole thing can make you blinkered. Carlton couldn't see that things had changed. It cost him his life. I just need to know you and Dakota are on the level."

"We're good," replied Jonas. He knew that Julie was worried about where they were going. It was only fair she question him. "Lukas too. He's solid. I can tell he has a soft spot for you."

"Lukas? Please, I hardly think so. I don't think he'd know what to do with me if he got hold of me. Which, by the way, *isn't* happening. I have no intention of hooking up with anyone. There's far too much to do before I start thinking about that shit."

As they approached the barrier that had been left across the road they paused. There was a large dark tarpaulin spread out over the road, and it crunched as they walked across it. Jonas noticed it was anchored down in two corners by some rubble, and in another by a tire. It flapped very gently as the wind began to pick up. There was some bad weather coming in, and Jonas wanted to be safely in Thunder Bay before it hit.

"Come on, Julie, cut him some slack. Why shouldn't he be interested in you? You're a good-looking woman. He's a good guy. Never say never." Jonas looked at Julie, and he could tell she was flattered. He could also tell from her face that she was serious about not getting involved with anyone. Her military training hadn't left her yet, and she was still planning, thinking ahead.

"Let's just get this thing moved, shall we? I think my love life can wait for another day," said Julie, smiling.

"You grab hold of the barrier, I'll get the other end. We can move it together," said Jonas. "Let's just get out of here."

They began walking over the tarpaulin, and Jonas wondered why it had been spread out over the road like that. Perhaps to cover a fatality? Perhaps in their haste to get away, someone had died here, run over or crushed by the cars. There was no sign of the police, nor any ambulance or fire trucks.

From the other side of the barrier, suddenly a zombie approached. It came running from behind a parked car, and the very ground seemed to tremble as it ran toward them. An obese man, rolls of fat still clinging to his dead body and jiggling around like jelly, thundered toward them. Pudgy fingers extended from huge arms where swathes of fat like wings swung, making it look like the man was trying to take off as he ran. Sores and boils ran down the man's legs, and stretch marks coursed his belly. Jonas assumed that somewhere underneath the man's belly fat was a pair of boxers, but either they had perished or were just hidden well.

"Jesus Christ," said Julie. "You'd think being dead you'd lose a few pounds."

Jonas knew it was dangerous to take on such a formidable zombie. One blow might not be enough to take it down, and if it landed on top of him, it would be a struggle to get out from underneath. He also didn't want Julie to go shooting the place up in case it alerted others to their presence. Where there was one, there was usually more.

"Hold up," said Julie taking aim, "I'll get it." She wanted to make sure she got a clean head shot, and walked forward over the tarp, letting the obese dead man get closer, waiting for the perfect moment to kill him.

"Okay, but hurry up. I don't like this." Jonas walked across to the barrier, and as he did so, he thought he felt the tarpaulin slide under his feet. It just slipped a couple of inches, but it was enough to make him concerned. He didn't want Julie falling on her ass just as she was about to shoot.

Julie watched the zombie come at her, bouncing off the vehicles, until it was finally in view, and she was staring straight down the barrel at it.

Jonas grabbed one end of the barrier, and when he put his hands on it, they came away wet. It hadn't been raining, and the ground was still dry, so why was the barrier wet? Jonas looked at his hands. They were covered in blood. The tarpaulin abruptly shifted beneath his feet again, slipping another couple of inches. Something strange was happening. It couldn't be moving of its own accord. He and Julie were standing still, so what was dragging it, and to where? Jonas took a step back and looked at the barrier. In bright red blood, words were painted on the rear. The writing wasn't visible from the truck, and it had obviously been put there on purpose. When he read those three simple words, Jonas felt like a sledgehammer hit him in the side of the head.

"Three, two, one..." Julie breathed in and lined up the zombie. It planted one foot on the tarpaulin, and she squeezed the trigger.

"Julie, wait!"

The tarpaulin was whipped out from beneath his feet, and Jonas was thrown forward. He tried to grab the barrier for support, but it fell with him, and he was pulled back with the moving ground. He heard the gun go off, but as he fell, he had no idea if Julie had hit her target. She screamed, and then Jonas found himself falling. Somehow the tarp had been set up over another hole, concealing it from view, and they had walked right on top of it. He saw the sky above him as he twisted and turned, and he caught a glimpse of Julie a few feet behind him. He thought he saw the body of the obese zombie fall, too, but he wasn't sure. It was all so quick.

It was only a short drop, but the impact knocked the wind out of him. With a thud, he crashed into the ground, and managed to look up just in time to see the barrier falling on top of him. Jonas knew that on any normal day it would've been just an unfortunate accident, but this was different. It was a trap. Those three simple words appeared in huge lettering above him as the barrier fell toward him.

'Sweetness and light.'

He caught sight of a crudely drawn smiley face on the tarpaulin as it gathered around him, and then the corner of the wooden barrier smacked into Jonas's head, sending him spiraling into unconsciousness. His last thought before he passed out was how odd the ground felt. It moved, as if it were alive; almost as if they had landed not on the ground, but in a pit filled with people.

CHAPTER TWELVE

"Get up, Hamsikker," shouted Julie. "Get the fuck up, now!" She fired at the approaching zombie, its fat arms dragging its immense weight over the tarpaulin toward her. She put two bullets in its skull, and the obese man finally stopped moving.

She had been as surprised as Hamsikker when she found the ground beneath her feet give way. One minute she was about to blow away a zombie, the next she was being sucked down into a hole, and her shot went wildly amiss. She reckoned the pit they had fallen into was maybe twelve feet long, and six feet wide. It had just appeared out of nowhere, and there had been no time to react. She was lucky she landed as she did and hadn't broken anything. The zombie that had been coming after her was dead, but it was quite obvious they weren't in the clear yet. The tarpaulin beneath her was moving as something or someone beneath it writhed around. Trying to stand was impossible.

She watched the edge of the tarp fall into the pit, and realized she was standing in another trench, probably dug by the workmen. A tearing sound ripped through the air, and then an arm appeared from the ground beneath her, forcing its way through the tarpaulin. The skin was pale, clammy, and the arm encrusted with dirt. Another arm swiftly followed it, and then a head appeared.

Julie fired at it, obliterating the head, only to see it replaced by another. A second zombie appeared in the opening, its face covered in sludge, its rotten mouth agape. It groaned as dirt and blood spilled from its mouth.

"What the fuck is this?" Julie fell to her knees, unable to stand as the tarpaulin bucked under her. It was being pulled apart, and she heard more tearing sounds behind her. Horrible clawing sounds came from below as more hands scratched at it, trying to find a way through.

Turning to Hamsikker, she screamed at him to get up, but he was out cold. Blood poured profusely from the wound on his head, and she knew she had to get him out of there quickly.

Cold fingers wrapped themselves around her ankle, and she whirled around to see a zombie about to sink its teeth into her flesh. Julie fired, sinking a succession of bullets into its head. The zombie fell back, and she recoiled from it, pulling the trigger until the chamber ran empty.

At the end of the trench, more zombies were rising. From the pit they rose up, one by one, clambering over one another, their ghastly faces caked with dirt. A girl emerged from the slime, clumps of mud falling from her body as she climbed faster than any of the others. Her once blonde hair was a tangled mess of filth, and her slim pale arms looked like they might snap at any moment. Her fingers splayed out before her as she pulled herself over another slow-moving zombie, and her eyes bore into Julie's. The once sparkling blue irises were dull and dark now, and as the girl got closer, Julie saw maggots pore from the girl's chest. It looked as if she had been blown apart, and her ribcage stuck out from her chest with flaps of pungent meat clinging to the bones.

As the foul stench of the dead reached Julie, she picked up the barrier and tried to position it in front of herself, trying to give herself and Hamsikker some kind of protection.

"Wake up," she shouted, and she slapped Hamsikker.

He murmured quietly, and she slapped him again, leaving a red mark across his cheek.

"Fucking wake up!" she screamed at Hamsikker.

"Reach up to me, Julie. Give me your hands, now!"

Julie looked up and saw Dakota leaning over the pit. Dakota's voice trembled as she spoke, and her eyes were wide with shock.

"Reach up, and I'll pull you out," said Dakota again, as calmly as she could. She stretched a hand out toward Julie. Though she tried to mask her fear, she knew she wasn't doing a very good job. There was a host of zombies ready to tear Julie and Jonas apart, and Dakota didn't know how to stop them.

"No," said Julie. "He's hurt. Take Hamsikker." There was still some part of her that wanted to protect first and foremost. These people were civilians, and it was her job to help them. Whilst she accepted the army was no longer in action, and in all likelihood gone forever, she still wore the uniform, and that meant something to her. There was no way she would leave anyone in harm's way.

Julie put her arms underneath Jonas and lifted him to his feet. He was stirring, and his eyes flickered briefly as she picked him up. She propped him up against the wall of the trench, and raised his arms so Dakota could reach him.

"Go!"

As Dakota began to pull Jonas up the smooth slide of the pit, Julie continued to lift him. She felt Jonas's weight lessen as he rose above her, and Dakota swept him up and over the edge onto the road. Looking up, Julie saw Dakota frantically pull her husband to safety.

Julie felt the wooden barrier crash into her back, and the moaning sounds of the dead right behind her. Whipping her body around, she propelled the barrier back, but the weight of the encroaching zombies was too much. She began to fall back with the barrier on her midriff, and the first of the zombies snapping at her arms as she fought them off. The little girl was first, clawing at Julie who batted the zombie away as best she could. Julie was pinned under the wooden barrier, and though she tried to wiggle free, she knew it was impossible. She was stuck fast.

"Get their heads up!" shouted Lukas.

Julie glanced upward, and she saw Lukas silhouetted against the blue-grey sky. He was holding a gun, pointing right at her.

"No, wait," cried Julie, fearing that Lukas would miss and shoot her by accident.

The little girl threw her head forward to bite Julie, and then her face exploded into a mist of gore and bone. Lukas blew the girl away, and then took aim at the next zombie.

"Can you get free?" he shouted as he shot another.

Julie tried to answer, but her face was covered by what was left of the little girl, and she knew if she opened her mouth she would get a mouthful of brain and rotten flesh. The weight on her legs increased as the zombies swarmed forward. She bit down on her lip to stop from crying out, but her feet were being crushed.

"Julie, reach up for me," said Dakota.

Dakota was leaning over the edge of the pit, stretching both arms down over the mud, and Julie reached an arm up. It was too far. There was at least two feet between them.

Julie screamed as the barrier began to punch its way into her stomach, and another zombie fell on top of her. It had been dead a long time, and its skin was rubbery and spongy to touch. Julie tried to push it away, but her fingers got lost in its spongy flesh, and she couldn't find purchase.

"Julie, get its head up," shouted Lukas.

Sweat poured down Julie's face, and she tried to force it up, but it was too much. The thing was pressing down on her, getting closer and closer to her face.

"Julie"! Jonas peered over the edge, and leant an arm down to her. "Reach up."

Julie screamed as a zombie began to rip out chunks of flesh from her leg. Another sank its teeth into her soft thigh, and another buried somewhere beneath the pile of zombies began to cut and dig its way through her leg. When its teeth hit her shinbone, she could take no more.

Julie held a zombie above her, and tears fell down her face. The pain was excruciating as the flesh was ripped from her body. Unable to hold the zombie above her anymore, and with her arms weakening every second, the zombie's face came closer to hers. Its bloody eyes stared at her, and its teeth nipped at her flesh. Screaming, Julie stuck her thumbs into its eyes, and gripped its skull. Her fingers sliced through its putrid flesh, and vile black liquid oozed from its eyes as she ground her thumbs around. The zombie was filthy, and though she kept its head from biting her, she could feel its sharp fingernails clawing at her arms. Green and brown fluid trickled from the zombie's mouth into hers as she screamed, choking her and drowning out her cries. More of the zombies in the pit began feasting on her legs and body, and she could take no more. Forcing the zombie's head to the side, she looked up into Lukas's face.

"Kill me, Lukas," she coughed. "Kill me."

"No way." Lukas shook his head, and fired randomly into the crowd.

"Kill the dead!" Jonas had grabbed another gun from the back of the truck, and was now trying to shoot them too. It seemed as though every time he took one down, another came crawling out of the pit, emerging from the depths of hell.

"Please," whispered Julie. She spewed a fountain of blood up over her face, and blinked it out of her eyes, desperately trying to get Lukas's attention.

The agony was unbearable. The skin was being flayed from her body as she lay there, unable to escape. Teeth sunk into her muscles, ripping her nerves and veins apart, and she could feel the wetness of her own warm blood begin to soak into the ground beneath her. An unseen hand raked across her left breast, and then began ripping it apart, pulling at the soft tissue and clawing inside of her.

Julie wailed, crying for release as she was eaten alive. She remembered summer vacations with her friends, she remembered Carlton and how close they had become, and she remembered thinking that they were supposed to be heading to Canada to find a safe place to live. Most of all, though, she felt the pain: white searing pain sweeping constantly through her body. It felt like the hands digging into her were sharp razors, slicing their way through her fragile body. Her pelvis was shattered, and she felt greedy hands pulling at her hips, threatening to pull her apart. She felt her left femur snap, and then her left foot was separated from her body, sheared off at the ankle where teeth had gnawed their way through to the bone. A rib cracked under her left breast and another popped as it was torn from her body.

"I'm so sorry," wept Lukas, and he put a bullet in Julie's brain.

The very second that Julie stopped struggling she was gone. It was like an invitation to the horde of zombies, and they swarmed over her, submerging her forever beneath their ravenous, disgusting bodies.

Lukas fell to his knees and turned away, unable to watch as Julie was devoured. He couldn't hold back the tears, and he cried out loud for her, frustrated that he couldn't save her. He was scared, too, scared that something like that could just have easily happened to him. His hands quivered as he looked at the gun in his hands. It wasn't enough. He had killed a few of them, but it wasn't enough. He could still hear the cracking of bones as the dead gorged on Julie's dead body. He could hear wet slurping sounds as they swallowed her piece by piece.

It wasn't enough.

Dakota pulled up her arms, rolled over onto her back away from the pit, and stared at the clouds hovering above her. She didn't cry. She couldn't. There were no tears left. How had it happened? She and Lukas were watching them, waiting for Jonas and Julie to move the barrier, when they suddenly disappeared into the ground. It was as if a sinkhole had opened up right beneath them. By the time they had realized what was happening, they were too late. Dakota rubbed her stomach. She felt sick. Her child was growing in side of her, waiting patiently until the day it would be born, and yet she felt nothing. Would motherhood kick in when she finally held it? Would she finally rediscover those maternal feelings when her daughter or son looked her in the eyes? Wasn't this supposed to come naturally? Why was it that she could only feel pain and death? She knew the answer, but hated herself for thinking it. She was glad it was Julie and not her.

Jonas crawled over the road, and took Dakota's hand. "Are you okay?"

Dakota shrugged. "We need to leave." She rolled over to look at him. Blood was clotting around the wound on his head, and the skin was already discolored from where a nasty bruise was forming.

Jonas nodded. "Now." He pulled Dakota up to her feet. The sound of Julie being consumed was more than he could take. He had led her to her death. He needed to get far away from here; far away from those noises. The zombies were louder now, their grunting and moaning only increasing as they fed. He knew he was partly responsible for her death. It could so easily have been him, and yet he was still alive. Julie had saved him; he was sure of that. He also knew that this was no accident. He was surer of that than anything. Rain was beginning to fall steadily, and they couldn't sit around grieving for Julie. It wasn't safe.

"Lukas. We're going," said Jonas. He glanced at the pit of writhing bodies. Julie was down there somewhere, at least what was left of her. He couldn't bring her back, couldn't thank her for saving his life, or even begin to explain it to Lukas. The only thing left to do was carry on.

Jonas put a hand on Lukas's shoulder. "Lukas, come on man, we need to—"

Lukas shrugged Jonas away. "We need to what? Bury her? There's nothing left to bury." Lukas stood up and shoved Jonas back. His eyes were teary, yet full of anger. "You couldn't do anything? You couldn't stop this?"

"It was so fast, what could I do? I didn't want for this to happen any more than you," said Jonas. "I didn't see what was coming until it was too late. I should've been on the lookout for something like this, but—"

"See what was coming?" Lukas wiped his face, and stepped toward Jonas. "What do you mean? You *knew* this was going to happen?"

"No, not really, I mean… Look, Lukas, I didn't know Javier would do something like this. It's not like he gave us a warning. I only saw the sign when we began falling. I couldn't stop it."

Lukas began to trudge back to the truck, waving his gun in the air. "You suspected this Javier guy might try something, and you did nothing? You didn't say anything?"

"It's not like that. Lukas…"

The truck door slammed, the engine revved, and Jonas turned to look at Dakota.

"He'll come round. Let's go." Dakota pulled Jonas to her, and examined the cut on his head. "If Lukas really thought this was on you, he would've taken your head off already."

Jonas closed the door as he and Dakota got in next to Lukas. Rain fell onto the truck's roof and drowned out everything except his thoughts. The seats were cold, and his damp clothes offered no warmth against the dropping temperature. The wind howled around them, and Jonas peered out of the window. Lake Superior was vast, bigger than he even imagined. He could only imagine how frigid it would feel in there. Julie's death clung to him like the damp, and there was no shaking it off. Another had died.

The atmosphere in the truck was icy cold, and Jonas said nothing as he sat next to Lukas. Dakota dabbed at the blood on Jonas's face, trying to clean him up as Lukas steered the truck away from the road. The only way forward now was to skirt around it. He reversed the truck carefully and then pointed it at the scrub before the lake. Lukas took it slowly, saying nothing, gripping the wheel, and eventually he got them past the roadblock. On the other side there was a slight gap between two cars, and he pushed through it until they were back on the road. When they were lined up again, he let the truck idle, and turned to face Jonas. Blood and tears streaked his face, but there was no sadness or pity on his features. His only emotion was anger.

"What else do I need to know?" he asked. "I need to know what the hell I'm getting myself into."

"Sweetness and light," said Jonas. "That's what it said on the rear of the barrier. Lukas, I swear I didn't know what was happening. But the moment I saw that sign, I knew it was him. He knew we would come this way, so he left it right there for us. We may have just been lucky up until this point. Maybe having Bishop with us was more than good luck. He knows how to read the land. He can see things coming before anyone else. I can't say for sure that there won't be any other nasty surprises up ahead, Lukas. I'd begun to let myself believe that he was gone. Javier is everything you don't want to be. He will lie, and cheat, and kill, and do whatever he can to stay alive."

"Not just that," said Dakota. "If he really set that trap for us back there, then he knows we're coming. It would've taken him some time to set that up, and he didn't even know for sure we would come along. He left us for dead, remember?"

"That sign was meant for us. Maybe he was just covering his tracks. I don't know. I'm through second guessing him." Jonas looked at the road ahead. Nothing had ostensibly changed. He still knew exactly what he had to do, where he had to go, and who he had to find. "All I can say, Lukas, is to watch your back. If Javier is out there, and if we find him, he'll kill you just for riding with us."

"I'll kill him first. Julie didn't deserve to go out like that." Lukas took in a deep breath. It wasn't Hamsikker's fault. If anything, Lukas shouldered some of the blame. Julie was in no state to go off with them. He should've made her go back with Bishop. She had spent months living like a prisoner, and he had expected her to just get back into it without thinking if she was really ready. Truth was he liked having her around. Julie was sweet, pretty, and knew how to wear a uniform. Lukas could've persuaded her to go with Bishop, but he hadn't wanted her to go. Now she was dead. The man responsible, Javier, was out there. He was the one who had lined up a pit of zombies for them. He was the one with a sinister agenda.

"Let's go find Janey," said Lukas exhaling slowly. He knew he couldn't afford to drive angry. There was still plenty of ground to cover, and he was going to keep his wits about him now more than ever. He couldn't afford to let thoughts of revenge or guilt or sorrow take over now. He was still driving the truck; still responsible for getting them all safely across the border.

"After we find Janey, we find Javier," said Dakota. "No matter what, we have to find him."

"Why?" asked Lukas. "Seems to me we're better off avoiding him."

"I want to make sure he's dead," replied Dakota.

Jonas looked at his wife and nodded. He felt it too. This wasn't a coincidence. Javier was making sure that if anyone was following him that it wasn't going to be easy. By rights, they should be dead, and if it hadn't been for Bishop finding them when he did, they would be. Javier had to think that, but still, he had gone out of his way to set that trap. He was vindictive, and manipulative, and probably hadn't even lifted a finger. Jonas could picture Javier barking orders from the safety of a car or van while Quinn and Erik did the hard work. And what of Freya? Was she still with them?

As they drove, a zombie appeared in the road, emerging from behind a stalled car. It growled, and then disappeared under the truck with a thud as Lukas ran it over.

"I ain't stopping for nothin'," said Lukas. The Lake to his right had vanished to be replaced by a line of trees. The road was headed inland, and as the lake receded, so did the sunlight. Lukas turned on the lights as dark clouds made the day become night. The air grew colder, and it wasn't long before spots of rain began to appear on the windshield. Lukas had to slow down a little, as the road became greasy. Soon the trees thinned out, and the lake reappeared. But as the view opened up, they could see the weather coming in from the east. Visibility was worsening as the rain intensified, and the sound of it hitting the truck drowned out any attempt at conversation.

Lukas pushed on, determined to not get caught up in anything else, and they saw no more zombies as they continued north. Small towns came up, communities built around bays on the lake, but they didn't stop. There were more road works sporadically spread out on the road, almost as if left there intentionally to slow them down. One caused them to lose almost an hour. An intersection outside of Illgen City was a mess, and the traffic had snarled up, leaving a line of cars across the road. Navigating a path around it was slow going, not least because they were being careful not to wander into any more traps. As it was, they made it through without any trouble. It was around late morning when they reached Taconite Harbor. A petrol tanker was blocking the road to the power station, and yet again Lukas had to be very careful as he drove off road. Jonas got out and helped point out where to go. The rain came down steadily, soaking him through.

"This is taking too long," said Jonas as he jumped back into the truck. His clothes were sodden, and there was no respite from the downpour. Dakota held him close to warm him up.

"Can't do much about it," said Lukas as he watched the power plant recede into the distance. "Just the way it is."

"I know. I'm just impatient. Knowing Javier was ahead of us has me worried. He might get to Janey before us."

Jonas blew on his hands for warmth. The day was utterly miserable, and the future was looking distinctly uncertain. Would Javier really waste time looking for Janey when his own brother was out there?

"Surely he would rather use Quinn and Erik to find his brother first," said Dakota. "I'm sure Janey's fine."

Dakota couldn't help but remember the sound of Julie's bones as they splintered and snapped. Yesterday had been full of hope. Bishop provided them with that. Now, with the wintry storm enveloping them, with Julie's death, and with the constant hold-ups along the highway, she had a horrible nagging feeling that the day might not end so well. At least, not for everyone.

"Sure she is," said Jonas. "I've got three nephews over the border, and ten to one Janey is with them right now waiting for me." He tried to sound upbeat, despite what he felt inside. It was as if he was back in that church about to bury his father. A sense of dread was eating away at him. Just as he had wanted to get his father's funeral over, so he wanted to get over that border to Thunder Bay. He felt like they were being watched. Everywhere he looked, every turn in the road they took, he expected to see Javier. Jonas wanted it over with once and for all.

Proceeding out of Taconite Harbor, it took them another couple of hours to reach the border crossing. When Grand Portage lay ahead of them, Lukas rolled the truck to a stop, and the three of them sat up front, staring through the glass, blinking through the raindrops that splattered against the windshield.

"Anyone hungry? There's still some food in back," said Dakota.

Jonas shook his head. It had been hours since they had eaten, but he couldn't eat. He couldn't think about anything but getting over that border.

"I say we just keep going, and hope for the best," said Lukas. He had no appetite either. The memory of Julie was still too fresh, too raw, and the thought of food only served to heighten the nausea creeping around his gut. It felt wrong going on without her. Lukas felt as if he had abandoned Julie, but he shook it off. It wasn't his fault. He just missed her.

"Let's go. Steer clear of Grand Portage, Lukas," said Jonas. "Just follow the road, and we'll find the border crossing soon enough."

It was only minutes before they saw the signs for Pigeon River and the Canadian border. As they neared, the road split into two. Both lanes were full of traffic, and in some places were three vehicles across, spreading right into the emergency lane. Between the road was a thin strip of land populated by trees blowing in the wind and lots of dead leaves. Clearly people had been trying to get in or out of the US long ago. The gloomy sky made it difficult to see far ahead, and it was obviously not going to be easy. Lukas had no choice but to head into the rough grass that grew at the roadside. The truck's wheels began to skid in the wet dirt, and they made it a few more feet before he gave up.

"This isn't happening," said Lukas as he stopped. "There's no way through. I think we're on foot from here. Once we get across, we can look for another vehicle, but there's no way we're going any further in this."

Jonas sighed, frustrated. They were so close. "I think the border crossing is right up ahead. After that there's a bridge across the river, and we're officially in Canada. There is no way in hell we're going on foot. It's a short journey to Thunder Bay in the truck, but on foot it'll take us the rest of the day at least. In this weather we'll catch pneumonia before we're even half way there. No, we have to find a way through."

"Hamsikker, I hear you, but if I go any further in this crap, we'll get stuck," said Lukas staring out at the near-black sky above. It was hard to believe it was the middle of the day. "The road is blocked. There *is* no way through."

"Lukas, trust me. Please. Just get us a bit closer so we can at least see what we're dealing with here. Try and stick as close to the road as you can. Have a little faith. You can do this."

"Fine. Just don't grumble at me when we get stuck."

They inched forward, each turn of the wheel threatening to leave them stranded. Lukas forced the truck to hug the road, but it was difficult. He scratched the side of every vehicle they passed and cursed on numerous occasions. Finally, to his surprise, he got them up onto the road. There was enough of a gap at the head of the traffic jam, except they were now sandwiched in between two station wagons. The border crossing was visible, but it was not all good news.

Jonas wiped the misty windshield and peered through it. If they could move the station wagon out of the way, they would be literally at the front of the queue and could get past. The problem was the crossing itself. It had been almost completely blocked. There were tanks, armored military jeeps, and even a helicopter stationed to the side of the crossing. It looked as if they had tried to stop an exodus; there were rotting bodies piled high either side of the tanks. The people had all been shot, a bullet in the head to ensure none returned. Jonas saw the path through the tanks was open. They could make it. If Javier could get through, then so could they. It would mean driving over some of the bodies, but it was feasible.

Jonas opened the passenger door. "Lukas, follow me. You and I are going to move this Goddamn car out of the way. Dakota, get behind the wheel. The second you're in the clear, get through that barricade onto the bridge. Lukas and I will come to you. Don't wait for us, okay? We're only going to be out there for thirty seconds. We move that car, and we're home free."

"Hurry back," said Dakota as Jonas and Lukas jumped out of the cab into the hurtling wind and rain.

"You can count on that," said Lukas drawing his jacket up to his chin. He grimaced as the harsh rain hit him, slapping his face like a scolding mother.

Together, Jonas and Lukas ran to one of the station wagons, and put their hands on the hood. Its icy coldness was shocking to touch, and every time they pushed, they slipped as the rain refused to let them get a good grip. The truck's headlights gave them plenty of light, and together they began to move the car slowly out of the way.

A clap of thunder was followed quickly by a snaking arc of lightening, and Jonas looked at the truck to make sure Dakota was ready. The lightening illuminated the road, and what he saw behind the truck froze him to the core. The road was clogged not just with vehicles, but zombies. Hundreds upon hundreds of them were pouring from the tree line, spilling onto the road, with their mutual murderous intent clear. Jonas saw them staggering, walking, running, their arms aloft, and their faces a picture of grotesque imagery that he would never forget. In seconds they would be all over the truck.

Jonas turned to Lukas and shouted. "They're coming. Push!"

CHAPTER THIRTEEN

Straining every aching muscle that he had, Jonas put his whole body weight against the car, and with the rain beating down on him pushed with as much energy as he could muster.

Lukas heard the thunder echoing through the sky and felt the car move. He saw the panic on Jonas's face, and knew something was wrong. With a surge of effort they got the station wagon off the road and out of the way.

"Go, go!" Jonas shouted to Dakota. He waved her on, and she immediately began to move the truck forward.

Unaware of the crowd amassing behind her, Dakota inched the truck forward through the gap in the cars and onto the crossing area. She then rapidly picked up some speed and hit the pile of bodies. As soon as it hit the first body the truck slowed as it churned its way through the sinking mound of rotten flesh and crumbling bones.

"Lukas, get…"

Lukas pointed and shot the first runner in the head. "I see them," he said. The red taillights of the truck had illuminated the crowd, and it was enough for him to see what had Jonas so worried. This was no trap. This was just the dead, seeking out the living, as they always did. He suspected a lot of them were people from the cars littering the highway they had passed on the way to this point. "Get after Dakota; make sure she gets through."

Jonas knew what Lukas was doing. He would take down as many as he could, but it wouldn't be enough. Lukas had reloaded his gun in the truck, but he wouldn't have enough to take them all down. No matter how he felt, this was not the way to end things.

"No," said Jonas, grabbing Lukas's shoulder. "Get going. We go together."

Both of them ran after Dakota. She made it over the mountain of corpses, and was waiting for them to join her. When she stopped the truck ahead of the border at the start of the bridge over Pigeon River, she opened the driver's door and looked behind her, expecting to see them jogging to catch her up. Instead, she saw the mob of zombies on the road with Jonas and Lukas only a few feet ahead of them.

"Run!" she screamed.

As they began to clamber over the stinking pile of bodies, their progress was slowed. The rain and the weight of the truck had created a sort of funnel through the bodies, but it was slippery underfoot, and it was difficult maintaining any momentum. Jonas watched as Lukas went down, and quickly scrambled to get up, away from the mangled people beneath him. Checking behind him, Jonas saw the zombies were now terrifyingly close. A runner broke from the pack and headed for Lukas. The stench was sickening, and Jonas knew they needed more time. He leapt from the bodies, and found himself sheltering against a tank. He had seen something glistening in the rain which should do the trick. If it didn't work then he was as good as dead.

"Keep going," he shouted to Lukas.

The two dead soldiers lying beneath the tanks wheels weren't moving. One's head was under the body of the tank, crushed to a pulp, while the other was riddled with bullets. Neither would be getting up again, and nor did Jonas care. It wasn't the men he was interested in. On the road between them lay a machine gun, its black body shining in the dim light. Jonas reached down and picked it up.

"This had better work."

Seeing the runner close in on Lukas, Jonas wasted no time in testing it out. A ripple of gunfire told him it did, and he watched as the runner fell. Lukas jumped off the bodies and ran for the truck.

"Time to kill the dead." Jonas opened up his body and let the machine gun do the work. The gun was lighter than he thought it might be, and it bristled with life as he held it. He wasn't a very good shot, but right now he didn't need to be. A tornado of bullets ripped through the advancing zombies. They twisted and turned, chest cavities bursting open and heads exploding into a red mist as they were torn apart. Jonas laughed as the dead fell one by one. He knew he wasn't getting headshots in every case, but they were at least being incapacitated. The machine gun was easy to handle, the bullets fast, and he was almost enjoying it. This was how it should be. He was in complete control now. There was nothing they could do to hurt him, nothing. The front of the pack had been decimated, and he had done enough to hold them off for a little while, to give himself some time to get to the truck safely and over the bridge. That was all had to do. Still, it was good to get some payback for Julie, and he decided he may as well shoot until the ammo ran out.

As he poured more and more bullets into the crowd of zombies, he failed to notice the lone zombie scrambling through the mud behind the tank. A fallen soldier, half his face missing, slowly began to claw at the ground. It scratched at the hull, snapping off its fingernails, until it hauled itself up onto its feet. Swirling blood and rainwater pooled in its one empty eye socket, and it groaned as it neared Jonas. It could hear him, see him, sense him, and with his back turned, Jonas was easy meat.

The machine gun finally clicked empty, and Jonas heard the clink of metal on metal close by. He turned, expecting to see Lukas, but instead found a zombie right in his face. The clinking sound had been the soldier's belt hitting the side of the tank, and Jonas raised the gun to bat the dead man away. The dead soldier's arm fumbled around the gun, and Jonas pushed it back. The soldier simply fell against the tank, dropped the gun, and resumed its attack. It rushed Jonas, and opened its mouth to bite him. Jonas saw only a few teeth in the man's head, and a huge hole where the left side of his face should be. As he prepared to dodge those deadly teeth and fight it, a single gunshot ran out, and the zombie's head exploded, cloaking the tank with the man's brains.

"Hamsikker, move it," shouted Lukas, lowering his gun.

Jonas ran to the truck, thanking Lukas for being such a good shot. "You should be in the truck with Dakota," said Jonas as he joined him.

"And so should you," replied Lukas.

They jumped into the cab, and Dakota took off. She checked the mirror. A few zombies were still standing and would undoubtedly follow, but they were far enough away now not to cause any problems. The bridge was short and relatively clear of traffic, so Dakota pressed on, speeding up as the road cleared. They passed a series of buildings to their right, some kind of border patrol station, and then the road turned northwest, away from the Lake, taking them inland.

Once they were over the border a sense of relief filled Jonas. It wasn't just a physical barrier they had overcome, but a mental one too. It was as if being in Canada was the last hurdle they had to get over, and now he felt closer to Janey, closer than he had in a long time. Nothing was going to prevent him from finding her now, not an army of zombies, and certainly not Javier. The zombies that had come from the woods were unfortunate. That station wagon blocking the way was either incredibly bad luck or conveniently positioned. Had Javier made sure it was there to foil anyone trying to follow him?

As they left Lake Superior behind, the trees flanked them on both sides, and the highway became clearer. The wind whipped the truck wickedly, battering it, and surface water flooded the road in parts, making driving difficult. The truck sent huge plumes of water onto the grass verge, and yet the rain did not stop. If anything, the storm seemed to intensify, and thick rain pelted the windshield. No more zombies appeared from the tree line, and the ones at the border were a distant memory. Dakota wished she could say the same about Julie.

Lukas offered to take over the driving again, but Dakota was happy behind the wheel. It gave her something to think about. Watching Julie suffer such a terrible death reminded her of Terry. He had been killed by the zombies, too, forsaken to be eaten alive. His death, just like Julie's, was on Javier's hands. Would he really be waiting for them? She wasn't sure of anything anymore. She knew that Jonas was desperate to get to Janey's. She could feel the tension in him; the urgency with which he did everything. She had no brothers or sisters, so couldn't put herself in his position, but if it were Jonas she was trying to reach, she would move Heaven and Hell to get to him. Right now, it felt like they were doing exactly that. She wasn't sure what to expect when they got to Thunder Bay. There were so many permutations, so many different outcomes to what they might find, that she had given up trying to second-guess it. It felt like things were coming to an end though. The journey they had been on after leaving Kentucky, after all they had been through to get to this point, was coming to a head. She had a baby to think about now, and in a few months she would be showing. Whatever happened after today, she needed to find somewhere safe; somewhere to raise her child with Jonas. She needed to be settled, not scurrying around trying to dodge bullets and zombies. The road ahead was grey and wet, and as she tried to focus on the driving, she wished she could turn the radio on. It would be so good to hear another voice, to know that they weren't alone. It was a thoroughly miserable day, and she needed a boost. They all did.

"There," said Jonas.

The truck shot past a dirty white sign that indicated Thunder Bay was coming up. Jonas thought he would be arriving under different circumstances. He was supposed to be with Erik, Pippa, Peter, and Freya, but Javier had torn that family apart. Instead of Lukas, Jonas should be sitting beside Terry, Mrs. Danick, and all the others who had put their faith in him. Quinn should be driving, not Dakota. It was hard to fathom how things had gone so wrong. Events just seemed to spiral out of control, and even when Jonas thought he was doing the right thing, the whole time Javier had been undermining him. Jonas was caught in two minds. Part of him wanted to find Javier. He wanted to find him and make him pay for what he'd done. He also wanted to find Quinn, Erik and Freya, and the two things went hand in hand. It was a daunting prospect, and he wasn't sure how things would work out if they did reunite. The other part of Jonas hoped to never see Javier again. What Jonas really wanted was peace. He wanted to find Janey, Mikey, Ritchie, and Chester. He wanted to build a new home with Dakota and his child. He wanted to keep anyone who fell under his custody, like Lukas, safe. It was so close now he could feel it.

The deluge continued, and Jonas peered up into the sky. The storm front was moving over them, dark wind swirling and blooming into thick clouds that looked like an erupting volcano, spewing out freezing cold, prickly rain and cavernous thunder. Was this what it had been like when Javier had crossed over the border? Had he been forced to take shelter? Were Quinn and Erik still helping him?

"There it is," said Lukas.

They crested a small hill, and then the city of Thunder Bay came into view. Jonas hadn't expected a welcoming party, but neither had he expected the grim sight that he was confronted with. The town looked like it hadn't escaped the plague of the zombies. He could see from the nearest buildings that they had been ransacked, destroyed, and there was no sign of life. No cars moved in the streets, no lights blinked on or off in the houses, and no people walked the streets. The quiet atmosphere of the city seemed apt somehow. It felt as if they had gone back in time to a place where there were no people or cars. The deep greens of the trees were the only evidence of life, and many of the buildings they approached had been burnt out. Between the fringes of the city and the lake, he saw Fort William rising through the parkland and the rain like a beacon. It instantly reminded him of Freya and the key chain he had given her. Did she still have it? Was she still clinging to it, waiting for him to save her from the monsters and the bad men? Jonas doubted that she had emerged from her self-induced bubble that she had wrapped around herself to protect her from the horrors that surrounded her daily. Javier had made sure she would grow up without a mother, and there was a fair chance that she would find herself without a father, too, before long. Freya hadn't spoken a word for months, and seeing Fort William only reinforced Jonas's feeling that they needed to hurry. It wasn't just Janey he had to reach.

Jonas took some comfort in that he couldn't see any zombies ahead in the city. That didn't mean they weren't there, though, and he knew they would have to proceed with caution. Going into any place where people had lived was a risky prospect these days.

"Dakota, slow it down a notch." Jonas felt his heart beat faster. Knowing Janey was here was hard to accept. It had been such a hard journey that it didn't feel real. "Let's cruise in, and try not to draw any attention to ourselves."

"Sure." Dakota drove carefully, methodically picking a way through the growing cars that had been abandoned on the highway.

Thunder Bay spread out before them beneath a covering of dark sky and heavy rain. Lake Superior appeared faintly in the distance, but the murky rain kept it hidden behind a blanket of water. Jonas had often wondered what this place was like where his sister lived. It had sounded much nicer when she had described it to him. Thunder Bay had been just a place he imagined in his head, a distant dream, but now that he was here the reality was very different. It was like everywhere else. Death hung over the place like a pollutant, gripping the city with its talons, like an evil toxin destined to ruin it forever. He couldn't accept it was too far gone. He couldn't accept Janey wouldn't be here either. She would be. She had promised him. Jonas looked at the buildings as they crept past them silently. He saw no lights on anywhere. Windows dark, doors closed, and cars immobile, lawns overgrown, and piles of rubbish unattended; it was like riding through a ghost town.

"Shoot," said Dakota, frowning.

Jonas brought his attention back to the road ahead, and saw the problem. Another blockage on the road, and this time there was no getting around it. He saw a black helicopter, a large military type, in the middle of the road, a charred husk of blackened, twisted metal. Its rotor blades had gouged out the road, and whoever had flown in it was long gone.

"Can't you squeeze us around the side?" asked Lukas.

Dakota pushed the truck onto the sidewalk, but she found it blocked by another pile of charred metal. The melted frames of cars surrounded the helicopter on both sides and stretched from one side of the road to the other. One and two storey buildings surrounded them making it impossible to get the truck any further.

"Leave it," said Jonas. "We're as close as we need to be. We'll go on foot from here."

Lukas looked at him with a furrowed brow, concern in his eyes. "I'm not so sure that's a good idea, Hamsikker. We don't know what's out there. We should stay in the truck. Let's find another route. There must be something."

"No." Jonas unclipped his seatbelt and opened the door. "We're close enough. I'm not waiting any longer. The place is deserted, you can see that. Janey's home isn't far from here. We need to proceed on foot down the hill, cross over that inlet, and we're as good as there. She lives this side of the city. We can do this. We'll get the guns from the back and go on foot. We'll come back for the truck if we need to."

Jonas disappeared around to the back of the truck, and Lukas looked at Dakota. "You think this is a good idea?"

"There aren't many other options open to us, Lukas. We could go back and find a way around, but I really don't think Jonas is going to wait while we do that. He's going down there whether we like it or not. We'll be better off if we stick together."

"I guess." Lukas wished Bishop was around. He would know what to do.

"Look, if you want to stay with the truck you can. I have to go with him. I want to go. You understand, don't you?"

Lukas nodded. "Yeah, I get it. I'm with you guys. I'm not going to pussy out now. Like you said, we're better off together."

Jonas handed out what weapons they had left. One gun each and some ammo. They decided not to take any food with them. It was a short trip and would only slow them down. Jonas knew there was food where they were going anyway. Janey would have enough supplies for them. The main point was to get to her. They didn't need to be thinking beyond that. The priority now was to reach her home.

Jonas knew progress would be slower on foot than if they had stayed in the truck, but there was no guarantee they would easily be able to find another route. The falling rain hit his face, and its icy coldness was like a slap. He pulled up his jacket, noticing Dakota and Lukas did the same. Each of them kept their guns at the ready. As quiet as it seemed to be, there were no guarantees anymore. After what had happened to Julie, Jonas warned them all to be careful. He took the lead, picking a way through the mangled pile of metal where helicopter and car had meshed and found a way through so they could continue on into the city. He vowed they would stop only when they had to. There was too much at stake to pause now for anything other than an emergency.

Once they were past the blockage, Jonas felt better. Although he hadn't been to Thunder Bay before, Janey had told him about it so many times that he felt as if he knew the area. With Lake Superior and the forest surrounding it, there was no reason why they couldn't make a go of it. Just as soon as he reconnected with Janey, they could start planning the future. There would be a lot to organize. They would need to erect fences for defense, and perhaps some sort of early warning system that could alert them to any zombies approaching the house. They would need to organize the food, too, and find a way of sustaining themselves off the land. North of the city it was just bedrock too barren to sustain any form of farming, but they only needed a small patch of land. Somewhere close to the house where they could grow vegetables. They could fish and chop firewood in summer to get them through the cold winters. Along with his nephews, they could all live here. He wasn't going to need to get ready for the baby, of course, and read up on childcare. He knew next to nothing about it which was why it was so important to get to Janey. She would be able to help Dakota with the pregnancy, the birth, everything. There was so much to do. Jonas picked up the pace, eager to find his sister again. He owed her so much, not least a huge apology. There was a lot to talk about.

"Hey, Jonas, look at this." Dakota picked up a baseball bat. "Could be useful, eh?"

Jonas looked at Dakota. Her wet hair stuck to her face, she was probably completely miserable and cold, and yet she was smiling. She held up the bat for him like a child seeking praise from a parent. "Maybe someone dropped it?"

She was stood by the back of a courier van, its rear doors closed. The van was a sleek black, with silver lettering down its side. Jonas approached the van, and took the bat from her. "Sweet. Let's hope we don't need to use it."

"Guys, give me a minute, can you?" asked Lukas. "I have a huge blister on my foot, and this rain isn't helping." Lukas hobbled over to the courier van, wincing as he walked, and flung back the doors. "I just want to sit down a second, and..."

The zombie inside the van thrust its face into Lukas's, and he screamed as it jumped on top of him. The dead man's face was smeared in gore, his hands bright red with blood. The zombie shook its face ferociously, like a hungry pig at a trough, guzzling down swill and gorging itself as if it hadn't eaten for weeks. Lukas pushed his hands into the man's chest, avoiding the dead hands that swiped at him, and shouted for help.

"Lukas, heads up!" Jonas smashed the bat into the side of the zombie's head. It lost its grip on Lukas and fell to its knees.

"What the fuck, man?" Lukas jumped up and backed away from the dead man. "That nasty fucker's been waiting in there for how long? Why isn't it, like, mummified or something?"

Jonas swung again, smashing the bat into the man's head. It rolled away, but was straight back up onto its feet. It was full of energy and showed no sign of stopping.

"Fuck it," said Lukas, and he shot the man three times in the head. It was finally still, blood seeping out of the bullet holes into the gutter where it mixed with the rainwater and drained away. Lukas looked the man over. From the uniform it wore, it appeared to be the courier driver. "Fucking animal."

"You okay?" Jonas looked at Lukas.

"Yeah, I'm okay. Just got a surprise. I should've checked first. I wasn't thinking."

"Forget it. You good to keep going?" asked Jonas.

Lukas wiped the rain and sweat from his face. "Yeah. Promise I won't go opening any more random doors."

Through the thunderous rain, Jonas went to Dakota. She was staring into the open courier van. Her eyes carried such pity that he almost dared not to speak for fear of her breaking down. When he spoke the rain flicked into his mouth. "Dakota? What is it?"

Dakota pointed through the open van doors. *"That's* why he was so animated."

Jonas stared at the inside of the van. What had once been filled with parcels and boxes was now filled with a half-eaten corpse. Blood was splashed up the walls, on the roof, and had soaked into what few cardboard boxes were inside. Scraps of clothing hung off the bones, and the skull had been licked clean. It was so white and striking against the van's bloody background that it almost looked fake. The ribcage had been dismantled, and if it wasn't for the skull, Jonas wasn't sure he would even be able to recognize what was left as a human being.

"How long do you think it took him to eat them? They must've been in there a while," said Dakota. Her faith was being sorely tested today. How long was He going to let this go on for? How many more had to die?

"Whoever it was, they're gone. God rest," said Jonas. There was no way back for whoever that poor soul had been. They were just lucky Lukas hadn't joined them. He took Dakota's hand and pressed the baseball bat into it. "Take this. Just in case. We should keep moving. Those gunshots will bring more out."

Dakota and Jonas headed toward Lukas. Without warning, Lukas raised his gun, pointing it at them. Even through the teeming rain, Jonas could see Lukas's face. His eyes were wide open, his hands trembling.

"Lukas, what are you doing?" asked Dakota. No way was this happening again. Lukas wouldn't do that to them. She gripped Jonas's hand in terror. She was so sure that Lukas was on their side, yet she had thought the same about Javier.

"Both of you…run!"

Lukas fired, and the bullet whistled past Jonas's ear. He instinctively ducked, and turned to see a zombie fall right behind him. That wasn't all he saw. As the lightening lit up the sky, he saw what Lukas had seen. A multitude of zombies was coming at them, pouring out of seemingly nowhere. They must have been inside the houses, dormant, waiting for something to bring them out. There was no way back now. It seemed as if the whole of Thunder Bay was after them.

"Come on, Dakota," Jonas shouted, as Lukas shot again, dropping a runner right behind them, "we've got to get out of here!"

CHAPTER FOURTEEN

Darting under the awning of a barbershop, Jonas pushed Dakota back and fired. He took out a runner and shot another in the leg which slowed it down. Lukas and Dakota shot back, too, firing at the advancing crowd. The brief shelter from the rain enabled them to aim more precisely, and by the size of the crowd, they needed to. Through the cloak of rain the zombies emerged as one. The courier van was quickly engulfed by the advancing mob, such was their number, and the street was filled by a chorus of groans that was audible even over the incessant rain.

"I thought this place looked quiet," said Dakota. "Shows what I know," she said, as she put a bullet between the eyes of a thin man.

"Let's keep moving," said Jonas. Thunder Bay had a population of thousands. He sincerely hoped they weren't all walking dead. "Downhill. We need to lose them in these shops. We can't risk going straight to Janey's and taking them with us."

Jonas fired once again, reloaded his gun, and then ran out into the road with Lukas and Dakota following him closely. Jonas knew where he wanted to go, but he was going to have to take the long way round. At the bottom of the hill was a small inlet. The bridge over it led into parkland, and Janey's house was somewhere inside along the edge of the lake. That little red house had never seemed so far away as it did now. If Jonas took them straight down the hill and over the bridge, the park would become infested with zombies. He had to make sure that didn't happen. If they ended up staying in Thunder Bay, they could worry about thinning out the number of dead later. Right now, he had to concentrate on leading them away from Janey's. Jonas dodged the outstretched hands of an old woman, and shot her in the face. Gristle and bone showered over his hands as the old woman fell, but Jonas had no time to clean it off. More were coming and fast. He turned to run, and slipped on a wet magazine. He tried to stay upright, but found his feet dancing away from under him as he ran straight onto more magazines.

His gun skipped out of his hands across the road as he landed with a firm thud, and his eyes caught on the adjacent travel store. Its large windows were empty of glass except for some sharp shards on the ground, and the main entranceway was exposed where a large red door flapped open in the wind. Racks of soggy brochures had fallen over, and many of the advertisements had blown out onto the street. Jonas jumped up quickly, and scooped up his gun just as another zombie reached him. Turning to shoot it, he was surprised to find it went right past him. Then he saw Dakota.

She pulled up her gun and fired, but only hit the zombie in the shoulder. It charged into her, knocking her off her feet, and Jonas watched them both tumble to the ground. Dakota's bat flew from her hands, rolling under a car.

"Dakota!" Jonas couldn't shoot with both of them so close. There was no clear shot, and he saw Lukas was too far ahead. He wouldn't be able to get back in time to help, so Jonas ran. He ran to save his wife, hoping he would be in time.

Bullets whistled past his head as he ran through the rain, and he knew Lukas was doing what he could, stopping the zombies behind him. He could see the zombie and Dakota rolling on the ground, locked in a tussle that neither seemed destined to win. The zombie was an old man, still dressed in a check shirt with scruffy black jeans. He wore an old cap, and would almost be able to pass as human if it weren't for the bloody hole in his neck.

"Dakota, hold on," Jonas shouted.

When he reached her, he could see that her arms were trembling with the effort of keeping the zombie off her. Jonas put his arms around it, and pulled the man back. Instantly the zombie's attention was turned, and Jonas found the man turning around, trying to bite him. They grappled briefly, but Jonas had the upper hand. He spun the man away from him, and fired quickly, blowing the man's head apart. Jonas grabbed Dakota's hand.

"You okay?"

"Yes, I'm fine," she said breathlessly.

They ran to join Lukas, careful not to skid over the slippery surface of the road.

"This is too much," he said as he fired his gun at another zombie. "We need to shake them off. I'm almost out."

"I'm almost out too. We need a short-cut." Dakota swept her hair from her face. "They must outnumber us fifty to one."

Jonas looked for a way out; a place they could go for shelter. They had to get off the street. It was acting like a funnel for the zombies, and if they continued going directly downhill they were never going to be rid of them. He shot at another runner, a young boy, and it spun in the swirling wind and rain before falling to the road, dead. Thunder boomed overhead, rattling the windowpanes, before lightening lit up the road again. Jonas shielded his eyes from the constant rain and saw the dead coming for them in droves. He saw old men and women, even children, oblivious to each other, but walking side by side down the hill to the three of them. Some zombies had missing limbs, some exposed their innards, and others had bones protruding from their bodies where skin and muscle had been torn asunder.

"This way," Jonas said, pointing to a side road. "We have to get off the main street and lose them."

They ran across a small intersection, weaving between the cars. Jonas ducked into the doorway of a toy shop. There was a plastic doll in the window, its face surrounded by thick wiry hair, and it wore a shabby white dress. Its eyes were black, and it stared out through the window at him unblinking. A small tattoo of a dragon had been etched onto its cheek, and it held a small bag in its hands. Jonas felt almost as creeped out by it as he did the zombies.

"Over there, past the arcade and over the lot, there's a sports center of some sort. See it? We're going for it. We'll try to lose them."

Lukas looked at the large sports center, its outline barely visible through the rain. "What if it's locked up, and we can't get in?"

"Then we'll keep running until we find something else. The horde will hopefully pass us by while we stay safe and dry, hidden behind those huge walls. It must be safer than somewhere small like this where we could get trapped," Jonas said, indicating the toy store.

"And the scary ass doll has got nothing to do with it, right?" asked Dakota, looking at it through the window. "Now *that* is fugly."

"Right," replied Jonas. "Look, it would be better to take our chances in the center than remain outside and have to battle this lot. You two okay? Dakota, are you up to this?" She nodded, but Jonas could see she was exhausted. He just needed her to get through this, and once they were at Janey's they could begin to relax. "We're almost there. This is just a quick diversion. We have to throw them off, all right?"

Dakota nodded again, and then Jonas was off, picking his way through the streets, ducking behind every car, trying to make it difficult for the zombies to track them. When he was halfway across the parking lot, he cast a glance behind him. Beyond Lukas and Dakota he could see the dead. Some were following, but not all. It was as if they were following a leader. It was if they simply followed the one in front of them. There was no way they could see clearly, not in this horrible weather.

Jonas ran up to the main entrance of the sports center. It was dark inside, and he pushed on the glass doors. They wouldn't budge, and he peered inside. There was a reception area and a turnstile, a couple of doors, and a stairway leading to an upper viewing area. At the far end of the foyer was a door that had been left open. Through it Jonas could see a swimming pool and a high diving board. It seemed perfectly empty, and the water was still. It was so dark, though, that he couldn't be sure.

"See if there's a side door." Jonas knew the quickest thing to do would be to shoot the lock or the glass, but then there would be no way of closing the doors behind them.

Seconds later he heard Dakota call out. "Here. It's open."

Racing to join her, he found Dakota standing in a doorway, one foot already inside. He ushered her in, then Lukas, and then he slammed the door behind him. Instantly the noise of the pelting rain died down, and he felt like he could breathe again. He looked around for something to block the doorway but there was nothing. They were in some sort of service corridor, its walls smooth and gray, and a green unlit emergency exit sign above the door.

"Come on," said Jonas as he wiped the water from his face and shook his head. "Let's just hope they don't figure out how to get in. I think we've a good chance of this working. We'll work our way slowly through the center and find another way out."

He held his gun out in front of him and began down the corridor. Reaching a door at the far end, Jonas pressed his ear against it. He was listening for sounds coming from within, anything at all that might suggest they weren't alone, but he couldn't hear a thing. Looking at Lukas, he indicated he was going to open the door.

"Ready?"

Lukas pressed himself against the wall. "Go for it."

Jonas pushed the door handle, but nothing happened. He pushed again, but still nothing. Dakota put her hand over his, and pulled the handle, easing the door open with a simple click.

"Ready?" she asked with a glint in her eye.

"I knew that," Jonas said, winking at Dakota. He looked at Lukas, and then pulled the door wide open. Nothing jumped out at them, no surge of zombies rushed them, and the door simply swung back with a faint squeak.

Lukas passed through into the center first. "It's fine. It's empty," he said, and Jonas and Dakota followed him in.

Their feet squeaked as they walked on the tiled floor, and Lukas proceeded to the first door he saw. Inside he found a large gym complete with running machines, weights, and a whole heap of trashed gear. The bar bells were scattered across the floor, and one huge mirror that stretched the entire length of the wall was cracked. On a gym mat were a couple of dead bodies, flies swarming around them indicating that they weren't going to be getting up again. There was no indication of anyone else inside. There was no sound either, just the faint regular sound of dripping water, and no other exit that he could see. There seemed little point in checking out the changing rooms, and he closed the door.

"Nothing," he said, looking back at the main entranceway. There were distant figures shambling through the parking lot. "I suggest we go upstairs. It's too open down here, and we're too visible. We need to put some space between us and them. Give ourselves a better chance of getting out of here. A couple of minutes, and we should be safe to come back down."

Lukas led them up a flight of stairs which indicated a seating area for non-swimmers. They passed a couple more dead bodies on the stairway, but the bodies were too far gone to be reanimated. It appeared as though most of them had been eaten. Lukas hoped they might find a food court or a kitchen. Despite everything, he was beginning to feel hungry. As they proceeded through the viewing area, Lukas found a vending machine. However, it had been completely emptied, and he kept going back into another corridor, looking for some place safe they could wait it out and maybe find a snack. Still, there was that sound of dripping water.

Jonas questioned the wisdom of going too deeply into the building. "We can just sit it out here, Lukas. There's no need to check out every room."

"I'm just saying that if we're going to spend some time here, we may as well check it out. We could find something useful: guns, weapons…food."

"We just need to stay put and hide for a while," said Dakota. "Let's stop here," she said, pointing to an empty office.

Lukas shook his head. "Look, we're here and we're safe. We may as well have a look around. The place is empty."

Lukas swung open a door, and stared into a gloomy exercise room lined with floor-to-ceiling mirrors. Gym equipment had been discarded and left strewn everywhere: dumbbells, towels, skip ropes, exercise mats, and large fitness balls. Each and every item was covered in blood. Lukas shook his head. He wasn't going to find anything here.

The dripping of water became louder, and it became apparent to Jonas that something was wrong. It sounded less like a dripping, and more like a gushing sound. As they walked down the narrow corridor, Jonas realized his feet were wet. There were two inches of water lining the corridor, yet he couldn't see the source of it. He looked up at the ceiling, trying to find a hole in the roof or a burst pipe, but there was nothing noticeable that would cause the flooding.

"Hey, Lukas, be careful," said Jonas. "We don't need to be in here for hours. We should go back down and see if they've passed. We might need to find another exit." They passed by another room, and Jonas took a look out of a small square window down into the parking lot. The horde of dead was right there, directly beneath them, and Jonas quickly pulled back out of sight. What pleased him was that they weren't hanging around the main entrance but moving past it. It looked like the zombies were passing them by, but he couldn't be sure, not yet. "Lukas, you hear me?"

"Yeah, yeah," replied Lukas. "Just stay away from the windows, Hamsikker. They're close, but they don't know we're here. I think we're safe up here."

Jonas kicked the water pooling at his feet and went back to the corridor. It sounded as if it was raining inside now. The air was damp, and he didn't think there was an inch of him still dry. His clothes were soaked through, and now his feet were too. There had to be a leak in the roof.

Lukas was stood in ankle deep water now up ahead of Dakota and Jonas. Pushing open a door carefully, he looked inside, turned around and smiled. "What did I tell you? There's a staff kitchen in here. Looks like we've hit the jack…"

With a huge cracking sound, Lukas suddenly disappeared. Jonas was looking at him, and the next he was simply gone. The cracking sound grew louder, and was replaced by what sounded like thunder. The water around Jonas's ankles began to rush forward, threatening to sweep him off his feet.

"Jonas?" Up ahead Dakota turned and reached out for her husband.

As Jonas tried to grab hold of her, she disappeared too. Her scream bounced off the walls as she fell, and then Jonas felt the floor beneath him give away too. Finally, he understood. The whole floor was giving away, probably weakened by the flooding, unable to withstand the weight of the three of them walking on it. A torrent of water cascaded over his head as he fell, and though it was only seconds, it seemed like an eternity before he landed. He tried to look for Dakota, but it wasn't just water that obscured his vision. Floor tiles and plaster bombarded him as he fell, and he became completely disorientated. Waiting for the inevitable impact that would surely kill them, or at least render them incapable of walking, he wished he could see Dakota one last time. He wished he could drag her out of this place and send her some place safe, perhaps back to stay with Bishop. He tried to call out for her, but his mouth filled with water. He flapped his arms as if he could fly, and then abruptly hit the water below.

It was like he had jumped into the ocean, so cold was the water that surrounded his body. He kicked furiously, trying to reach the surface, desperate for oxygen to replace the water he had swallowed. He blinked his eyes open, but as soon as he did they stung, and he caught only a glimpse of light before he had to close them again. Kicking his legs out, and trying to swim upwards, he finally broke the surface of the water and coughed.

"Dakota? Dakota, where are you?" Jonas retched, and spat out the foul water that had gotten into his mouth. It tasted like a foul cocktail of chemicals and blood. Was there chlorine in there or bleach? He spat again, and wiped his eyes.

"Dakota!" Jonas shouted for her, wishing she would scream. At least then he would know she was all right.

Jonas looked around, trying to find her, trying to figure out where the hell they were. Evidently the floor they had been walking on was directly above the center's vast swimming pool, and they had landed directly in the middle of the main pool. To one side of the huge room they were now in Jonas saw a row of seats. To the other side he saw two open doors that led to change rooms. There was a high diving board beneath a clock that had stopped at three o'clock. A tearing sound filled his ears, and then more plaster rained down on him. The ceiling was giving way, and more of it was coming down. They had to get out of there quickly. He was treading water as best he could, unable to feel the bottom of the pool. He knew Dakota could swim, but in this mess, with the roof caving in on them, anything could happen. He had to get her out of there.

Jonas became aware of a body slipping by him. It was face down, and not moving. The brown hair was wrapped around the woman's face, and the skin on her arms pale and wrinkled.

"Dakota?" He pushed the body over, preying it wasn't her. When he saw the face, grossly disfigured, the skin covered in teeth marks, the eyes pulpy and creamy white, he wished it had been her.

The zombie reached out an arm, and began to thrash around, trying to get to Jonas. Its rotten teeth clacked together, and its eyeballs rolled in its head.

"Fuck." Jonas tried to push it away, but every time he did, it just seemed to bring the creature closer. He aimed a punch at the zombie's head, and he succeeded in hitting in cleanly on the side of the head. Unfortunately, the zombie had spent so long in the pool that its skin had become nothing but a rubbery soft mush, and Jonas only succeeded in cleaving off its skin, leaving him with a gooey pink mush enveloped around his fist.

"Get the fuck off me," he shouted, as he tried to swim away from the zombie.

"Jonas?"

Suddenly she was behind him coughing and spluttering.

"Dakota...get out of here."

A floor tile that had fallen down with them floated within reach, and Jonas grabbed it. He kicked upward, got himself a couple of inches extra height, and brought the tile down on the zombie's head. Swathes of hair and skin came away with the tile, exposing the dead woman's pure white skull, but the zombie kept coming. It had no idea how to actually swim, but the way it kept flailing its arms around kept it afloat, and Jonas knew it was next to impossible to get away from it.

"Dakota, get the hell out of here." Jonas swung the tile down again, hoping he could smash through the thing's skull, but the tile broke in half, and the zombie just kept on coming. Its hands grazed Jonas's face, its pudgy, dead fingers clawing at his skin, touching his cheeks, his jaw, and his nose. Jonas shuddered. It was disgusting, and it needed putting down. Kicking as frantically as he could, he tried to put some distance between himself and the zombie. He tried swimming after Dakota toward the edge of the pool, but every time he thought he was going to get away, the thing wrapped its fingers around his ankles and pulled him back. Putrid water rushed into his mouth as he gurgled and coughed, trying to get away from the zombie's deadly clutches. He spat the gross water out, and took in a breath before he was pulled under the surface.

With the zombie grasping him tightly, Jonas had no choice but to let it pull him down, and he twisted to face his adversary. Under the water Jonas had no momentum, and though he tried to push the zombie away, all he succeeded in doing was slicing off more foul skin. They were slowly sinking, further and further down toward the bottom of the pool. Jonas tried to stop it, but the pressure in his ears grew, and no matter what he did, they were sinking inexorably, inescapably, to the bottom. The zombie continued to pull at his legs, and Jonas felt a burning in his chest as he struggled for air. His eyes felt like they were on fire as chlorine and stagnant water stung them. His feet touched the bottom of the pool, and he realized they weren't going any further. The zombie was trying to pull him toward it, toward its gaping open mouth where a rubbery tongue was flicking in and out of its engorged mouth, darting in and out like a small pink fish in a dark cave. Jonas tried to get himself around the back of the woman, to keep himself away from her mouth, but it wasn't easy. He managed to maneuver himself away from the zombie's head, but it kept twisting and turning, just as he did, and he knew very shortly the dance they were doing was going to stop. His lungs felt like they were exploding, so desperate was he for air, and he tried to use the bottom of the pool to kick upward. The zombie kept dragging him down, though, and Jonas could feel himself weakening. He looked around for anything he could use as a weapon, hoping to spot a piece of piping, perhaps something that had fallen from the upper floor that he could use to leverage himself free.

There was nothing.

The bottom of the pool was lined with square blue tiles, and all Jonas could see were more bodies. All of them were in varying stages of putrefaction, some appearing to be perfectly preserved, whilst others were ragged corpses held together only because they had not had time to decompose. The zombie's faces were swollen, their stomachs were burst open, and exposed entrails bobbed around in the water like a fleshy seaweed. Jonas noticed movement amongst the bodies, and thought that his fight with the zombie must have disturbed the water. Some of the arms and legs of the bodies were moving, swaying irregularly, undoubtedly disturbed by his macabre dance with the dead woman. Jonas heaved with all his might, and pulled the zombie toward him. It was all he could think to do, and the last chance he had to escape its clutches. He used the zombie's forward momentum to make it go over his head, and the zombie passed above him like the hull of a ship. Its hands lost their grip on him, and he was finally free. The problem he had now was that the dead body was floating directly above him, and he was going to have to swim out sideways to avoid it.

With his body aching, he placed his feet flat against the bottom of the pool and pushed. He was aware of a distant noise, of shouting and screaming, but he couldn't make out what was being said. The shouting was probably coming from Dakota on the poolside, but he had to trust she was safe. All he could do now was get himself to the surface. He longed to take in a long deep breath, and knew he couldn't last more than a few more seconds underwater. As he pushed off, a body slipped beneath him, and he looked at its face. The thing blinked, and reached up for him, its clammy hands grabbing hold of his belt. They weren't just bodies in the pool, they were zombies. When he had seen their hands and legs waving around, it hadn't been the fight disturbing them in the water. They were trying to get to him, and he glanced around, noticing more and more of them all heading toward him.

Startled, Jonas opened his mouth. His scream was muted by the water, and as the last of the oxygen in his lungs rushed out, filthy, bloody water rushed in.

The zombie beneath him kept hold of his belt, and all of Jonas's impetus was lost. His legs buckled as he felt himself being pulled back down again. The zombie beneath him was once a man, and long black hair flowed around his face like an octopus's arms. Thick strands of hair on the dead man's head writhed around in the water like spindly hungry worms. The man wore only a pair of board shorts, and they were straining to be freed from the man's extended gut. Jonas felt the zombie that had been above him grab his left leg, and though he fought it, he couldn't shake off two of them. He wriggled around, trying to get free, but drained of energy and air, the game was up. He tried to suck in more air, but all he could do was swallow the water that continued to burn its way down his throat. The zombie beneath him was getting closer and closer, and he could see straight into its eyes. The man had bite marks all over his face and neck, and as he opened his mouth to bite, Jonas thought of Janey. She was waiting for him with her three kids. She was less than a mile away, and he wasn't going to make it. He wasn't going to see her. He wasn't going to get his chance to tell her how sorry he was.

Jonas didn't have time to dwell on his thoughts, as the world around him began to turn black. It felt like his blood was bubbling, and his brain was freezing, and he desperately kicked out, praying he would finally be able to kick the zombies away and get out of this pool.

His feet connected with the zombie that held his left leg, but the dead woman grabbed his other leg. The zombie beneath him had one arm wrapped around Jonas's right arm now, and was close enough to taste. He was trapped like a fish in a net. Jonas looked at the others crawling across the bottom of the pool toward him, their revolting faces staring at him, and he swallowed one last mouthful of sickening water. He could feel his body tensing up, and his brain was screaming at him to get out of this, to get back up to Dakota, to get out of the pool, to find air, to find freedom, to find Janey.

But he couldn't do it.

Jonas felt his life ebbing away. Grey spots flashed in front of his eyes, and they merged together, growing larger until he saw nothing but a dim, dark blackness. He prayed that Dakota was at least safe. He wanted more than anything to be a father, to spend his life with her, but he couldn't fight it anymore. His eyes closed, and his body went limp as the life drained out of him beneath the turgid water. Jonas slipped into a horrible blackness that engulfed his entire being, and the zombies claimed their victim.

CHAPTER FIFTEEN

Lukas ripped off his shirt, revealing a smooth chest and muscled physique that surprised Dakota. He was so young, so quiet and unassuming, that seeing him spring into action was unexpected. She thought he was more likely to have his head in a book than be found at a gym.

"Stay here, and get ready," said Lukas as he looked into Dakota's eyes. "If I don't come back up with Hamsikker, you need to get the hell out of here."

Lukas looked at the pool, the water sloshing around as the zombies tossed and turned in the water, thrashing like dying animals. There were so many of them. When he had landed in the water, he had been surprised. The floor above had given way so quickly that there had been no time to plan what to do, so he had gone with it, and waited for his body to smash into the lower level. He knew with two broken legs it would be the end of him, but when he fell into the soft landing of the swimming pool, he took his chance and got out quickly. He hadn't even noticed the dead bodies as he swam away. It was only when he crawled out and turned around that he had seen them. There were a dozen or more bobbing in the water, and he saw even more were beneath the surface. He wasn't sure if they could get out, but he didn't intend to wait to find out. He had heard two more loud splashes behind him as he got out of the pool, and knew it must be Dakota and Hamsikker. As he looked at the pool now, its churning water turning red, he feared the worst. He had helped pull Dakota out of the water, but when they had gone back to pull Hamsikker out he was gone, sucked beneath the surface by a zombie. So much time had passed as they waited for him to resurface, that Lukas knew something was wrong. There was no way Hamsikker would be able to hold his breath this long.

"I'll get him, I promise," said Lukas. Dakota was shivering, yet through fear or cold Lukas wasn't sure. The whole place was like a huge fridge. Going back into the cold water wasn't an appealing prospect, but he couldn't just leave Hamsikker to drown, not like this. He grabbed a jagged, broken piece of piping that had come down from the ceiling, and braced himself.

"Lukas, be careful. Don't…" Dakota's words were lost as he dove into the water.

For a moment time seemed to stand still. Dakota watched as Lukas disappeared beneath the water. It didn't make sense. One moment Jonas was there, helping her, the next he was gone. He was a good swimmer, but something had gone wrong, she knew it. She couldn't see what was going on down there, but in her gut she just knew something bad was happening. The prospect of Jonas not making it was unbelievable. She couldn't lose him, not now.

Dakota needed to do something to distract her from what she suspected was happening, and she looked around for something she could use to help. There was a lifesaver on the wall, and she plucked it from its case. She looked eagerly back at the pool, but there was still no sign of Lukas or Jonas. Dropping the round lifesaver at her feet, she realized it would be of little use. Down at the shallow end of the huge pool Dakota saw a form stumbling up the steps and out of the water. It slipped as it took its first tentative steps on the poolside, and landed on its back. Like a crab, it wriggled for a moment, arms and legs waving in the air, before it found traction on the slippery tiles, and stood again. The zombie was thin and weak, yet Dakota knew it would find her quickly. She looked at the water again, peering beneath the surface, trying to find them, hoping they would come up and tell her everything was fine, that they were going to all be fine, and that this was just a horrible dream. The surface of the pool was covered in parts of the roof, and more kept falling as she watched.

Dakota couldn't convince herself that everything was fine, and her heart pounded fast. *Please God, not Jonas, not now*, she thought. She knelt down at the edge of the pool, but through the murky water she couldn't see anything. There were lots of bodies down there, but who was living, and who was dead was impossible to tell.

"Come on, damn you, come on."

There was a gurgling noise behind her, and Dakota spun to see a zombie stood right behind her. Her heart lurched, as the thing reached out for her. It couldn't have come from the pool, as it was dry, so must've found another way in. Dakota was through screaming, and as it attempted to grab her, she sidestepped quickly out of the way. Teetering on the edge of the pool, she did the only thing she could think to do, and pushed it in, hoping it wouldn't get in Lukas's way.

The rake thin zombie from the shallow end was halfway around the pool now. Dakota knew she couldn't sit around waiting for it to get to her. When Lukas brought Jonas out, they were going to need to move quickly, and she looked around for something to use as a weapon. When she'd fallen she had dropped her gun, and presumed it was now somewhere at the bottom of the swimming pool. Dakota noticed a pole of some sort on the tiled floor, and ran to pick it up. It was a telescopic pool cleaner, and she flipped it around so the net was in her hands, and the main blunt end of the pole was pointed at the zombie. She approached it carefully, and then whacked the side of it, intending to knock it off balance and into the pool. The rod was too long, and didn't carry enough weight to dislodge the zombie, though, so the dead man kept coming, batting away the rod with ease. It opened its mouth to moan as it neared Dakota, but only water came out and dribbled down its dislocated jaw.

Bending it over her knee, Dakota quickly grasped the cam and snapped the rod in half. Now it was much shorter, but she had the equivalent of a javelin, and as the zombie threw itself at her, she raised it quickly at the dead man. With a sickening crunch, the zombie impaled itself on the rod, and Dakota was thrown beneath it as she held onto the broken rod. It had entered the zombie's chest, and Dakota knew it wasn't going to be enough to stop it. She kept a firm hold on the rod, not wanting to let go for fear of the zombie freeing itself. She was sandwiched between the cold tiles under her back and the zombie above. Only the rod kept it at bay, yet the zombie was slowly, so slowly, sliding down the pole toward her. As it kept coming toward her, more water spewed from its mouth, and she could smell its foul innards mixed with the chlorine. There was shouting coming from the pool, too, and she knew Lukas had found Jonas. They needed help, and she'd had enough of fighting this zombie. With a surge of energy she slid out from under it, letting the zombie fall where she had been lying. Darting away from its groping hands, she grabbed the other end of the discarded broken rod.

Dakota let the zombie roll over and stand up. She dare not push it into the water for fear of simply pushing it toward Lukas or Jonas. The zombie uttered a groan, and then Dakota jammed the rod into the zombie's eye, ramming it through the socket and up to the hilt. Blood trickled down her forearm, and began gushing from the exploded eye. She shoved the zombie backward until it was pressed up against the wall, and then she pulled the rod out before quickly ramming it into the other eye.

"Fucking die!" she screamed.

Now blinded, the zombie fumbled for her, but Dakota could tell it was weakening. She twisted the road around until it hit the tiled floor, carving up the zombie's face like a Christmas ham. Smearing the zombie's brains onto the tiles, Dakota thrust the rod into its skull into it finally stopped moving.

"Dakota, come quickly."

She dropped the rod. Turning to see Lukas bent over her husband on the side of the pool, she ran to them.

"What happened? Is he going to be all right?" Dakota looked at Jonas knowing full well he wasn't all right at all. His face was pale, and his lips blue. "What do we do? I don't—"

"He's not breathing," said Lukas calmly. "I need to clear his airway." Lukas began to blow into Jonas's mouth.

"Oh God." Dakota looked on horrified, and clutched Jonas's lifeless hands. He couldn't leave her now, not when they were so close. She watched Lukas breathe for Jonas, and then pump his chest in an attempt to restart his heart. Nothing seemed to happen, and Jonas lay motionless.

A clatter behind her forced Dakota to turn around, and she saw a zombie stumble from the change rooms. It immediately began to head for her, and then she saw another behind it. The place had a seriously bad zombie infestation.

"Lukas, please…" Dakota rubbed Jonas's hand, trying to get some warmth back into him. She squeezed his fingers, and ran her hand up his forearm, hoping he might respond. His skin was cold, and as Lukas kept giving him CPR, she saw nothing was happening. She had to give Lukas more time, and the zombies weren't waiting.

Lukas rocked back on his heels. "Dakota, I'm sorry, but he's not responding." Lukas saw the zombies approaching, two men with bite marks all over their bodies, and he prepared to get up and fight. "Dakota, Hamsikker is go—"

"*Don't* you say it, Lukas, don't you *dare* fucking say it. I'll deal with them. *Keep going.*"

Dakota got to her feet and faced the zombies. "He's not gone yet, Lukas."

Though he felt like it was a waste of time, Lukas resumed CPR. He could hear the zombies splashing around in the pool, and knew that some would eventually get out. It wouldn't be long before they were surrounded. They couldn't afford to hang around much longer if they wanted to get out.

"Keep going," shouted Dakota as she ran toward the two zombies. She plucked the broken rod from the skull of the one she had just killed, and skewered the first zombie she came to. She thrust the rod into its neck, and the zombie's hands flailed as it tried to reach her.

"Not today, motherfucker," she screamed, and with all her might she yanked the rod to the side, sending the zombie into the small children's play pool. The zombie floundered in the shallow water, surrounded by inflatable penguins and bloody armbands. Dakota was angry. She was not going out like this, and neither was Jonas. The aching in her bones, the coldness that seeped through her damp clothes to her skin, and the constant tiredness and headaches had been a drain before. She had a child inside her, and a husband at death's door, and she was fucking pissed. She summoned up all her energy and used her anger to spur her on.

"Throw what you can at me, 'cause I'm not stopping now," she said, and she charged at the oncoming zombie. Dakota had no more weapons. The guns were gone. She had nothing left but her own hands, and she grabbed the dead man by the hair as she shoved him to the ground. The dead man was young, and his hair was long and curly. With both hands she began to smash his head back onto the tiled floor. What had been a clean white floor was soon a dark bloody red color. Dakota kept smashing his head back until the bone cracked, and his brain was exposed.

"Dakota, stop, it's okay," said Lukas.

Still, she kept going, her face contorted with rage, her eyes burning with tears as she killed the man. She was oblivious to everything else around her. Why did they think they could take Jonas away from her? Who did they think they were, these stinking walking corpses? They deserved to die. They should be rotting in hell.

"Dakota, come on," said Lukas gently. He put a hand on her shoulder. "We have to get out of here."

When the zombie beneath Dakota stopped moving, she kept smashing his skull back until his face was obliterated and there was nothing but a pinky-white pile of mushed brain and bone. She pulled her hands up to smash his head again, but there was nothing left to hold onto, and she stared at her hands that clutched nothing but strands of coarse hair. Blood trickled through her fingers, and only as she began to accept the monster was truly dead did she realize Lukas was beside her. She looked into his eyes, scared what she might see. She didn't want to know Jonas was dead. She didn't need to see the sympathy in Lukas's eyes or feel his consoling touch. She needed her husband.

"Dakota, he's okay."

A ripple of relief washed over Dakota, and as Lukas stepped aside, she saw Jonas sitting upright coughing painfully. She was surprised and elated at the same time to see him sitting up, and she ran to him.

"Oh, Jonas, I thought…"

Dakota wept as she held Jonas, and she tried to hold him close to her, to give him some of her little body warmth. He was ice cold, and she looked him over. "Jonas, are you okay? What happened?"

"I'll be okay, thanks to Lukas. I remember being at the bottom of the pool, and then it's all a blur. They were down there. There were too many."

Dakota embraced her husband tightly. "You're okay now, I've got you. You're okay, Jonas. We're okay."

"Um, guys, I hate to break up the reunion, but we really do have to go," said Lukas. He spotted a zombie crawling from the pool at the far end near where the ceiling had collapsed. "We can get out the main entrance. The parking lot looks clear, and we need to get away from this pool as soon as we can."

"Can you walk?" asked Dakota, as she helped Jonas to his feet.

Jonas nodded. "I feel like I've gone ten rounds with Tyson, but I'll be okay."

Dakota put an arm around Jonas to support him. "Lukas, how do you know CPR?"

"First aid course. My employer made us take it last year. I thought it was pointless, but turns out it was the only good thing that came out of me working there. Good job my Mom made me learn to swim at high school, too, huh?"

They walked back into the foyer, leaving the swimming pool behind. It was quieter away from the zombies, and Lukas was right. The parking lot was clear, and it looked as if the plan had worked. The rain had eased up slightly, but was still coming down in a constant drizzle. The storm had passed over them, and the sky was beginning to get lighter.

Lukas rattled the glass doors, but they were locked tight. "Well, we have no guns anymore, so I guess shooting our way out is out of the question," he said. He could see a few zombies back at the pool begin to find their way around the edge and toward the foyer. "Any bright ideas?"

Dakota looked around and saw two plants by the reception desk. The leaves were still a lush green, and yellow flowers adorned the uppermost branches. She yanked one of the artificial plants from its pot, and lifted it up. The pot was four feet high, and appeared to be ceramic. "This should do," she said, and then she threw it at the glass doors.

At first only a slight crack appeared, and she picked up the pot for another go. Lukas grabbed the second, discarding the artificial plant, and both he and Dakota began battering at the glass. Within a minute they managed to get one of the panes out, enough to squeeze through. One by one they filed back outside into the rain. After the stench of the swimming pool, it was refreshing, and no longer the same annoying cold rain that had drenched them earlier.

"What now?" asked Lukas. "Back the way we came? We don't know where that horde went."

"Yeah. We go back to the main street and down the hill. We need to get over the bridge," said Jonas. He looked at Lukas's face and could read what he was thinking. "I know, sounds too easy, right?"

They retraced their steps back to the crash site unhindered by the dead. Jonas didn't care where they had gone, he was just glad they had. Images of them still floated around his mind, and it was as if he could taste them, as if they were a part of him. He had bad memories of the sports center and was pleased to be out of there. He knew if Lukas hadn't been there, he would most likely be dead. Dakota too. Jonas's head was swimming. There was so much to do, so much to think about, to prepare for; Janey was waiting, his nephews were relying on him, and Dakota needed him. Yet the images of the zombies reaching for him and pulling him underwater kept resurfacing, kept confusing him, and it felt like his lungs were bursting again, full of deadly dark water.

As Jonas's knees buckled, Dakota held him upright. "Lukas, help me."

Lukas immediately helped her lower Jonas to the ground. "Hamsikker, you okay buddy, you still with us?"

Dakota watched as Jonas blinked his eyes, looking at her as if she was nothing but a stranger. His head seemed to sway slightly, as if he were drunk. "There's no way he can do this on foot. We could probably carry him between us."

"Hey, Hamsikker, come on, this is no time to go sitting down." Lukas patted Jonas's back. He kept his tone light, but was concerned. Jonas was weak, and would undoubtedly slow them down if they carried on as they were.

"I'll be okay. Sorry. I just need a minute." Jonas felt dizzy, and despite the lightness of Lukas's questioning, it was clear they were worried about him.

"We need wheels," said Lukas.

"We'll never get the truck past the crash site," replied Dakota. "I don't see as we have many options. The chances of finding a working vehicle with the keys left conveniently inside are slim to nil. Not to mention, we don't have the time to go looking for one."

"We don't need to. All we need is something to get us down to that bridge. Like Hamsikker said, once we're over the bridge we're in the clear. You can see the park from here. The trees are just beyond, and I'm guessing Jonas's sister lives close by."

Dakota watched as Lukas wandered over to a jeep and opened the driver's door. He fumbled inside for a moment, and then closed the door. "No good."

Lukas went to another vehicle, a red pick-up, and opened the door. As he did so, Dakota heard a scraping noise, as if something were dragging itself along the ground. There was movement coming from the crash site; something crawling out from underneath the helicopter. Dakota stared as a man pulled himself along the ground using only his hands. The lower half of his body was missing, and his legs ended in bloody stumps that left a wet slick trail of blood as he crawled across the road to her. His eyes appeared to be jet black, utterly devoid of life, of compassion, of feeling anything. The zombie sickened her. Was this what man had come to? Was this what they had been reduced to?

"I'll get it," said Jonas as he stumbled to his feet. "I'll just..."

"No, I've got this." Dakota needed Jonas to save his energy. They weren't safe until they were all stood in Janey's house in front of a roaring fire, and Jonas was going to need all his energy for what lay ahead.

Dakota found a brick and picked it up. She strode over to the man crawling on his hands and swung the brick at his head, raking it across his face, and taking off large swathes off skin. The zombie kept coming, and Dakota ignored its feeble attempts to grab her ankles. She swung again. The brick smashed into the dead man's face, his nose disintegrating with a satisfying crunching noise. Dakota hit it again, pulverizing its head until it finally stopped moving.

"Okay?" asked Jonas, as Dakota returned to him.

"Yeah, I'm just ready to go. I've over it. I've had enough of the killing. I just want to lie down and sleep for a long, long time," she replied.

"I know the feeling," said Jonas. He kissed Dakota as the rain fell on them, and he felt a little better. They weren't done yet. "I love you, Mrs. Hamsikker."

"All right, Jonas, no time to get mushy now. Save it for later," said Dakota as she kissed him back.

"When you two are ready, I've got one," shouted Lukas.

The red truck had been dinged up pretty badly, and the windows had been smashed, but the main thing was it wasn't locked up. Lukas was beckoning them over from the driver's seat, ready to go.

"Does it work?" asked Jonas.

"Not a chance." Lukas grinned. "But it doesn't need too. It's pointed in the right direction, see? Downhill, you said. All I need is a little push, and gravity will take care of the rest. We'll be down and over that bridge in one minute."

Dakota smiled, impressed at Lukas's ingenuity. "Then what are we waiting for?"

Jonas and Dakota went to the back of the truck and began to push. It moved slowly, reluctantly, but then began to pick up speed.

"Jump in!" shouted Lukas, and Jonas and Dakota ran to get into the truck.

Jonas checked his mirror and noticed the gathering crowd. They were back. He saw them just behind the crash, their putrid bodies shuffling around, arms flailing wildly, teeth gnashing together, and pale eyes searching for their next meal.

The dead.

Even if they noticed the moving truck, would it be enough to draw them out? He doubted it. There was no noise as the engine was off, and they would be out of sight within seconds. He said a quiet prayer, and glued his eyes to the road ahead. It was time to put some distance between them and the zombies.

The truck moved slowly at first, but soon picked up speed. Lukas felt the truck pulling to the left, and as they gained more speed, he felt the drag even more. Lukas cursed quietly.

"What is it?" asked Dakota.

"I think we have a flat."

"Well, we can't stop to change it, we don't have time. We've got to get over the river, Lukas. Can we make it?"

"We'll let physics help us out," said Jonas. "The truck should be fine until we get down the hill, at least. When we reach the bottom, we'll bale and go through the trees on foot. It's no more than a couple minutes' walk through to the lake, and that's where we'll find Janey. This will give us some breathing space to get ahead of any zombies who try to follow. We'll lose them in the park."

The natural gradient of the hill made the truck speed up without Lukas having to do anything, and he pulled on the wheel to keep them as straight on the road as he could. The road was flanked by quiet, dark buildings, and the dead. Not the walking kind, but the dead kind, the ones who didn't get up. Pieces of bodies, hunks of meat that had been left to rot and be picked at by rats and crows lay scattered in the gutters. There were police cars and ambulances, an illusion of safety that had meant Thunder Bay had turned from a safe haven into a slaughterhouse almost overnight.

"Those poor people," said Dakota as she counted the bodies littering the road. "They stood no chance. I can't imagine what it must've been like."

"Then don't. Let's focus on what we need to do," said Jonas. He kept checking his mirror. The crowd of zombies had reached the top of the hill, and some were beginning to follow them down. He couldn't afford to bring them to Janey. It was a mile to the river, but it was a long straight road, and there was no hiding. They had to make it over or they would be torn apart like Julie. "Don't think about it. What happened has happened, and feeling bad for them isn't going to change anything."

"I know. I still feel bad though."

"I don't," said Lukas. "I don't think about things like that. I'm just thinking about what I'm going to do when we meet Janey. You think she's got plenty of food? I'm still hungry."

Jonas wondered how Janey was doing. Did she have enough food? Were the kids okay? He had so many questions. No doubt, she did too. This was it. No going back now. The road veered to the east, but they were going into the park and through to Janey's house. He could hardly wait to see her little red house. The dark clouds were retreating, and more sunlight began to filter through the thin rain. It was clearing up. The storm had passed. They had made it through Thunder Bay. The three of them were going to make it.

"I'm sure she can rustle up something for you, Lukas," said Dakota. She looked at Jonas and saw something in his eyes that she hadn't seen in a long time. Hope. There were lots of variables as to what could happen, but at least he had found something to believe in. She knew he desperately wanted to see his sister again. She just hoped Jonas's faith in her wasn't misguided.

Suddenly the buildings at her side seemed to be rushing past way too fast, and the bridge was coming up quickly. She pulled the belt around her, and clipped it in. "Just in case," she said as Lukas looked at her. To the side of the bridge grew long grass and thick, tall weeds. From there, the grass petered out into the river, and then led to the cold water of Lake Superior.

"Dakota, don't worry, the bridge is right ahead of us. We're fine."

Just as they were about to cross onto the bridge, the front left tire blew out completely. Along with the flat at the rear, the truck was wrenched from Lukas's control. It slewed across the road, and the steering column was pulled from Lukas's grasp. The truck hit a drain cover and bounced wildly. Lukas fought to keep them under control, but the flat tires were useless on the wet road, and they were being pulled violently to the side. If they didn't slam into the side of the bridge, they might just make it, and they could slide to a halt on the other side. As the truck bounced up and down, its wheels clinging to the edge of the road, Lukas could feel it trying to mount the verge. If they did that they were history. The entrance to the bridge was so close, yet the truck was rapidly veering away from them, and Lukas found himself looking not at the road ahead, but a very hard, very solid, low wall. They were going to crash.

Lukas steered them into the slide, taking them away from the bridge, and heading away from the wall. Now it looked like he had avoided crashing, but the wheels of the truck were sliding over dirt and grass, spinning wildly out of control. Lukas looked through the rain spattered windshield and braced himself. He could hear Jonas and Dakota shouting and screaming, but there was nothing he could do. He stared at the cold river that was suddenly coming up to meet them. The bridge was gone. The road was gone. Instead of watching events unfold slowly, it actually all happened fast, as if time had sped up.

One side of the truck scraped the bridge wall, leaving huge scratches in the side, and gouging out a deep furrow in the driver's door. The scraping sound made Lukas's skin crawl, but there was no time to react. They were on the sloping riverbank, and the truck's tires lost all traction. The front left wheel, reduced to metal rims and pieces of flapping tire spun around uselessly in the grass, and the truck began to tilt alarmingly.

A split-second later, and Lukas saw the Kaministiquia River before him. At such high speed there was nothing he could do but to let fate take its course. The truck spun around a full 360 degrees, and then they were facing the river again. He was aware of Dakota next to him screaming, but it was more of an aside. His head was full of thunder, amazed that they were still alive, and it was the crunching sound of the zombie they hit that really brought him to his senses.

A zombie lying in the grass, unable to walk on its legs that had been eaten away by rats, reared its head up in surprise at the approaching noise. The truck hit the zombie as it took off, taking its head clean off it shoulders as the truck began to fly through the air. Hidden in the tall grass behind the zombie was a police motorcycle, and the front of the truck rammed into it, sending them into a tailspin. The ground dropped away beneath the truck, and then it was turning over and over as it flew up into the air. Flashes of water, of a pale blue sky, and of the disappearing bridge all flitted before Lukas's eyes, and then the river suddenly filled his vision entirely. He'd thought he could control it, but he should've known it wouldn't be that simple. The wet road was too slippery, and the truck took on a life of its own.

As they flipped over, Lukas felt something slicing through his arm, and wondered if he had been cut by the broken glass. The last thing he saw before they hit the water was his bone sticking out of his right arm.

The truck smashed into the water with a huge roar and a tremendous splash. The roof of the truck smacked into the surface of the water, and they landed in the river completely inverted. Bracing, cold water rushed into the open windows, and they instantly began to sink.

"Get out," was all Lukas managed to shout, before he felt the water swirling around his head, and he could see nothing but blackness.

CHAPTER SIXTEEN

Dakota coughed and spluttered until she had cleared her throat. The marshy bank was cold, and as she crawled up it, her fingers digging into the soft dirt, she spat out a lump of stringy blood. The impact when they had hit the water had thrown her clear of the truck, and for a moment she thought she was going to drown. The swirling water of the Kaministiquia River had sucked her from the truck, and it was all she could do to get to the surface. Now, freezing cold, she was trying to get out of the river, up away from the sluggish swollen river that had swallowed the truck whole. She looked over her shoulder and saw only water. The truck was gone, somewhere beneath the surface, its tires now sinking into the silt at the bottom of the river. Looking back up at Thunder Bay, at the hill they had just descended, she could see movement in the distance. Shadowy figures moved through the grim city, far enough away to not put her in any immediate danger, but close enough to pose a threat should she stay there much longer.

"Jonas?" Dakota rolled over onto her stomach and threw up. Bile burnt her throat as she retched, unable to bring up anything solid. She realized she was shaking, and not just because of the cold. She was terrified.

"Dakota? Dakota!"

She heard a voice calling for her, and she raised her head to find its source.

"Jonas? Lukas?" She rolled onto her back, propped herself up on her elbows, and coughed once more. "Where are you?"

She looked up at the bridge, hoping she might see Jonas standing up there, but the bridge was empty. She knew she couldn't sit around waiting for help; she had to do something. She had to find Jonas and Lukas. The accident had been so fast, there had been little time to do anything. She remembered unclipping her belt just before they flew into the river, thinking she was going to need to get out quickly, and it was probably that which had saved her. What if Jonas hadn't got out? He was still weak, and she hadn't seen what had happened to him. What if he had gone down with the truck? Dakota felt sick again, but forced herself to get up. Despite her legs feeling like lumps of concrete, she had to stand. She had to move.

"Jonas?" Dakota scanned the riverbank, but there was no sign of him. Knowing that she was seconds away from descending into a complete panic, she summoned up all her energy, and screamed. "Jonas!"

Dakota screamed again. Where the truck had entered the water there was now nothing but a few bubbles, and then nothing. It was as if they hadn't even been there. As she stared at the spot where the truck had gone down, she saw movement in the grass to her left. She looked closer, and then saw a figure lying in the grass.

"Lukas?"

Dakota made her way across the muddy riverbank carefully, clutching at the long grass to stop herself from falling and sliding down back into the river. Her fingers wrapped around slim slithers of coarse grass that cut into her, slicing through her skin, and leaving droplets of blood behind. She didn't care if she was cut, she was just glad to be alive. It was nothing short of a miracle that she was still standing, and she knew it.

She knelt over the figure in the grass, and began to sob. "Jonas, I thought I'd lost you."

"Drown twice in one day? You don't get rid of me that easily." Jonas pulled Dakota into him, and looked her over. "How are you?"

"I'm okay. I've felt better, but...oh, God, I thought I'd really lost you that time. Are you hurt?"

"Nothing major. I don't know what happened, but I managed to get myself clear before the truck went down. I'm banged up, but I'll be okay." Jonas sat up and held Dakota, noticing that she was shaking, and he tried to rub some warmth into her. He was freezing cold himself though, and didn't have much warmth to offer. "Dakota, we have to get going. I know, this is fucked up, but we have to go." He looked up the hill. A few of the zombies had seen the crash, and were heading toward the river. Jonas wanted to slip into the park and use the cover of the trees to disappear. He couldn't afford to let them follow him to Janey's place. "They're still coming."

Dakota looked at Jonas and brushed her wet hair behind her ears. "Where's Lukas? Have you seen him? Did he get out?"

Jonas had been dreading this moment. He bit his lip, and then parted the long grass behind him. Lukas's body lay perfectly still, and Dakota collapsed when she saw him. The river was lapping at his feet, his eyes were wide open, and the rain was gently washing the blood from his face.

"No," she sobbed, "oh, God, no." Dakota wept freely as she looked at Lukas's body. One arm was bent back behind his shoulder, and she saw a huge piece of metal protruding from his chest where the steering column had pierced his ribcage. Part of his skull had caved in where something had hit it, exposing and destroying his brain.

"I dragged him out," said Jonas, "but it was too late. There was nothing I could do. At least he won't be coming back."

A faint moaning sound carried across the water, and Jonas saw two zombies stumbling down the hill. They were getting closer, and he knew they had to get going. There was never a moment to pause, to reflect, or to plan; the world was rushing toward death and taking everyone with it.

"Help me?" Jonas put his arms under Lukas, and Dakota bent down to do the same. "Let's lower him into the river. I don't want to leave him here for those animals to butcher him. It's the least we can do."

Together they gently pushed Lukas into the river, and he was dragged out and away by the current.

"God bless you, Lukas," muttered Dakota.

"Thank you for saving my life." Jonas could feel his jaw trembling as he watched Lukas slip away. It wasn't fair. Lukas had given them everything, and now he was dead. One minute they were planning for the future, and the next it was all taken away from them. He didn't know how Dakota kept her faith. It really did seem as if God had abandoned them. Lukas could have easily gone back with Bishop, made his own way, found another path, but he had chosen to stick with them, believing in Canada. Where was the justice in what had happened to him?

"Come on." Jonas put his hand in Dakota's, and they staggered up the riverbank. When their feet were on solid ground, they began to jog over the road toward the park. It wasn't lost on Jonas that he was alone with Dakota now. It had been a long time since it was just the two of them. With any luck, he would be reunited with Janey, but even if she wasn't there, even if the worst had happened, as long as he had Dakota, he thought he could cope. She was his future. His child was his future. Running into the trees with Dakota, he didn't care that he was cold and hungry. He missed Lukas already. The boy had a positive vibe about him and a smile that seemed to stretch from ear to ear. Jonas missed his friends, all of them. Days ago he had thought he would be pulling up to Janey's house with Erik, Tyler, Mrs. Danick, Peter, and so many others. Even Julie had been a part of them for a short while, and now she was gone like all the others. He wasn't even sure where they were going. All he knew was that Janey's house was somewhere on the other side of the trees, somewhere along the border of the lake.

The ground was soft and squelched as they walked. Their wet clothes stuck to them, and Jonas knew they needed to find a change of clothes and get dry. The rain had almost stopped, but the air was bitterly cold, and there was precious little sunshine to warm them. Jonas began to see more of the lake. Patches of it became visible as the trees thinned out, and then suddenly they were clear of the park, standing on the foreshore. There was a pathway around the lake's edge and a small driveway. Jonas put his hands on the twisted trunk of a small pine and let his eyes follow the pathway. To the south it bent around a curve and disappeared from view, obscured by the park. Jonas pushed aside the large wet leaves of a sycamore, and looked north at the pathway that led to a little red house by the lake.

"Janey," he said, barely able to believe he had made it. The house was just as Janey had described. Cute square windows hugged its small frame, and ivy climbed its walls. It was the ivy that made the house appear to be red. Patches of it were dead and brittle, but it still grew in places, auburn and crimson leaves covering up the brickwork. The house was surrounded by tall grass, and it backed onto the lake. Jonas could see a small wooden jetty with a rowboat moored up and what looked like a couple of fishing rods poking out of it.

When Dakota saw the crooked path leading from the driveway to the front door, she felt relieved. There were no vehicles parked out front, and nobody came out to see them. The windows of the house were dark, and she saw no evidence of life. That didn't mean Janey wasn't there, but it also suggested Javier hadn't made it this far.

Jonas approached the house, crossing the pathway, and then he swung open the small gate that bordered the driveway. He could still scarcely believe he was actually here. It had been so long since he had spoken to Janey that he could hardly remember her voice. It had been even longer since he had seen her. Months had passed since they had last had any sort of communication. He just knew that she had kept her promise. She was here, he could sense it.

"Stay behind me." Dakota followed Jonas through the gate and nervously walked behind her husband. This was it. There was nowhere else to turn. She looked around the grounds. Barbed wire surrounded the house, aside from a small clear patch by the front door. It looked as though it had been set up with the intention of stopping intruders. There were a few zombies who had been snared in it. They were dead now. None moved. Dakota was impressed. Janey must've set it up to protect the house. It was a smart move. It was thinking like that that kept you alive.

Almost oblivious to the zombies trapped in the barbwire, Jonas raised his hand to knock on the front door. Should he just go in? Should he wait for her to answer? What was the correct etiquette when approaching your estranged sister's house in the middle of a zombie apocalypse? He didn't want to admit it, but he was nervous. This was the culmination of everything they had been trying for. This is what Lukas had died for, what Pippa and Peter had died for, what he had almost died for himself. He could still taste that foul water from the swimming pool, still see Cliff's battered face, still feel the sore wound on his arm where Javier had shot him. Jonas rapped three times and waited.

He listened patiently, but there was no answer. Nobody came to the door, and he couldn't hear footsteps or children.

"Maybe they're out fishing or something," suggested Dakota.

"No," said Jonas shaking his head. "She wouldn't risk going out in this weather. Plus the boat was still out back."

Jonas tried the door handle, and it clicked quietly as he opened the door. It wasn't locked. Wouldn't Janey keep it locked? It felt as if his heart was beating so fast it was going to explode, but he couldn't wait any longer.

"Be careful," said Dakota, as she watched Jonas push the door open.

Stepping into the little house, Jonas was struck by how cold it was. Maybe Janey couldn't risk having the fire going in case the smoke attracted the dead. He would probably find her upstairs in bed, the kids buried beneath a pile of warm blankets. That was it. Janey was smart. She would do the right thing, and do what she had to in order to protect her children. The room was just a small foyer cluttered with small boots and coats piled up in the corner. There was a pair of sneakers with penguins on the side, and a jacket with a dinosaur on the sleeves. Jonas could imagine the kids playing outside in the open spaces. They must love living here, he thought. There was a frosted glass door ahead of him, and he put his hand on it. Jonas looked back at Dakota.

"Go ahead." Dakota looked at Jonas's eyes, so full of excitement and nervousness. "I'm right behind you," she said closing the front door softly.

Jonas pushed the glass door open and walked into a small kitchen. The room was gloomy, cold, and barely any warmer than outside. The floor was covered in a black and white checkered vinyl, whilst the cupboards were painted white. In the middle of the room was a small wooden table, four chairs around it, and a high chair to one side. In one of the chairs sat a figure.

"Come on in, sit down."

Jonas gritted his teeth, and tried to keep Dakota positioned behind him. It wasn't fair. "Why? Why here?" he asked the figure. "Why the fuck don't you just leave us alone."

Javier pointed a gun at Jonas. "And miss out on all the fun?" He drew the gun through the air toward Dakota, and then back to Jonas. "Both of you sit down, I think we should have a little chat. Remember now, you do right by me, and you'll find I'm all sweetness and light." Javier grinned. "This is going to be interesting."

CHAPTER SEVENTEEN

"How did you get through Thunder Bay?" asked Jonas. "How did you manage to get past that horde of dead that's hanging around the city? The road was blocked, so don't tell me you drove past them."

"Them? It wasn't so hard. I just had to give them something to play with, keep their attention off me." Javier's eyes drifted up and right as he recalled what happened. "The road being blocked was a pain in the ass, true. Who leaves a damn helicopter parked across the main street? I guess the dead just hang around hoping for someone to come along. Must be pretty quiet around these parts usually. We were hoping for an easy passage once we were past that helicopter, but as soon as I saw them, I knew I had to keep them busy. I didn't want them following me here."

Jonas was pleased Javier had at least had the foresight not to drag the army of dead with him to Janey's. He remembered thinking the same thing which is how they had ended up in the sports center. He didn't know the layout of Janey's house, but there couldn't be too many rooms, too many places to hide. Perhaps Janey had seen Javier coming and hidden with the children.

"Where's Quinn? Where's Erik and Freya? Are they here?" asked Dakota.

"One question at a time, people. Now, Hamsikker asked how I got here. I'd be delighted to tell you. You can't just stroll through a city these days, not with so many dead people around. And Thunder Bay has its fair share, as I'm sure you noticed." Javier rested his gun on the table, but kept it pointed at Jonas and Dakota. He was under no illusions that if he gave them half a chance they would try to overpower him and get the gun for themselves.

"There was really only one logical way of making sure they didn't follow us," said Javier.

"Yeah, you said you gave them something to play with," said Jonas. "Get on with it. We want to see Janey. We're not here for your amusement, you asshole."

Javier smiled. "All in good time. You asked where Quinn was? Well, I'm surprised you didn't see her."

"How would we have seen her? When would we…" A shiver ran up Jonas's spine. Suddenly he knew exactly what Javier meant.

"I shot her in the leg. Just enough to incapacitate her. She screamed blue murder which was quite convenient actually. Lots of blood too. I think I hit a major artery. It made them focus on her, and gave us the chance to slip away. Last I saw her she was trying to pull herself up into a black courier van to hide. I don't suppose you know if she's still there? I figured there wasn't much chance she would evade the dead, but I left her with a baseball bat. Didn't seem like a fair fight otherwise, you know, a thousand of them against poor little Quinn?"

Jonas had seen Quinn. He also knew she was dead. Javier hadn't given her a chance. She had gotten herself into that courier van all right, but unluckily for her she hadn't been the only one to make it in. Jonas hoped she had died quickly. The alternative was too horrifying to think about.

"You fucker. We saw her. Quinn's dead."

Dakota closed her eyes. She had held that baseball bat. She had thought nothing of it, but now she wished she had kept it. She could bash Javier's brains in with it. Quinn would like that.

Javier shrugged. "Anyway, I knew Quinn would come in handy at some point. I mean her driving skills were fine, but really, once we were over the border there was little point in having her hanging around."

Dakota looked at the kitchen bench. Beside the sink was a microwave, and next to that a knife rack. If she could just get close enough to it without Javier noticing, she could pull one out. It was no match for a gun, but she didn't intend to get into a fight with Javier. All she needed was three seconds. She needed Javier's attention solely on Jonas. "Who the hell do you think you are? You can't go around killing people just because you have no use for

188

them." Dakota wanted to grieve for Quinn, but she had nothing left in her. After Julie, after Lukas, she felt immune to it. Death was too commonplace now. Until Javier was taken care of, any thoughts of Quinn would have to wait.

"Sit down, both of you, you're making me nervous. And when I get nervous, I get clumsy. It wouldn't do for me to shoot you before you even found out what happened to Janey, would it?"

"You're unbelievable," said Jonas. "Quinn's dead. What about Erik and Freya? You kill them too? Where's Janey? My nephews? If you've hurt them in any way at all, I *will* kill you, Javier."

"Of course you will. All in time, Hamsikker, all in good time. Now *sit down*," said Javier.

Jonas fully intended to kill Javier anyway, but knowing Quinn was dead filled him with rage. This monster wouldn't stop until everyone was dead.

Javier motioned with the gun for Jonas and Dakota to sit down and kicked forward a chair with his feet.

"No. We don't need to sit. We're here for our family and friends. We're not going anywhere."

"Is that so? Seems to me, Hamsikker, that you're in no position to bargain with me. You have lots of questions, and I have the answers."

"You're not going to shoot me. If you wanted to, you would've killed me already. You like playing games. You like the feeling of power it gives you. You want me to know. You're desperate to show me, so let's get this charade over with. What do you say we go and find out now?" Jonas walked over to a door that led further into the cottage. "This way?"

Javier couldn't help but chuckle. He nodded. "Go ahead. You'll find what you need to know in there."

Dakota went to follow Jonas, but Javier told her to sit down.

"I'm not leaving her alone with you," said Jonas. "Dakota's with me."

"Am I invisible? Am I talking to myself?" Javier sighed and stood up. He walked around the table so that he was next to Dakota, blocking her from the knife block she had been inching toward. He had noticed her looking at it despite the dim light in the kitchen. Her motives were obvious. "Fine, have it your way.

Hamsikker, go on into the dining room, and come back when you're ready. In the meantime…"

Javier smashed the butt of his gun across Dakota's face, breaking her nose. She immediately screamed out in pain, and Javier pushed her over the table, forcing her arms out in front of her. He leant on her back, and then put the gun to the back of her head. Jonas rushed to help her but was stopped in his tracks.

"Try it, Hamsikker. One more step, and I'll put a fucking bullet through your wife's skull."

"Okay, okay," said Jonas backing off. He knew better than to test Javier. Jonas couldn't see Dakota's face, but he knew she was in pain. He had to find a way to get them both out of this mess. "What do you want? Why don't you let Dakota go? You and I can sort this out. Whatever you want, Javier, we'll work it out."

"We'll work it out? I'm through working things out. Get into the dining room before I run out of patience completely. When you're back, we'll talk more. I'm not going to do anything to Dakota. She'll be fine as long as you behave. We'll be in here when you're done."

Jonas turned around and faced the door. He wondered if Javier was going to shoot him in the back, but there was not much he could do about it if he was. As Jonas stepped through the doorway, he braced himself, but there was no movement behind him, no bullet tearing into his body. Jonas swung the door back cautiously, nervous about what he was about to find. Javier wanted him to go into this room, that much was certain. What he might find, though, was a mystery. Javier might have Janey tied up or locked up in one of the upstairs rooms. Maybe Javier was going to give Jonas a chance to save them, and then he'd kill them all together. Jonas knew he was going to have to be careful. He would keep an eye out for any weapon he could get his hands on.

Jonas entered the room and looked around. It was cold and gloomy. Soft rain cascaded down the large bay window at the end of the room, and long drapes partially obscured the faint light outside, leaving the room in near darkness. He looked around at the furniture. There were toys scattered about the floor and a large, dark television set in the corner with DVD boxes stacked up on a shelf. The room appeared to be empty, when suddenly Jonas heard a groan come from behind a lazy-boy in front of the TV. He looked closer and then saw a pair of feet sticking out. They were moving, drawing themselves back, and then all of a sudden someone was standing behind the chair looking at him.

Erik.

Jonas had hoped to find Janey, but this was the next best thing. "Erik, thank God, I didn't know if I would see you again." Jonas felt a rush of blood, and a surge of adrenalin as he suddenly realized he now held a numerical advantage over Javier. Together with Erik he could formulate a plan to overpower Javier. The man might have a gun, but he didn't have the desire that Jonas did. When he looked at Erik a sense of relief that he wasn't alone came over Jonas. Together again with his best friend, he could do something about this. "Erik, where's Freya? Is she okay? Have you seen Janey?"

Erik groaned and lifted an arm to the lazy-boy to steady himself.

"Are you hurt?" Jonas stepped forward and saw blood on Erik's head. The man was large, twice the size of Javier, but was still capable of being hurt. "Erik, let me see. I'm here now. I can help."

Erik took a step out into the middle of the room and raised his arms. Jonas saw the familiar whiteness of the eyes, the tightness of the limbs, and a large slit across Erik's neck.

"Oh no. Oh no, Erik, not you. Not…"

Erik lunged forward, and Jonas stepped back out of the way. Erik's large cumbersome frame caught the edge of the sofa and fell to the ground.

Jonas wished things were different. He wished he could've been there for his friend. He wished he could turn back the clock and not drag him or his family into this whole sorry mess. Javier had let Jonas come into this room on purpose. He had killed Erik and was now making Jonas clear up the mess. The elation that Jonas felt was replaced instantly by a sense of loss. Erik couldn't be dead. He had saved Jonas on countless occasions, and was such an integral part of Jonas's thoughts, that it just didn't seem real. How could he be dead? This was just a bad joke, a trick. It was as if he had wandered into an obscure play, and was waiting for everyone to jump out and yell surprise.

Jonas strode over to the fireplace where dry coals and damp wood lay collected in a large basket beside the fireplace. Jonas picked up a poker, the metal handle cold to touch, and he leant over Erik's body. Erik was trying to get up, but Jonas held him down. He looked into his old friend's dead eyes. There was no mistaking it. Javier had slit his throat and let him bleed to death. How could he do that? Was it out of spite? Was it to goad Jonas for fun, or just because he could?

With his lips trembling, and tears threatening to roll from his eyes, Jonas plunged the poker into Erik's temple. "I'm sorry, my friend. I'm so sorry." He thrust the temple through Erik's brain, and the man's body shuddered before settling into a permanent, final stillness. Erik slumped to the floor, and Jonas carefully let him go. This wasn't just a game anymore. Javier had to be stopped. Had he killed Freya too? Jonas retrieved the poker. There was no time to think, no time to search for Janey, no time to do anything but get Dakota out of harm's way. The only way he could ensure Dakota would be safe was if Javier was dead. Christ, it had all gone so horribly wrong. Jonas ran his hands over his head, and looked at Erik. He looked peaceful now, and Jonas hoped he was with Pippa and Peter. Jonas desperately hoped that Erik *wasn't* with Freya.

Jonas slipped the poker into a loop on the back of his pants, and then went back to the kitchen.

"Get the answers you were looking for?" asked Javier. He was still stood exactly where Jonas had left him, the gun still at Dakota's head, still with the same inane, malicious grin on his face.

"Why the fuck did you kill Erik? What did he ever do to anyone?"

"Sit down, Hamsikker."

Jonas pulled out a chair, but was reluctant to sit down. He pulled the poker out from his belt loop discreetly, and held it behind his back. He knew if he tried to attack Javier then Dakota was dead. Janey could be bleeding out right now, and there was no telling what Javier had done to her three kids. Jonas needed this to be over, and quickly.

"*Sit.*"

Jonas sat down opposite Javier, and slid the poker underneath the table, careful not to let Javier see it. He stretched out a hand to Dakota and caressed the back of one of her hands.

"Where's the jolly green giant?" asked Javier. There was a glint in his eye as he asked. "Erik not joining us?"

"What's it to you? You don't care. You know full well Erik's dead."

"Erik had to be put out of his misery. After Quinn was gone, he was a real pain in the ass, and when I saw you coming, I had no use for him anymore. Just like this kid I met once, Noah. Letting him live would've just prolonged the agony. Sometimes you just have to get things done. Erik was past his sell by date, so I put him down."

"So you killed him, just like you killed Quinn and everyone else you've met."

Javier laughed. "Not quite *everyone*, but well, you're mostly right. I'm going to assume you and Dakota are on your own? It would be reckless of you to think that I haven't thought about some sort of surprise attack. I care very much about what happens to the beautiful Mrs. Hamsikker. If you have a friend perhaps working their way around this house trying to find a way in and shoot me in the back I would suggest you tell me now. I would hate to be startled. When I'm jumpy my fingers get sweaty, and then accidents can happen, you know?"

"We're on our own," said Dakota. "There's no one else left."

Jonas stared at Javier. "There were others, but they didn't make it. Julie, and a young man named Lukas. They should be here, but thanks to you, they're dead. Julie was ripped apart by your little game at the border. Lukas died back in Thunder Bay when we were trying to get here. They're not coming back any more than Quinn, Erik, or anyone else you've murdered."

Javier looked at Jonas. He was telling the truth. "I was curious about that. I set it up very much on the spur of the moment. Those trenches at the road works just seemed like too good an opportunity to resist. I wish I could've been there to see the look on your face. So you and Dakota didn't fall in?"

"I did. I got out thanks to Julie."

"Then I guess she got what was coming to her."

Jonas saw her being torn apart all over again and shuddered. "I knew it was you when I saw that message you left for me on the sign."

"Clever, huh? I wasn't sure you would pick up on it. I wasn't sure you would even fall into my little trap, much less so, even get that far."

"Why, Javier? You just said so yourself you didn't even know we would be coming. You left us for dead, remember?"

"That's true. It was more Quinn to be honest. She kept telling me that you would come; that somehow you would find a way. I guess on some level she got through to me. Besides, even if it hadn't been you, it would've been someone else."

"You're insane, Javier. You've lost it. I'm not sure that you ever had it. People are dead because of you. Doesn't that mean anything?"

"It never did, so why would it now? Nothing's changed. I haven't changed. And your problem is that *you* haven't changed. You still think the world is a nice place; that one day the army is going to come marching over the hill to save the world. You still think the shops are going to re-open, and you can go for brunch while the kids watch cartoons. America is a very different place to the one little Jonas Hamsikker grew up in. The streets aren't safe anymore. You can't hide anywhere. They *will* find you eventually, Hamsikker. Why can't you see that? Why don't you give up? Accept the way it is now. The Wild West is back, and this time it's a mean son of a bitch. You think I'm responsible for this. You want to blame me for Julie, and Quinn, and Pippa, and everyone else who died. But all I did was use the tools at my disposal to survive. That is what your America has taught me. You've finally lost, Hamsikker. You couldn't protect them because you were too wrapped up with your own lies. You couldn't see the truth even when it was standing in front of you with a semi-automatic about to blow you and yours away. That's on you, Hamsikker."

"On me? Maybe a little. I'm not perfect, I have my own demons, and maybe sometimes I lose sight of the bigger picture. But I try. I try to be a man, and that's more than you will ever be. A man doesn't think of other people as things he can use for his own end. A man doesn't leave his woman behind in the dirt full of bullets. A man doesn't hold a gun to another man's wife. That's what a *coward* does, and I refuse to accept that there is nothing left to believe in. I still believe that there are people out there on the right side, who still think that America can grow again."

Jonas looked at Dakota. Her nose had stopped bleeding, but she looked like she was giving up. She couldn't fight back, and she knew that no matter what Jonas said, Javier was the one with the gun. He still had control. Jonas was supposed to protect her, but it was Javier that was forcing them into this position.

"I don't have the faith that my wife does. She's stronger than you think. I do know one thing, Javier. You're going to rot in Hell for what you've done."

"Oh yes, Hell. I'm fairly certain that we're there already, so it doesn't quite have the same threat as it used to. As for your America, well, what a tragedy. You still talk to me as if I have no feelings, as if I didn't care about anything. Let me remind you, I'm here to find my brother. He's here somewhere. I just wanted to get some local information about the area, and about where he could be holed up. I'm not the one in the way here, you are. You're interfering in my plans, Hamsikker. I'm here for my brother. I'm not a robot."

"Not a robot? What about that psycho, Rose? Don't make me laugh. You didn't give a fuck about her. You left her on the ground to be eaten."

Jonas could see Javier bristle when he brought up Rose's name. Jonas wanted to push the man's buttons. He needed to get a reaction, to get this over with. He had to get Javier out of the way so he could free Dakota and find Janey and her children. "I heard them dismantling her body, you know," said Jonas, lying. "They pulled her head off her shoulders first. Scooped out her brains before they began on the rest of her."

Javier clenched his teeth and then sighed, annoyed. "All right, Hamsikker, let's just—"

"They ripped open her stomach and stuck their greedy mouths right into her. By the end there was nothing left of her. I watched them devour Rose, and I was glad. I enjoyed it. I wish you had been there to see it, Javier. I've never seen them enjoy a meal as much as they did Rose."

"Enough!" shouted Javier. "I know what you're doing, but it's not going to work. You think I'm going to crack? You think that you can get me to cry like a little girl? Telling me about Rose doesn't change a thing. You can dream of revenge, Hamsikker, but you're a long way off."

"I'm past revenge, Javier. I just want to see you dead," said Jonas. It was his time to smile. "I'm sure that's not too far away now."

Javier tapped the gun on the wooden table three times, recomposed himself, and then pointed the gun across the table, all the while keeping one hand firmly on Dakota's back. "I could just shoot you, you realize? Then you'll never know what happened to Freya, or Janey, or those three precious nephews of yours. How about I put one between your eyes right now, Hamsikker?"

"Go ahead. I know you better than that, Javier. You're not going to shoot me."

"Maybe not." Javier exhaled slowly and stepped back into the shadows. "But I can shoot her."

With Javier off her back, Dakota felt the weight lift, and she looked up into Jonas's eyes. She reached out her hands, and Jonas took them in his. A cold shiver rippled through her, and the hairs on her arms stood up on end. "Jonas?"

The gunshot echoed loudly around the small kitchen, and Dakota's body convulsed. Fresh warm blood splattered Jonas's face, and he watched as Dakota's face disintegrated. The bullet entered the back of her head and buried itself in the table beneath, sending sharp splinters flying through the air. Dakota's body slumped forward onto the table, and Jonas jumped up, his chair scraping against the floor as it flew backwards. He leant over the table, frantically pulling Dakota toward him. Jonas turned her head over. The back of her skull had been blown wide open, and as he looked at her face, he saw where the bullet had left through her forehead. Her eyes were still wide open, a mixture of confusion, fear, and love. Javier had finally killed the last thing Jonas loved. His child was dead. His wife was dead.

"No." Jonas felt his eyes stinging, and he buried his face into Dakota's neck. There was still warmth there, but no movement, no pulse. He couldn't believe she was gone.

Dakota was dead.

CHAPTER EIGHTEEN

Jonas kissed his wife's cold cheek, and then rocked back in his chair. This sort of thing happened to other people. Dakota wasn't supposed to die like this. She was going to raise their child with him, and death was not on the agenda, not for a long time. They had a future. Despite everything, they still had a future to plan, to live together; was it all supposed to end so suddenly, so violently?

"Are you going to listen to me now, Hamsikker? Can you still not see it?"

Jonas stood up, and grabbed the poker. He calmly began to walk around the table to Javier.

"Step back, Hamsikker," said Javier pointing the gun at him. "Take a moment, and…"

Jonas ignored Javier. It was easy now. The rantings of a madman paled into insignificance now that Dakota was dead. It was as if he couldn't feel anything, couldn't hear anything. All Jonas thought about was Dakota, how her future had been so crudely ripped away from her. Javier may as well have been waving a comic in front of him instead of a gun. He raised the poker to strike, when Javier suddenly shoved the gun into a back pocket, and rushed him.

Jonas was knocked back as Javier crashed into him, and the two men scuffled around the table. The poker went rolling away under the table, and Javier shoved Jonas to the floor. He was much stronger, and Jonas was weak. He tried to throw punches at Javier, but there was no power behind them, and Javier easily repelled him. Jonas tried kicking out at him from the floor, but Javier just dodged his kicks like a boxer dancing around the ring. Soon Javier was able to retaliate, and began kicking Jonas. He booted Jonas all over, wherever he could, striking Jonas's head, sides, arms, and legs.

As he lay on the floor taking a beating from Javier again, Jonas felt no pain. All he could think about was Dakota. He still pictured her full of life, still laughing and smiling as she used to do before the world changed irrevocably. His body was so used to being beaten that it had stopped bothering sending messages to his brain that he was suffering. No amount of pain could top the anguish he felt when he thought about a future without Dakota. The tears he shed were not from pain, but the realization he had lost his child and the woman he loved.

As he accepted his suffering, the cold hard floor offered up a chance. Beneath the table lay the poker, silent and unassuming. Jonas stretched out a hand, and wrapped his fingers around it. With his right hand he brought it swiftly out from underneath the table, and jammed it horizontally through Javier's standing leg, just above the ankle. Javier roared with pain, and Jonas pulled it back out, this time stabbing it downward through Javier's foot, embedding it into the floor beneath. Blood spurted from Javier's boot, and Jonas scrambled to his feet. He hoped to bundle Javier over, to pulverize him out of existence, but as Jonas got up, he found himself staring down the barrel of a gun.

"You'd better move real slow, Hamsikker," said Javier through gritted teeth, "or you're going to be joining Dakota sooner than you think. Maybe you should start to think about your sister and your nephews before you make any more rash moves."

Jonas stood up straight, and looked Javier in the eye. "Where are they?" Without Dakota or his child, he only had Janey and his three little nephews left. If they were gone, what was there? He had to know. He had to find a reason to keep going. He had to make sure Javier hadn't killed them, too, or worse still, have them locked up somewhere.

"You know why I'm here? You think you know me?" Javier bent down and pulled the poker from his foot. He grimaced with pain as it slid up through his foot, scraping along the bone as he took it out. "Fuck. I've got to say that really does sting." Javier threw the poker aside, and shoved Jonas toward the dining room. "Put your hands on your head, and get in there. Move it."

Jonas slowly raised his hands, and placed them on his head. He took a look at Dakota's lifeless body, and then turned and walked into the next room. Erik's body was still where he had left it. Everywhere he looked there was death. He couldn't block it out anymore. Dakota wasn't coming back. She wasn't going to smile at him, kiss him, hold him, or fight with him ever again. He would rather she hated him and be alive than be cold and dead.

Javier shoved the gun into Jonas's back. "Across the room you'll find a staircase. We're going to meet your sister."

With the gun at his back, Jonas crossed the room and found the stairs. Was Janey really up there? Had Javier killed her like he had Erik? Had he tied her up just so he could kill her in front of Jonas? The steps were covered in a thin, worn brown carpet, and the staircase creaked as he ascended. Reaching the upper floor, Jonas began to detect a change in the air. It was cloying, thicker, and just smelt wrong. It wasn't just the dampness. A powerful smell permeated the air infusing the house with a heavy atmosphere that was both sweet and sickly at the same time. It was then that Jonas knew Janey was dead. Javier wasn't bringing him up here to be reunited with her. Javier wanted to show him, to destroy any last semblance of hope that Jonas still clung to.

"In there." Javier pushed open a door, and Jonas stepped inside.

Instantly they were hit by the smell. Lazy flies, idling in the still air, buzzed around the corpse's head, and Jonas put a hand over his mouth.

Janey's hands were still wrapped around the shotgun. On the floor, her body was slumped against a wall, her legs spread-eagled, and behind where her head should be just the splattered remnants of her brain. Hair and bone decorated the wall, and the blood splatter reached up to the ceiling. The white bedspread had soaked in much of the spray, and Jonas didn't need to examine the body to know it was her. The photographs around the room told him he was in the right place. It was a woman's room, and her clothes were still piled on a chair, a dress hanging on a lonely hanger above the drapes. There was a picture on the bedside table of her with Jonas and Erik when they were younger. All three of them were smiling, and the sun was shining. Jonas could still remember when his mother had taken that photo. He could still remember when they were happy, but it was a long time ago. At least his mother hadn't lived to see Janey like this.

Jonas had never felt more wretched. In the space of five minutes he had lost his wife, his child, and his sister. There was a part of him that couldn't process it all, that refused to accept what he was seeing; yet he knew it was all too real, and that he had not only been too slow to save Dakota, but too late to save Janey. He had failed them all. He had come here to start again. It was supposed to be a new start for him and Dakota. He thought they would be safe here, but he was wrong. Javier was right. The world he thought he knew was long gone. It wasn't just America, nor Canada, but everything, and every person; God had truly abandoned his children.

"I can't claim credit for her," said Javier. "She was like that before I came along."

For once Javier was telling the truth. Jonas could tell Janey had been dead a long time. Several weeks, probably, if not months. A cobweb stretched from the tip of the shotgun to Janey's chest where a thin legged spider fed on a bluebottle it had recently captured.

How long had she held out? How long had she thought about killing herself? What was so bad that she had felt compelled to end it instead of taking her chances? Jonas wanted to pick her up, to tell her it was okay, and that he would never leave her again. He wanted so much to tell her that their father was dead, and that he was here for her now. He wanted her to meet Dakota and tell her that he was finally going to be a father.

But he couldn't say a word. Jonas could only stare at his dead sister and wonder how it had come to this. Where was the girl he grew up with who used to pull his hair? Where was the awkward teenager who used to flirt with Erik? Where was the beautiful girl who had become a mother and raised three sons.

The children.

Jonas turned around and faced Javier. "Where are they? Have you seen them?"

"I assume you're talking about the boys from the photographs? They were Janey's then?"

"Yes. Look, just tell me where they are. You can do what you like with me, I don't care anymore, Javier. You're right. I can't fight you. I can't win. But please, *please*, just let me get my three nephews out of here. Christ, how have they survived on their own?"

Javier stood clear of the doorway and hurried Jonas through, back to the top of the staircase. He had known grief, and could see Hamsikker was hurting. That was just how he needed him: weak and vulnerable. "They're outside. Go back down through the kitchen and skirt around the house to the left. You'll find them in the garden." His foot was still bleeding, and Javier was in pain. He knew Hamsikker wasn't about to run off. "I'll catch up with you."

Jonas saw that Javier had lowered his gun. He could use this opportunity to fight back. He could ambush Javier and get some payback for everything that he'd done.

Heading down the steps, Jonas decided that Javier would wait. He needed to make things right first. This little red house had not been the safe haven he had hoped it would be. It harbored death and disease in every room. What had Ritchie, Mike, and Chester gone through? How had they coped with their mother gone?

Heading back through the kitchen, Jonas couldn't help but glance at Dakota. She was exactly as he had left her, still slumped over the table. He would bury her before the day was over. She deserved at least that.

Back outside, the air was cool and fresh. The sky was cloudy, and still the rain fell softly, turning the soaked ground into a swamp. Jonas looked across at the park. A couple of zombies were heading through it toward the house. It didn't matter. The barbwire would soon stop them; even if they found a way through, there were only two of them and could be easily dealt with. Jonas looked at Lake Superior, its vastness imposing, its natural power making him feel less than insignificant. Maybe this was the way it should be. Maybe once everyone had gone, the world could start again, but this time without people to interfere with it. Jonas shook his head. No, that wasn't right. Dakota had taught him that he shouldn't lose his faith; should never give up. He had fought for her, killed for her; to give up now would be to throw that all away. Had Lukas died for nothing? Had Erik and Tyler died for nothing? Mrs. Danick, Julie, Quinn? Jonas was going to carry on. He couldn't afford to waver now, not when he still had a chance. Not while his three nephews still needed him.

Turning around the corner of the house, Jonas came upon a small garden area bordered by a low picket fence. There were shrubs and flowers surrounding it, and a large spade and fork leaning against a huge mound of dirt. The jetty lay just ahead of him, down a curved mossy path that led down to the lake. The small rowboat that he had seen earlier was still anchored up, and it moved slightly on the water. Closer to the house, Jonas recognized the combi van parked around the back. It was the same van that they had travelled in with Javier; the same one that Javier had left him and Dakota for dead in. Javier had positioned it carefully, making sure it wasn't visible from the road. Jonas looked for his nephews, but there was no sign of them. He tried to see if Javier had them tied up, either in the garden or in the van, but both looked deserted. Jonas looked closer at the garden, specifically around the large pile of mud. Taking a deep breath, he walked slowly up to three smaller mounds of dirt. Each one was about two feet across, and three or four feet long. At the head of each mound were crudely made crosses held together with twine, and upon each separate pile of raised dirt were mementos. On the first grave was a toy truck, its red paint glistening and wet. On the second was a book, its pages swollen with water, its cover faded into obscurity, and on the third Jonas saw a teddy. Its smiling face seemed at odds with where it was. Each was held in place with a small garden stake.

Jonas sank to his knees and clawed at the ground. He felt utterly empty, devoid of emotion, unable to cry or scream or do anything but stare morosely at the three small graves that held his nephews. His fingers gouged out narrow lines in the ground as his frustration grew. He had been too slow. He had left it too long. Janey had promised she would wait for him, and she had. How long had she waited while her three boys were dead and cold in the ground? How long had he made her wait with that unbearable grief and guilt weighing on her? How long had she tormented herself waiting for Jonas to come, only to finally give in and take her own life with the shotgun upstairs? Jonas kept seeing them all in his mind, seeing them laughing and smiling. He imagined Dakota was still with him, stood by his side as he introduced them all. This was supposed to be a family reunion, not a wake.

The soft patter of rain on the ground hid Javier's approach, not that Jonas held any fear of him now. He had nothing left to offer, nothing more he could tease Jonas with. It was over. Everything had been in vain.

"We both came here looking for something; looking for answers." Javier walked up beside Jonas. "I guess you found yours. It might not be what you want, but it's the way it is. If it counts for anything, I'm sorry. Those three little boys never had a chance. I can understand why Janey killed herself. She was responsible for them, and she let them down."

"Shut your God damn mouth," said Jonas. He ran his fingers through the dirt of the third grave until he found the teddy. He plucked out the stake holding it in place and looked at it. Was this Ritchie's, Andy's, or Chester's? Jonas wished he knew. He wished he could be holding his nephews instead of a soggy teddy bear.

"You're a new man, Hamsikker. You've shown you can fight; you've proven yourself. You can stop now. Janey let her kids down, but you don't have to go the same way. There's nothing you could do for them or for any of your friends. They made their own choices. I can help you. I can give you a choice. You can join me. I came here looking for help. My brother is out there somewhere, and I needed someone who knew the area. I needed Janey just like you. She's left us both on our own. You're my brother now, Hamsikker. You can help me. You can help me find Diego. You've got no ties anymore; nothing holding you back. I saw how they dragged you down. The others you travelled with, Erik, Quinn, Dakota – they stopped you from being the man you could be. *Now* is the time to do something useful, something really meaningful. I need a second pair of eyes out there. Join me."

Join Javier? Jonas stared at the grave, one hand planted firmly on the sodden ground, one still clutching the teddy. He put it carefully back on the grave, but held onto the stake. It was no more than a foot in length, but it was sharp. Water ran down his back and inside his collar, but it was no more than a minor irritant. He wanted no part of this anymore. Faced with so much death, how could he contemplate going on? How could Javier still expect him to think rationally after this, to still want to go on? "No. Leave me alone."

"You can't stay here grieving for the rest of your life. Those three kids are gone. I'm sorry, truly. But you have to decide now, Hamsikker. What do you want to do?"

"What are you talking about? I don't have to make a choice. Everyone's dead. My family are dead." Jonas stood up to face Javier.

Javier was still holding the gun, but he held something else, too; something in his other hand that dangled and shimmered in the faint light. It was a key chain. Jonas looked closer and saw the familiar metallic square, the picture of the building in green, set inside a golden yellow circle. Jonas recognized it as Fort William, and he knew what it meant.

"Everyone?" Javier looked at the van, and smiled. "You sure about that, Hamsikker?"

Jonas followed Javier's eyes and saw what he meant. There in the van, with her cherub-like face peering through a window, was Freya. She was still alive!

"Now," said Javier, "you really *do* have a choice. You can join me." Javier looked at the three graves as he walked up to Jonas, so they were only inches apart. He jabbed the gun into Jonas's chest.

"Or you can join your family."

CHAPTER NINETEEN

Jonas had clean forgotten about Freya. What the hell was Javier doing with her? Jonas ignored the gun pointed at him and stared at the van. Freya was waving at him, her face barely visible behind the steamy window. She looked pleased to see him, but she wasn't smiling. She was pointing at the back of the van as if trying to show him something. Jonas looked and saw the approaching dead coming from the park. There weren't just two of them anymore. Around a dozen or so trudged across the wet ground, and more were following from the shelter of the trees. Had the horde found them? Had Lukas's death brought them down the hill? Was it the truck crash, the gunshots when Javier had killed Dakota, or the shouting when they had fought? It didn't matter what the cause was. The barbwire would only hold so many back. He couldn't just leave Freya like that. He owed Erik that much.

"You know what separates us from the monkeys?" asked Jonas, turning back to Javier.

"Say what?" Javier was expecting Hamsikker to give in, to accept he had no choice but to help him. He thought he had finally won. "That's hardly—"

"I said, do you know what separates us from the monkeys?" asked Jonas calmly. "You know? Like, chimpanzees and apes?"

Javier rolled his eyes in his head and sighed. "Like I give a shit. I don't know. Opposable thumbs?"

Jonas tapped the side of his head with his index finger. "Cognitive reasoning. We learn from our mistakes. We can do it in a nano-second; realize the implications of what we're doing before we've done it." Jonas remembered a conversation he'd had with Dakota when she had asked him to renege on his promise to her. What were her words? "I want you to kill that bastard."

Javier smirked, confident now that Hamsikker had lost it. "So?"

"So, Javier, you seem to have skipped that part. You still think you can do whatever you like and get away with it."

Jonas raised the stake in his hand and raked it across Javier's face. Instantly Javier put his hands up in defense. Jonas took his opportunity, stamped on Javier's wounded foot, and then grabbed him. Both men slipped over on the wet grass, and Javier's gun skidded away to rest beside the three graves. The men began to fight, Jonas pounding Javier relentlessly. He screwed up his hands into fists and hit Javier with everything he had. Using both left and right hands, he straddled him, smacking him in the face over and over.

Javier tried to stop him, but it was like fighting an animal. There was a deep cut running from his chin up to his right eyebrow where the garden stake had torn open his skin, and he was lucky not to have lost an eye. Jonas had gained the upper hand, but Javier had no intention of letting this pathetic man beat him to death. Bringing up a knee, Javier caught Jonas in the gut, and it threw Jonas off balance. All Javier needed was a second's respite from the attack, and he ducked his head to one side, letting Jonas punch the ground. Javier reared up and head-butted Jonas square on.

Jonas saw stars and suddenly found himself falling back as Javier crawled out from under him. Through the blood falling down his forehead, Jonas saw the gun at the same time as Javier. Both men tried to reach it, but it was just out of their reach. Jonas pulled Javier back, and punched him on the back of the head.

Javier whipped around, and kicked Jonas in the face, desperate to shrug him off. There was to be no redemption for Hamsikker. He couldn't see the bigger picture. Javier thought he might be able to convince him that there could still be a future, that together they could find Diego, but it was obvious Hamsikker couldn't see past his own blinkered grief. So be it.

Hamsikker had to die.

Javier twisted over and wrapped his legs around Jonas, but the man fought back, punching Javier in the thigh and groin.

"Fuck you, Hamsikker." Javier crawled out of Hamsikker's reach and sprung up. Like a lioness attacking a springbok, Javier jumped on Jonas and forced him down to the ground. Hamsikker was tiring already. So much for Hamsikker trying to protect Freya. So much for revenge. Javier had the strength and the inner-belief to see it through. He doubted that Hamsikker had anything left, and as he held him down, he could see the strength disappearing from Hamsikker's eyes.

"Seems you didn't listen to your own advice, Hamsikker," said Javier as he moved his hands up to Jonas's face. "You're supposed to learn from your own mistakes, right?"

Javier put his hands on Jonas's head, and dug his thumbs into Jonas's eyes. He could feel the warm soft eyeballs give way as he dug in deeper. He was going to enjoy killing Hamsikker.

Jonas cried out in anguish, and he put his hands on Javier's wrists, trying to stop him, but Javier was putting all his weight behind his attempt to blind him. He wanted to crush Jonas, to force him into the ground where he would die. Javier wanted to push his hands right through Jonas's face into his brain, and watch the life drain out of him.

Jonas opened his mouth to scream, to plead for mercy, but no sound came out. He was blind, and he could sense Javier laughing, knowing he was about to win. Death was everywhere, and now it had come for Jonas. That was what it was about now. It wasn't about survival or mercy, it was about death. It was about killing.

"I want you to kill that bastard."

Jonas felt his left eye pop, and Javier's thick thumb continued to gouge out his eye. The man wasn't going to stop until one of them was dead. Jonas saw Dakota's dead face looking at him. He remembered Erik with his throat slit and the eaten corpse of Quinn in the courier van. He remembered Peter's lifeless corpse attacking him, and he remembered Julie being torn apart while he watched. He remembered Freya's scared face in the van, no more than twenty feet away, and he knew he couldn't give in. Javier was the devil, determined to destroy everything and everyone. He wouldn't stop until the world was dead and gone. Killing was the only way left. Hamsikker had one last promise to keep to his wife, and he only needed one good eye to ensure he kept it.

Overcome with rage and desire, suddenly Jonas shoved his head up and bit down on Javier's ear. Javier released his blood covered hands from around Jonas's head, and grabbed the side of his face.

"What the fu…?"

Jonas pulled back, ripping off Javier's ear in the process. He spat it out, and punched Javier on the side of the head where there was now a bloody hole instead of an ear.

Javier screamed and jumped up clutching his torn face. Blood spewed between his splayed fingers, and he stumbled back in shock.

Jonas stamped on the decapitated ear, grinding it into the ground. He spat Javier's warm blood out as he spoke. "I made a promise to my wife, Javier. I'm going to kill you," Jonas grunted. The effort to speak made him feel woozy, but he found a surge of energy just when he didn't think he had any left. His right eye was a searing white-hot ball of pain, and his left eye was useless. He knew he would never regain sight in it, but through the blood that dripped over his one good eye he could see Javier. Jonas advanced upon him with his hands balled into hard fists.

Javier whirled around looking for the gun he had lost. It was only a few feet away, still lying beside the graves, and he ran for it. Better to shoot now than get into another pointless fight. Jonas had maimed him for life, and he was going to pay. Javier would shoot Jonas in the gut and let him bleed to death. He intended to make Jonas watch as he throttled the life out of Freya. Now that everyone else was gone and Hamsikker had shown he would rather die than join Javier, Freya had no use. She was his last bargaining chip, and Jonas had refused it, ensuring they would both die.

As Javier bent down and picked up the gun he felt a sharp jolt in his back between his shoulder blades. The pain was brief but all too real, and he cried out. It shot through him twice, and he spun around to see Jonas towering over him with the garden stake.

Jonas aimed for Javier's heart as he rammed the stake into his chest, but the metal stake hit a rib. It sliced through Javier's flesh and ended up piercing a lung. Javier's eyes grew wide, and he frowned in confusion as the cold metal punctured his lung, and he began to gasp for air.

"Hamsikker, stop this, we can…"

Jonas shoved the garden stake in as far as he could so there was nothing but the tip of it sticking out. He watched with pleasure as Javier tried to prise the stake free, but there was little to get hold of, and his hands were slippery with blood. As Jonas bent down and scooped up the gun, he saw the zombies approaching. Janey's house was safe no more, and Jonas saw lots of dead bodies wandering from the tree line. He wanted to run, but his business wasn't done yet. Staggering toward the combi van, Jonas aimed the gun at Javier who was trying to go the other way. With one eye dead, his vision was poor, and Jonas fired wildly, just hoping he would hit Javier.

He missed, and the bullet spat up wet dirt at Javier's feet. Jonas didn't know how many rounds he had left, and with the approaching zombies, he couldn't afford to waste a single one. He marched over to Javier who was struggling for breath and punched him in the jaw, sending Javier to his knees. Jonas kicked him in the chest, and Javier was sent onto his back, clutching at thin air as he tried to stop Jonas.

It was all he could do to stop himself from putting a bullet in Javier's head, but the man didn't deserve to have it ended that quickly. Jonas was disgusted as he looked at Javier on the ground. He was no man. He was barely even human. He was pathetic.

"Please," said Javier, coughing up blood. "Hamsikker?"

Jonas nodded, and then retrieved the spade with which Janey had dug the graves for her three children. He marched over to the nearest section of fencing to him, quickly digging out a shallow fence post. He hacked at a piece of barbwire, and it rapidly came free. Jonas dropped the spade to carry it back with him to Javier. The house was almost surrounded now by the dead, but he wasn't finished with him just yet.

When Jonas reached Javier's body, he shoved him up into a sitting position, and drew his arms behind his back. Jonas began to wrap the barbwire tightly around Javier's arms. It gouged into his skin, tearing open his flesh, but Jonas didn't care. He wanted to make sure Javier didn't find some way out, some escape from this place that was saturated in death.

"Stop." Javier's breath was ragged and short. "Stop, Hamsikker, think about this. Please, you're not supposed to—"

"I'm not *supposed* to do what?" Jonas finished wrapping the wire around Javier and looked proudly at his work. Javier looked as if he was on the verge of tears. Jonas had surpassed anger and was now completely in control. "Well? You want me to take the moral high ground? Show mercy? Let you go? Join you?" Jonas raised the gun and pointed it at Javier's head.

Javier began to plead for his life. "God, Hamsikker, don't..."

"Don't what? You expect me to show you some leniency? Like you did when you took my wife away from me? Fuck that. Fuck God. And *fuck you*."

Jonas pulled the trigger, and Javier's neck erupted in a shower of bright red blood that spurted from his exposed artery. A single stream of blood flew in an arc over the garden as the bullet passed through Javier's neck just above the shoulder.

"See? I can show mercy. I'm not going to kill you," said Jonas as he spat on Javier's writhing body. "I'm going to let *them* do that."

Jonas picked something up from the ground by Javier's feet and then walked away. Leaving Javier with his hands tied, unable to stem the flow of blood from his neck, Jonas went to the combi van and threw back the door. Freya was sat in a forward seat, her knees up to her chin, and her pale arms wrapped around them. Jonas leant into the van, but Freya backed away. She looked scared, and Jonas guessed his appearance wasn't helping. He must look like one of the dead. Could Freya even recognize him?

"Take my hand, Freya. It's me, it's Jonas." He leant his hand in and tried to take hers, but she backed away, her demeanor that of a cornered mouse left with nowhere to run. She reminded him of Pippa, but Jonas could see Erik in those blue eyes of hers. There was a defiance that suggested no matter how afraid she was, she wasn't going to meekly surrender. He brought out the item he had picked up from the garden and held it out to her.

"It's me, Uncle Jonas. I found your key chain. Remember? The bad man has gone now. He won't bother you anymore. I'll look after you, okay, honey?"

Freya tentatively reached out for the key chain in Jonas's hand. She took it and looked at it. Her eyes went from it to him, and then back again, confusion spreading to amazement, and then finally acceptance. She smiled when she looked at the sparkling key chain, and then she shoved it into a pocket. She took Jonas's hand, and he scooped her up into his arms.

"It's okay, Freya, it's okay." Jonas took her out of the van, and looked around. The zombies were everywhere. Some were in the house now, some in the garden, and more approaching the van. How was he supposed to stop this? How was he supposed to keep on fighting, to find a way of surviving with a nine-year-old girl with him?

"Thank you," said Freya quietly.

Those two words made Jonas realize how much he still had left in him. His body ached with a fierceness he didn't know was possible, yet hearing Freya speak for the first time in months gave him a belief he hadn't felt for a long time. He gently lowered her to the ground and passed her the gun.

"Can you do me a favor, please? I need you to hold onto this for me. It's very dangerous, so you mustn't play with it, you understand? I'll get it from you when we're out of here." Jonas had no idea if it even had any bullets left, and it wasn't much use in a fight against a swarm of zombies.

"Okay, Uncle Jonas." Freya took the gun carefully, holding it as if it were precious china. She pushed it into her other pocket, and smiled. "Are we going home now? Are we going to get Daddy?"

The words stung Jonas more than any of the blows he had taken from Javier. "Sure, Freya. In a bit."

Jonas could only deal with one thing at a time. If he told Freya that Erik was dead, there was no way of knowing how she was going to react. Right now he needed her focused and positive.

"We're going on a little trip. Have you ever been on a boat?"

Freya nodded. "Once, but I didn't like it much. My tummy felt funny."

"Okay, okay, well this time will be better. You're with me now, so I'll look after you."

Jonas could see no way back to Janey's house. The only way was to go where the zombies couldn't follow. He picked up the spade and then looked at Freya. "See that boat over there? We're going to go on that, okay?" Jonas pointed to the jetty. "I want you to run and jump in it. I'll be right behind you. We'll make it a race. Ready, steady…"

Freya took off, running straight for the jetty. "Go!" shouted Jonas. He had no intention of racing Freya, but he needed her to get to the boat as fast as possible. He had seen two runners emerge from the park, and he had to make sure they didn't get to the jetty before he had a chance to get Freya to safety.

Jonas jogged away from the van and stood between it and the jetty. There was no way in hell they were getting past him. As he waited for the first runner to meet him, he looked back at Javier. Blood was trickling down the man's face, filling Javier's open mouth as he screamed and tried to push the dead off him. Jonas watched with satisfaction as Javier was eviscerated. The zombies clawed their way into his body, ripping his skin from his bones, shredding his flesh, and burying their teeth into him. As the dead dismantled Javier's body piece by piece, Jonas caught Javier's eyes. They were full of terror and pain, and Jonas couldn't help but smile.

"That was for you, Dakota."

Jonas gritted his teeth, raised the garden spade, and swung. He caught the first runner square in the face. With a resounding clang, it fell to the ground. The woman was barely out of her teens, but Jonas saw only the zombie. He brought the spade down on her head, the blade slicing through her scalp, decapitating her head from her body. The next runner was a thin girl with dark blue hair, a ring through her nose, and studs through her ears from top to bottom. Her upper lip appeared to have been peeled back as if in a snarl, but the reality was that it had been ripped off. Her skin was pale, mottled with a blue-green hue, and as Jonas swung the spade at her, she tripped. At the final moment, when he should've been lopping her head from her shoulders, she fell down at his feet, and he swung through thin air. The dead girl grabbed a leg, and Jonas stumbled back, desperately trying to get away from her gnashing teeth. He brought the spade down on her head, smacking the flattened metal over and over until the girl finally lay still. He had been seconds away from becoming one of them, and as he looked up, he knew he couldn't fight any more. There was just enough time for him to make the boat, and he dropped the spade and ran.

"I beat you," announced Freya as Jonas ran up to her. She was proudly sat in the boat, holding the gun. "I got this back out in case I had to shoot the bad people."

"That's great," said Jonas jumping down into the boat. He quickly untied the mooring and began to push them away from the jetty, aware that the zombies were chasing him, some of them already running down the wooden jetty. He had to get the boat out onto the lake quickly. If even just one of those zombies got into the boat with him and Freya, he didn't know how he would deal with it. "Just hold on to it for me, okay? Sit down and hold on, Freya."

Jonas used the oar to push them out into the lake and dropped the fishing rods into the water. He heard Freya yelp, and saw the zombies running straight off the jetty into the water. He prayed they hadn't worked out how to swim, and he sat down to row them further away from land. He wanted to rest, to drop the oars and hope the boat would navigate itself, but he couldn't risk it. He forced his weary arms to work, pulling on the oars, and getting them further away from shore. More zombies dropped into the frigid water, and then they stopped. They began to crowd on the jetty and on the shoreline all around the lake, obscuring Janey's house from view.

When they were far enough away, Jonas sat back in the boat and took the chance to regain some breath. His broken eye socket was causing him immense pain, and he couldn't keep going. It was all catching up with him. It wasn't just the physical effort but the mental effort it took to keep going.

Dakota was dead. His unborn child was dead. Janey was dead. Everyone he had ever known was dead. He hadn't even been able to say goodbye. The one crumb of comfort was that Javier was dead too. It had been so good watching him die, and Jonas was quite sure that Dakota was watching, too, from wherever she was now.

As Jonas sat back in the boat it floated effortlessly on the lake, and he was pleased Freya was quiet. He needed a moment to gather his thoughts. The shoreline was teeming with the dead. It seemed as if the whole of Thunder Bay had come out to see them off. Probably drawn by the firefight, the dead came in all shapes and sizes. Some staggered around the shore watching them; some even wading into the water. Unable to swim, the dead who ventured into the water never resurfaced. Hundreds of them lined the shore, their groans drifting across the calm water to him. Jonas slumped back, and let the rain wash his face. He just needed to sit and do nothing for a moment. He remembered so much no matter how much he tried to forget. He thought of how he had got to this point, and what had led to him becoming the man he had. Dakota, who had come with him on this journey only to die when they had been so close, was at the forefront of his thoughts. Erik, Quinn, Javier – all dead.

Dead.

All that was left, all that he had in the world, was Freya, a boat, and a gun. As rain beaded down his forehead and dripped from the tip of his nose, he remembered his father's funeral. He should've buried him in a decent coffin. Why did that matter? Why did stupid thoughts like that pop into his mind? Hamsikker knew that this was the end of the line somehow. Where were they going to go from here? Everybody he had cared about was gone. Why was *he* left alive when everyone else had perished? What made *him* special? He didn't want this and certainly hadn't chosen it.

Life.

He didn't even know what to do with it anymore. Dakota was looking down on him, he knew that, but he couldn't feel her presence. He would give anything to see her one last time. He remembered making love to her, the trust and love he'd seen in her eyes when he'd proposed, and he wished he had the energy left to weep. More than Janey and her three boys, more than Freya, more than anything, he wanted Dakota back. He wanted her back so much it literally hurt. His heart pounded with pain, he missed her so much, but he couldn't do a damn thing about it. There was no going back and no way of seeing her ever again. God, he needed to be with her. He didn't want to talk about Dakota in the past tense. To do so would be an admission she was gone forever, and his mind was not ready to accept that yet. He could still feel her, and he wanted to hold onto that as long as he could.

"Uncle Jonas, are you okay? I can still see the bad people."

Freya's question snapped Jonas out of his dreams, and he looked at her. She was so precious, so delicate and full of sorrow, that he hated to see her like this. Looking at her, her blue eyes so very much like her parent's, he knew he couldn't give up now. In the second that it took to look into her eyes, he felt something stir. It was a hope that life hadn't given up on him just yet. This little girl needed protecting, and giving up on her was not an option. He just needed to figure out where to go next.

"I'm okay, Freya. I'm just a bit tired. I'll be okay in a minute. The bad people can't reach us here. Try and ignore them."

Jonas let his head fall back, and he closed his eyes. He was exhausted, and he knew he was bleeding all over the boat. He had been drowned, beaten up, blinded, and left for dead. Freya would understand if Uncle Jonas needed a rest. She could...

A loud crack startled Jonas, and he sat bolt upright. "What was that?" He saw Freya sitting upright, the gun held in both hands in front of her.

"The bad people. I thought they were going to get you. I wanted to shoot them, but-"

"Don't worry, Freya, just put the gun down. The bad people can't get you, I told you that. We're in the middle of a lake, and they can't...swim. I think...I think..."

Jonas felt sleepy suddenly, and he looked down at his shirt where red blood was blossoming. It was blooming in a circle from somewhere under his collarbone. There was a burning sensation coming from his chest, and all of a sudden he felt more tired than ever.

"I'm sorry, Uncle Jonas."

Freya burst into tears, and Jonas watched as she threw the gun into the icy water.

"No, Freya, we might..." Jonas tried to sit up and grab the gun, but it was too late. He saw it slip beneath the water, and as he reached for it, he knocked the oar out of the boat. It, too, began to slip beneath the surface.

"Damn it." Twinkling lights danced in front of his one good eye, and Jonas slumped back into the boat. He knew they needed the oar, but he felt utterly devoid of strength. He looked down at his shirt where the blood continued to flow. He understood why Freya was sorry. She had been aiming for the zombies on the shore. It was an accident. For some reason, he wasn't worried, and didn't even feel much pain. It was almost comical. They had come so far since Kentucky, been through so much and lost so much, that it was ironic he should die now at the hands of an innocent child. There was still a chance the bullet had only scratched him, and Jonas couldn't bring himself to get upset about it. With Dakota gone, and only Freya left, he had other things on his mind. "Don't worry, Freya, it's not your fault."

"I'm sorry, it was an accident," said Freya between her tears.

Jonas smiled at her as blood trickled from the corner of his mouth. "Not your fault, Freya, I shouldn't…I shouldn't have… I…"

Jonas felt Dakota whisper in his ear. She was telling him that she loved him, and he let his remaining eyelid close. This was just a flesh wound, he told himself, just an accident. He had survived worse. He could recover from this. He always did. He sank back and tried to think. His thoughts were lucid, but he was slipping into a euphoric state. Voices at the back of his mind were foggy, distant, as if calling to him from some place far away. Dakota's was the clearest. She was calling to him; telling him to relax. All he had to do was close his eyes and sleep. The pain would be gone soon. A blissful white light settled over him, surrounding him from all sides, like the gentle touch of his wife from before any of this trouble started. He knew he had to wake up, to help Freya, but it felt so good, he just wanted to relax for a moment longer.

Freya watched the bad people from the boat. They didn't look like they could swim. If they could, wouldn't they have all started by now instead of standing there waving at her? She stopped crying, and wiped her face. Daddy always told her not to cry, but to think about *why* she was crying, and then find a way to solve it. If only Daddy was here now, he would know what to do. Freya reached over the side of the boat and ducked her hand into the water. It was icy cold, and she pulled her hand out quickly. She was *not* going to swim in that. She didn't even have her swimsuit with her.

"Uncle Jonas? You don't look so good." Freya was glad he was here in the boat with her, but he was asleep now, and she wasn't sure what to do. She supposed she was going to have to row the boat herself. She looked at the water. The paddle thingy that Jonas had used to get them away from the bad people was gone. She looked around the boat, but it was empty. There was nothing but herself and her Uncle. It was quite nice out on the lake, and her tummy didn't hurt like it did last time she had gone on a boat. If it stopped raining, she actually wouldn't mind it. It was quite peaceful, and she started humming a little tune, something she remembered from school. After a minute of that, she was bored though. When she stopped humming it was silent, and she'd had enough of that too. She didn't have any toys anymore, and now the stupid boat was drifting away from the shore. How were they going to get back to Daddy if they kept going the wrong way?

"Can we go now?" Freya kicked Jonas's shoe. "Uncle Jonas?"

Jonas groaned, and slowly opened his one good eye. He stared at Freya and said nothing.

Freya drew her knees up to her chin, and fished in her pocket for the key chain he had given her. "Uncle Jonas?" He didn't look very good, not at all, and the way he looked at her was funny, as if he didn't recognize her. Her murmured something but she couldn't make out what he was saying and it just sounded like a groan.

"Uncle Jonas, are you okay?"

THE END

Acknowledgements

I hope you enjoyed being dragged along with Hamsikker on his tortuous route through America. If reading it was hard at times, then trust me, so was writing it. There is a lot we could learn from Hamsikker and Javier, both good and bad. If nothing else, then at least we know how to dispose of a zombie, right?

I urge you to check out my publisher Severed Press, and the fantastic novels they have produced at www.severedpress.com

Finally, if you have enjoyed this, then please consider leaving a review, and pay a visit to my website www.russwatts.co or look at my other titles:

The Afflicted
The Grave
Devouring the Dead
Devouring the Dead 2: Nemesis
The Grave
Hamsikker
Hamsikker 2

13206075R00126

Printed in Great Britain
by Amazon.co.uk, Ltd.,
Marston Gate.